a Piece of the Sky

a Piece of the Sky

a novel

MICHELLE BUCKMAN

RIVEROAK®

Good News in Fiction

COOK COMMUNICATIONS MINISTRIES
Colorado Springs, Colorado • Paris, Ontario
KINGSWAY COMMUNICATIONS LTD
Eastbourne, England

RiverOak® is an imprint of
Cook Communications Ministries, Colorado Springs, CO 80918
Cook Communications, Paris, Ontario
Kingsway Communications, Eastbourne, England

A PIECE OF THE SKY
© 2005 by Michelle Buckman

Published in association with the literary agency of Yates and Yates, LLP,
1100 Town & Country Road, Ste. 1300, Orange, CA 92868.

Cover Design and Illustration: Jeffrey P. Barnes
Cover Photo (sky): ©PhotoDisc
Cover Photo (car): ©Bruce Adair

This story is a work of fiction. All characters and events are the product of the author's imagination. Any resemblance to any person, living or dead, is coincidental.

First Printing, 2005
Printed in the United States of America
1 2 3 4 5 6 7 8 9 10 Printing/Year 09 08 07 06 05

ISBN: 1589190505

To
Tommy, Ty, Arielle, Cierra, and Bridget.
You are my everything.

Acknowledgments

I did not know at the outset that this story was about infertility. Carla came to me as a desolate woman, and I had to discover why. While on vacation in Florida, I went to retrieve something from my car late one night. Across the parking lot, through the glass block windows of a shower stall, I glimpsed a couple in a passionate embrace. I hurried back to my family's rental unit wondering if a different woman might have stood her ground and watched the couple. "I would," came Carla's voice in the mysterious way that characters often speak to writers. I took up a pencil and began scratching down what she had to say. By the time we returned home, I knew her secrets, and I was ready to write her story. Her character was not based upon a particular person but was influenced by two women I knew who were going through their own personal struggles with fertility treatments. To those two women, I extend deep gratitude for sharing the pain and trauma of injections, tests, and schedules. I would also like to thank Hale H. Stephenson, M.D., for verifying that I got the medical details right. I know I cheated in a few spots, but it *is* fiction.

I have to thank my husband for his patience through this venture—for bringing home the bacon and cooking it, too, and for not complaining about the many nights I crept back to my desk in the wee hours to capture inspiration.

My children, my sweet blessings from God, you are the

real troupers. Thanks for tolerating my deep concentration and long hours of writing. Ty for installing everything on the new computer, thinking it would be yours and then not grumbling *too* much when I took it over; Arielle for your professional can-do attitude and singing your songs on any ol' stage; Cierra for cuddling up to me while I wrote in bed and setting up a small table beside my desk so you could tap your own stories in to my cast-off computer; and Bridget, my baby chick, for sitting in my lap and reminding me that being a mommy is the most important job of all.

Thanks across the miles to my sister Karen Parkes for encouragement. Mega thanks to my mother-in-law, Melanie Buckman, for the loan of her beach condo and for the sweetest weeks of writing on retreat. Thanks and a hug to my dad for the fantastic new laptop.

This list wouldn't be complete without inclusion of Gizmo, Honey, and Shadow, my own "dust cloud of poodles," who slept at my side and sometimes in my lap throughout the entire writing process. And to my dear friend Kristen Bethea for setting off a chain of events that had huge results.

I extend sincere thanks to my circle of critique partners who have become dear friends: Terry Burns for kicking me back into gear one more time. Sylvia Roller for being my number one reader—you're a gem. Francis Porretto—you're the brainiest writer I know; thanks for sharing your wisdom. Alan Jackson, my Canadian buddy—keep dreaming about the south of France and enjoying those pancakes with maple syrup.

There are many people in publishing who have helped me along the way and to each I am grateful, but there are several I must thank personally: Delin Cormeny for giving me confidence in my work. Michael Morris for long phone conversations and for opening doors. Jeana Ledbetter for believing in me and selling my book. Jeff Dunn and all the staff at RiverOak and Cook Communications Ministries— you made a dream become a reality.

In the end, I am naught without God. All glory be to the Father and to the Son and to the Holy Spirit.

One

I am barren.

The old-fashioned word flashed to mind as I pressed the phone receiver to my chest. The nurse on the other end continued talking, repeating my name: "Carla? Carla, are you there?" I couldn't respond. She, as bearer of the news, the harbinger of a childless life, had proclaimed my latest attempt at conception a failure. I hung up the phone and pressed my forehead against the wall.

Barren.

Infertile, my doctor, my mother, the entire world said, but that term didn't adequately project the emptiness—the great bleakness of a desert that stretches beyond eyesight.

I ached with the need to cry but resisted. The knot in my stomach tightened. I couldn't let the disappointment get the best of me. Crying wouldn't change the fact that children abounded everywhere except in my home. Life carried on despite my anguish: sunshine flickered on the ripples of Lake Norman; a man jogged by; a bird soared across the cloudless blue sky. Even my own home lacked any indication of the turmoil burning within me; my kitchen gleamed, not a thing out of place. Total serenity.

My eyes paused on the crystal vase on the counter. I'd meant to fill it with roses from my garden in celebration of the life I thought was blooming within me. Instead, the vase stood there, an empty vessel. I ran my finger down the crystal ... tall, cylindrical, perfect.

My dime-store youth passed before me—plastic plates and thick stoneware mugs, cheap glasses with visible seams. My mother's motto: *Buy nothing that isn't a bargain—shop two-for-one sales and clearance racks; quantity over quality in kitchenware and clothes.* I wouldn't own anything plastic now. I'd left all that behind me. I had crawled away to college and metamorphosed. I had developed wings of splendid new ideas and tasted the nectar of the better things in life. Material things.

I cradled the vase gingerly in my hands. The crystal warmed in my clasp. A beautiful piece, a pattern etched in heavy, angular cuts intended to reflect the candlelight of romantic dinners like a woman's diamond ring set center stage on the table. When filled with roses, the vase overflowed with petals' perfume sweeter than any imitation scent the seductress plies from a bottle. But it was empty.

Oh, God, why have you done this to me, left me as empty as this vase?

I didn't expect an answer. Despite my husband's preaching, God had ceased to exist in my world. I was alone in my misery.

I tightened my grip around the crystal and squeezed. It didn't yield to my pitiful human strength. I hurled it across the room. With a satisfying smack against the wall, the vase exploded into an array of brilliant shards and tinkled to the floor by the door.

I stared at the mess but didn't move to clean it up. The shattered glass didn't ease my pain. Nothing could ease the pain. A tiny voice whispered in my head: *Pray.* But I ignored it. Prayer was something only my sanctimonious husband could indulge in.

The roar of a car in the lane interrupted my self-absorption. I knew it was him, my husband in his red Z3, and I feared the words building in me.

He would never understand why I destroyed my most treasured vase. He couldn't understand that my once-upon-a-time goals—reached and surpassed—were no longer enough. I wanted so much more. I wanted an infant in my womb. I wanted a child by my side to teach me to see things once again through the eyes of innocence instead of scorn, to fill our house with laughter, and to refocus our marriage on life instead of work and the bristling tension rising between us.

I pictured him in the garage, parking the car squarely without a glance toward the waterfront we'd paid so much to live on. He would step out, straighten his suit, pause, and as always, touch the BMW hood ornament—but not the way a true sports-car enthusiast would. I know. My dad lived for his cars. My husband admired his as a status symbol.

Outwardly, the car didn't suit Simon. I didn't look at him and think *sports car*. He didn't wear macho clothes or walk with the leisurely swagger such a driver has. Simon was what my grandma would have called *upstanding*, like my grandpa. He dressed properly: a suit and tie for work, tailored clothes for leisure. He was precise in his speech and movements to ensure he presented the right public image. That was what first attracted me to him. I loved his self-control and mani-cured style.

But when Simon was driving, I saw a change in him. He melded into the car. He took curves as if he were born on a racetrack. So cool. So easy. A second nature ascended full of daring and spontaneity, drawn to the surface by the car's magnetism. He became more like me, more adventurous. Then he stepped out of the car into his reserved self again as if he could reveal that inner spirit only when it was shielded from view or tapped into by some outer force.

I loved him most when he was driving.

Yet initially, it was his outward reserved nature that attracted me. He looked dependable, mature, settled. He had a stable job and a solid nature. I knew he would never change. I could count on him.

I was right. He hadn't changed one iota from the day I met him. Not even the part in his hair. I think it's because he's a Taurus; they hate change.

Let me rephrase that. He never would have said he *hated* change. He would have said he didn't *tolerate change well.*

Simon didn't tolerate attempts at change either, including my obsession to conceive. Whenever I tried to discuss the infertility issue, he would shut me out.

Silently, I wished I were the outside force—like the car— that could pull him out, shed his skin of caution, and bring that impulsive side laughing to the surface. I loved his conservative nature, but he often hid emotions and braced himself against letting go and having fun.

He grew up the oldest of three children. His father ran off when he was ten years old, and he assumed the role of man of the house—caring for his younger brother and sister after school and taking on the yard work and other such chores his father had always done. His childhood was cut short. He'd had to be serious about school and life in general. The day he told me his life story, I imagined him as a little fellow donning a miniature suit and marching off to elementary school, briefcase in hand.

The experience developed him into a loving man with a profound sense of responsibility, but one so controlled I had come to feel suffocated at times. Somewhere inside him, there was a carefree little boy who needed to be released to laugh and frolic and jump headlong into life without accounting for every step he took.

His footfalls sounded on the garage doorstep.

"Carla, you beat me home this evening."

"I've been home most of the day. I wanted to get the call here, not at the office."

He nodded. There was no need for explanation. If the news had been good, I would have knocked him to the floor in my excitement. Instead, I stood there before him, a failure at the one thing that came naturally to most women. I had conquered the world, but I couldn't conceive a child.

"I'm sorry," he said. It was a limp offering. I don't know what I wanted him to say, but not that. What other response was left? It had been the same result month after month.

My cell phone rang. A work issue, no doubt. I knew that a new customer's carton order was scheduled for startup that afternoon—an account of major proportions—and I needed to check the department's progress. But I didn't even glance at the phone.

"Aren't you going to get that?" he asked.

I shrugged. I had struggled against all the old female biases to become plant manager, without children to distract me. I had reached for the golden ring and grasped it on my own. Now, none of it mattered. The rest of life remained detached. Nothing existed but the disappointment of the moment; I was a mere human surrounded by a vast black hole of despair.

We stared uncomfortably at each other. I wanted him to

hug me right then, to acknowledge my hurt and anger and to offer me his support and love. I wanted him to hold me the way he had after our first attempts, when he'd embraced me and dried my tears and reminded me that we had enough love to fill each other up for the rest of our lives. I don't think he understood that his love alone wasn't enough for me anymore. He couldn't see the hole inside of me growing larger with each negative result, with the uncontrollable, innate longing for children. I had to carry the weight of it alone.

His shoe crunched down on the shards of crystal, and he looked up at me again, his annoyance plain in the narrowing of his eyes and the set of his mouth. But for once he didn't reprimand me for disrupting our home's perfection.

I wanted him to recognize *why* I smashed the vase. I didn't have any tears left. Only pain. And anger. I wanted him to see both.

He didn't. He shook his foot, casting off bits of glass, then set his briefcase by the desk in the corner. "I guess I'll change and go to the club for a while. Care to join me?"

"No."

Simon always asked but would have been shocked if I had said yes. I never went to the club. Exercising in a room with a dozen sweaty people held zero appeal to me. I'm not perfect, but I am naturally slender, bordering on skinny, which is good enough for me. The ladies there spent more time on their nails than I spent on my entire makeup routine; I kept my blonde hair short and my nails blunt, and I minimized blush and lipstick. Anything more looked garish.

Simon headed out of the room with me shadowing him.

He paused and turned to look at me. "Aren't you going to clean up that mess?"

"Not yet."

He pursed his lips and turned away.

I followed him through the house, up the steps to our room. The house was ridiculously large for two people. The walls laughed at me, scorning me for the quiet. Silly, considering if it hadn't been for the house, Simon and I would never have met. We bumped into each other while touring this house—while inspecting the master bathroom, actually. Habitat for Humanity had convinced Charlotte-area builders to hold a special open-house presentation of their most prestigious homes and to donate a portion of all resulting sales to the Habitat charity. The builders showcased and sold some of their favorite upscale waterfront homes and raised a wad of money for the Habitat folks.

The house was built with two fronts: one facing the lake and one facing the street. The street side was brick with impressive white columns, narrow double-hung windows, and a heavy oak door with a brass knocker hung at eye-level. The lake side was glass with stair-stepped decks leading down to a pool edged in by boxwoods. The pool was an extravagance. The lake lay a hundred feet beyond its edge, at the bottom of the sloped yard.

Inside, the house was nothing special. Just an open floor plan combining kitchen and family room. Formal areas to the road front. Three bedrooms upstairs.

The funny thing was the urinal in the master bath. Of course I had seen one before, but I had never considered having one. That day on the tour, I wasn't seriously considering purchasing the house. I mean, I had a fat enough paycheck to buy the house, but I hadn't really settled on the idea until I saw the urinal and felt this surge of disappointment—like the house would have been perfect and I would have bought it if it weren't for this one huge flaw. I didn't want a urinal in my bathroom.

I was standing there, arms crossed, staring at the dumb thing when Simon walked in. He lounged in the doorway with that thin-lipped smile of his, so confident and serene—a man who meant business but who had all the time in the world, none of the nervous rushing so many businessmen twitched with. No chatter. No fast come-on lines or ogling eyes. He leaned against the doorjamb a moment, then pulled himself erect, introduced himself with a handshake, and asked me what I thought of the house. He was as impressive as the house: tall, lean, gray eyed, short haired, and dressed in some classy sportswear. I beheld him with fascination, a man devoid of all my previous dates' irritations.

We talked, which led to dating, and the rest followed. We got married and bought the yet unsold house, urinal and all.

That was four years ago.

I plopped backward on the bed while he went through his routine: shoes into the closet; socks, shirt, and pants into the hamper. His bare feet slapped on the ceramic tiles as he crossed the bathroom to use, no doubt, the urinal, not the toilet.

I had to make one final effort. When he returned to pull on his jogging shorts, I spoke, not even bothering to sit up. "Dr. Freeman wants to know if we're ready to progress to the next step."

I didn't dare say *artificial insemination* aloud. I didn't want to push it in his face. He knew what I meant by *the next step*. And I knew what his answer would be.

His voice was flat, matter-of-fact. "We've already discussed that."

Discussion had amounted to him saying no. He refused

to say why. Some days I suspected it had more to do with his newfound Christianity than anything; but other times I put it down to him having an ego the size of a hot-air balloon that made him too high and mighty to admit he couldn't father a child the normal way. I stared at him and imagined a never-ending row of men who wouldn't have a problem with it. It would be so easy to find another man willing and able.

I shoved the thought aside. "It will increase our chances—"

He didn't even look at me. He grabbed a polo shirt out of his dresser, sniffed it (as if Abigail might have put it away dirty), and pulled it over his head.

"Well?" I said. "Are we going to?"

Still, he ignored me. He snatched sneakers from his closet and sat on the bed to put them on. Conflicting emotions crossed his face.

I didn't know whether to scream or cry.

I had tolerated blood tests, ultrasounds, internal exams, and daily injections, yet he wouldn't let go of his ego and agree to artificial insemination.

Despite my determination to remain strong, tears welled in my eyes and I sniffled. He turned to me. His expression softened. He reached out and laid his hand on my leg. "We've talked about it, Love. It's one thing to take medications to resolve an imbalance in your system, but that's as far as I'm willing to go."

"The medications don't fix an imbalance. They control my ovulation cycle. What we need to do now is make sure sperm reach the egg on time."

"We do that. Right on schedule the natural way, the way God intended."

"But it hasn't worked. The doctor can make sure.

Insemination just inserts your semen directly at the egg. I don't see what the big deal is."

He sighed, tied his laces, and stood. Discussion was over. "So you won't need help with an injection tonight?"

I closed my eyes and swallowed. The injections jump-started my ovulation to make sure my uterus was primed and the eggs were released on schedule. No injection after a negative test. Not till the fertility drugs wore off and my cycle started over again. Three days of cramping, of feeling mentally beaten, followed by days of being hollowed out—the self-draining of bloody life-giving nourishment. "No. No injection tonight."

He squeezed my shoulder and nodded. "Right. We'll talk later then." He tried to kiss me, but I turned and gave him my cheek. "Let's pray about it, okay?" he said.

Pray about it. The words made me clench my teeth. My newly saved husband constantly tried to get me to pray. I had nothing left to say to God. I had a grievance against God I couldn't resolve.

Simon stared at me a moment more, a need to say something playing across his face in the way he chewed his lower lip. Despite our years of marriage, I realized there were things we would never know about each other. I wondered what ate at him that he couldn't blurt out. I waited, hoping words would spill forth.

No words came. He gently stroked my hair, then turned and left.

Somewhere along this trek I had devolved from an independent career woman seeking an equal mate, to a sniveling wife begging to be heard. We weren't a couple anymore. In this, we were opposing teams. I had to find a way to win.

I hadn't always wanted children. I had been as career oriented as Simon when we first married, but then I began to sense something missing from our lives. One day I stopped at a park to eat my lunch. I sat on a cracked wooden bench warmed by the spring sunshine. A vanload of children cavorted around the swings and slides while two young women leaned against the outer fence and gossiped with barely an eye on their charges.

One of the smallest children, a tiny girl, headed toward the fifteen-foot-high slide. She skipped along, all prissy in a frilly skirt. Her shoulder-length golden blonde ringlets, held back from her face by two pink bows, swayed with each bounce. The two women didn't even glance at her. I kept watching, wondering if I should yell, but the women were laughing at some private joke.

The little girl started up the rungs. I opened my mouth to call out, but two boys began fighting in front of the teachers and I knew the noise would have drowned me out. I set down my yogurt and perched on the edge of my seat. I don't know why I felt so concerned. She wasn't my child.

For an instant, I wished I hadn't come to the park. It was out of character for me. I usually ate at my desk. I had been bombarded with phone call after phone call—problems in production, materials delayed, and personnel hassles. I'd simply escaped to save myself a roaring headache. Otherwise, I would never have been there. But there I was, watching that little girl take step after step up the ladder. She got to the top rung, and I held my breath as she climbed awkwardly onto the platform. I stood, not knowing what to do. I wanted to charge over and demand she get down, but I hesitated.

She slipped. Tummy down, hands outstretched, she sped

down the slide, flew off the end, landed face first in the dirt, and flipped over sideways. Her scream rose around us, high pitched, full of fright and pain.

I couldn't hold myself back. I rushed to her side. I would have made her lie still, but she pushed herself to a sitting position and began wailing. Dirt coated her face, stuck to her eyelashes, and crusted her lips, teeth, and tongue. I scooped her into my arms and carried her the twenty feet to my bench, not caring that the two gossipy teachers were trotting up behind me.

I pulled tissues from my purse and wiped at her eyes and cheeks. "You poor dear," I murmured.

She opened her teary angel eyes, a deep blue perfect enough to rival the sky above. I saw everything in life rise up in that instant—the misery of the world with peace trying to shine through. As I held her in my arms, a calling rose within me, a revelation, an image of completeness within my grasp. Here was all the softness in life I lacked, the clarity of purpose, the simplicity of existence. All my pettiness fled in this aura of solace. Before then, a child had been the next logical step in my progression through life. That moment, it became my urgent passion.

I dried her tears and used the moisture to rub at her mud-mottled cheeks, her quivering mouth, and even her teeth, then reached for my water bottle. She took a swig, and I leaned her over to spit out the mud and grime, letting it splatter at the feet of the useless teachers, then continued with fresh tissues to finish the job.

I looked at her one last time—a little girl I knew nothing of, whom I would never see again despite many trips to the park—and engraved her image in my heart.

She slipped from my lap and secured her hand in the

waiting palm of the nervous teacher who stood there fussing, making excuses, while the other teacher gathered the rest of the children and herded them back to the swings.

I held the image of that child in my heart ever after, through all the long trials of fertility treatments, with her expression molded into visions of my own child. *Our* own child, except Simon couldn't understand my longing.

For more than two years, on specific nights, on a schedule of stopwatch precision, I had begged for conception from God and husband and whatever ova roamed my fallopian tubes.

What a paradox. I desperately wanted to have a baby with Simon, and yet I felt myself stepping away from him. In the recesses of my mind, I imagined shedding my life of him, which scared me to death.

I didn't want to go back to being single. I simply couldn't love my husband the way I once did. What had happened to those feelings of delirious love? The nights of dancing and sweet lovemaking, the passion of whispered words, fantasies fulfilled under satin sheets, and secret dreams confessed? Once, his touch had sent shivers up my spine with anticipation; the caress of his lips had lit my most intimate desires. I tried to grasp the bits of memory, but they seemed like another lifetime. Had they ever existed, or had I just wished them into being?

I thought back to our beginnings. I remembered our first anniversary, rising at the crack of dawn that morning and rushing off to a meeting at a plant in Greensboro, two hours away. There wasn't time to snuggle up to Simon in those blissful early hours to tenderly renew our vows. Work demanded my full attention.

The business meeting wasn't long, but with the travel it was midafternoon by the time I returned to my facility. I was tired from fighting freeway traffic and had so much left to do, I doubted I would get home on time, let alone early enough to serve up a nice anniversary supper. I snapped at my secretary when she handed me a stack of phone messages, and stomped into my office. There, I stood in shock. The heady aroma of twenty pots of roses in bloom assaulted me. My favorite flower, my dream of starting a rose garden handed to me in the most romantic of ways. I melted into my desk chair in amazement and breathed deeply. Each rose spoke to me like a kiss from his lips.

Simon acted nonchalant about it that night. He kissed me sweetly, smiled his laid-back little-boy smile, and shrugged. "I had to make sure you know how much I love you. I hope I can fulfill all your dreams the way you fulfill mine." I fulfilled his dreams that night.

The next morning, when it was his turn to dash out in the wee hours, he left me a note on his pillow: *You are my everything.*

I wondered if he still felt that way.

A tear rolled down my cheek. He *had* to still feel that way. Deep inside, I knew I felt that way about him. It was just buried, dormant, like my roses in the winter. But if spring never arrived to warm the roots, our love would never bloom again.

I was left with one hope to pull our life together: the baby that now seemed an impossibility.

I couldn't surrender to Mother Nature's declaration.

The urgency to bear a child welled in me again. It raged in my brain and consumed me. It had long overshadowed my sound reasoning. Nothing else mattered but succeeding. I shoved all loving thoughts away. I was a woman obsessed with motherhood. I knew I would do whatever it took to reach my goal.

Two

I listened to the garage door close behind Simon and pounded the bed with my fists. I'd been through a lot of pain and discomfort trying to get pregnant, and he hadn't done a thing other than fill a cup with semen. Even *that* he had to do in private at home and drop it off later. Maybe all men are that way, unable to ejaculate in a doctor's office, but it seemed to me they could do it every other place on earth if there was a girl willing and able. Simon had this problem, though. He embarrassed easily, especially about his genitals because of missing one testicle. Dr. Freeman said having a single testicle wasn't a problem since Simon's sperm count fell within workable range. Slightly low, but high enough to get the job done. I don't think he would ever have given a sperm sample if he'd had to go to the doctor's office to do it.

I sat on the bed for ages, staring into space. I tried to look at our problem from every angle, as a couple and as individuals.

Simon. He flooded me with conflicting emotions. I set my anger aside and concentrated on his endearing idiosyncrasies. He used his hands when he talked; his long fingers played a melody in the air in rhythm to his voice. He chewed on pencils when deep in thought and crunched on ice when he was nervous. He deftly prepared the most complicated menus for an ordinary meal. When he swam laps, his body glided smoothly through the water like a dolphin. He loved jogging and taking long walks on starlit nights. We often met for lunch as if we were secret lovers instead of a married couple.

I loved him.

But what would our lives be like in five years if I gave up the whole fertility ordeal and accepted a childless existence? Too quiet. Too lonely. Too aimless.

I thought about adoption and sighed at the implication of starting down a new path of paperwork, checkpoints, and evaluations, of waiting for adoption possibilities and enduring new disappointments. The little girl in the park filled my mind, and I tried to picture someone like her sitting in a dark corner of some orphanage waiting for me to find her. But in my heart I was sure she wasn't there. I didn't want to take on another struggle. I wanted to finish the fight I had started and achieve the goal I had set for myself—a successful conception.

I considered setting everything aside. If I gave up on having a child, I was afraid I would give up on Simon, too, which would leave me standing on a long road with no destination in sight.

I came full circle to Simon again. I pictured him holding that little semen cup in his hand and shaking his head no to insemination. Behind him stood a long line of men grinning and saying yes. *Yes.*

Being inseminated with a donor's sperm instead of Simon's wasn't a new idea. Rose, Dr. Freeman's nurse, had planted the suggestion in my mind almost a half a year earlier, citing from past cases that an anonymous donor with proven sperm could increase the chances of conception. The possibility had been nagging at me ever since. The scheme had become a more serious option every time Simon said no to insemination with his sperm. Now I was at the point of grasping it as my last hope.

I had only mentioned it once to Simon. The conversation didn't go well.

"Let's pick out a sperm donor. That way if it's the whole God's plan thing that's bugging you, you won't have any liability in it," I said.

"Don't talk about God like he's a joke."

"I didn't say he was a joke. I'm just trying to figure out how to make a baby without you getting into trouble with him, if that's what's bothering you. I'm not ignorant, you know. I used to go to Sunday school. Abraham used a concubine to increase his family. I'm not even suggesting I sleep with somebody, like he did. It'll all be a medical procedure."

"Now there's a perfect example of what I'm talking about. God had promised to make Abraham's descendants as numerous as the stars, but after ten years, Sarah gave up hope on God's promise and took things into her own hands. She asked Abraham to beget a child with her maid, Hagar, which he did. But God said the lineage he promised Abraham would not come from Ishmael, the illegitimate child; he said Abraham and Sarah were to have their own child. He made them wait thirteen years longer, until Abraham was ninety-eight and long past being biologically able to impregnate Sarah, before he blessed them with Isaac. Everything is in God's time, not ours, Carla."

"Unfortunately, God hasn't appeared and made us any promises, Simon, and I don't intend to wait until I'm an old woman to see if that's what God has in mind."

He looked at the floor a moment, then at me. "Maybe God doesn't want us to have children. He doesn't promise to give us what we want as much as what we need. Sometimes those aren't the same things."

"Oh, so now you're saying I should accept being childless without a fight? Being infertile is part of God's great plan for me?"

"I have no idea what God's plan is. I'm just trying to put things in perspective."

I relayed volumes of what I thought of his opinion with the look I gave him.

"Shoot, Carla, forget all that. What it comes down to is this: Jesus taught us to love one another. Having a child is the ultimate display of God's love for us. It should be the same for you and me: the result of love in our marriage. Natural procreation in a marriage fulfills the covenant between husband, wife, and God."

"But we can't have a child the normal way, Simon. Don't you get it? It can still be about love if you love me enough to get off your high horse and let me be inseminated with your sperm or a donor's." I paused. How did we manage to fight even about love? I had to put us back on a factual level. "Just come with me to the doctor's office and talk to Dr. Freeman about it."

"Dr. Freeman can't tell me anything I don't already know."

"That's right. You know everything."

"I don't know everything, but I know it's time we took a break from this. Let's get back to the way things were."

Things couldn't go back to the way they were. We had great memories together, but there was a piece missing in our marriage. We weren't a complete family. I needed that missing piece even if Simon didn't. "I couldn't have a child the way things were."

Frustration shattered his reserve. "Why can't you give it up? We don't have time for a child anyway. We work all sorts of hours. We have the club and dinners and parties. We travel. Just keeping your roses cared for is an issue. How would we manage a child? I think God knows we couldn't."

His remark opened an old wound, reminding me of how well-wishers had explained my father's death as part of God's plan to deliver him to his heavenly reward. I wanted no part of a God who caused such misery. If God thought I was incapable of raising a child, I would show him differently. No one controlled my life except me. I kept my response calm. "I run an entire plant. I think I can handle one very small person in my life."

"Babies cry all the time. They stay up all night. And they don't stay small. They grow into rebellious teenagers."

"You weren't rebellious and neither was I."

"They get sick, Carla. Kids get sick."

That statement stopped me. I couldn't even think of a time Simon had been sick except with a cold and one brief bout with the flu. What scared him about kids getting sick?

His voice dropped to a whisper. "Let's just keep praying. All things are possible through God."

I sat on the bed, staring into the early evening shadows stretching across the room, and thought back over that conversation. I figured things were only possible through God if it suited him: God's will and all that. God hadn't promised me a child, as he had Abraham. And if God was waiting until I hit ninety as he had done with Abraham's wife, Sarah, I didn't think I would be up to it. I wanted a child right away.

What did I care about God anyhow? What in my life proved his existence? I slammed the door on my conscience. The nurse's urging echoed within me. A sperm donor. A sperm donor would solve everything.

I shuddered with apprehension.

Despite my brave mind-set, I wavered at challenging God. I rationalized. If God did exist, maybe it was his will for me to take things into my own hands. Maybe it was his will that Rose suggested a sperm donor and that I follow through on her advice.

My heart pounded as I contemplated it seriously, not just as a vague hope, but as a reality. Despite months upon months of living with the idea, it was almost too daring to really step out and do. So many things could go wrong. What if Simon found out? What if I actually got pregnant?

In place of the bleak quiet of the two of us, childless, I envisioned a new life: Simon and I walking hand in hand with a child between us, a family laughing and trekking through the park or hiking the path he now jogged alone, having picnics and boat rides, and splashing in the pool. A child would complete us.

If I used a sperm donor, Simon would never be the wiser. I could just go on as usual and never tell him. If I conceived, he would never know it wasn't his child.

My spine tingled at the thought. I had never lied to Simon.

It wouldn't be a lie, though. It would just be an omission. That wouldn't be the same thing, would it? In the end, it would be for our good. If it was God he was worried about, God would want us to stay together rather than divorce, and I had decided it would take a child to keep us married. I didn't want a child simply to keep us together—my desire to have a child went far beyond my relationship with Simon—but that excuse made the ends justify the means in my head.

I stretched out flat on the bed and let the reality of the decision settle on me. I knew I could do it. I'd been through enough medical procedures to not even flinch at insemination. And I knew I had the self-determination to make the decision without Simon; independence was my trademark. I had done everything on my own as far back as I could remember.

It wasn't a slapdash decision. It was a step I'd been building up to for ages. I'd had part of my mind set on it ever since the nurse first mentioned it. A year of treatments, of having sex on a schedule, of ordering my life around injections and medications and ovulation charts—I had done all that without Simon helping more than minimally. It was ridiculous not to take the final step.

I was resolved. There was no other option left. The realization electrified me and set me in motion.

I pounded down the stairs, then paced around the living room. I dragged my finger along the spines of the collection of classics lining the pickled shelves, across the damask print of the sofa, and down the piano keys, dispelling the interminable silence with a clunking, erratic scale. I needed noise in my life. I wanted a child's laughter echoing around me. I wanted nursery rhymes and Brahms lullabies stacked among our many CDs.

I circled through the dining room where I paused to gaze out at the azaleas blooming around the Taylors' house next door. Many days I'd sat at the table sipping tea while watching their two boys play out some new version of cops and robbers in a modern sci-fi format with whoops and kicks and plastic laser guns. They also had a daughter at the awkward twelve-year-old age, wanting to act grown up but still drawn to the boys' antics. I wanted that in my life: children playing games in my yard and running through the house.

Their yard, like mine, lay silent in the evening gloom.

I passed through the kitchen doorway and stared at the phone. It would only take a phone call, a simple reply to the nurse: *Please inform Dr. Freeman that Carla Rochwell will proceed using an anonymous donor.* A simple decision. The only sane decision.

I touched the phone and considered how I would feel actually making the call.

My hand was still on the receiver when the phone rang. "Hello?"

The voice on the other end was crisp, decisive. "Hello! I just knew I'd catch you at home. I felt it in my bones."

It had been ages since I'd heard the voice, but I placed it immediately: Phyllis Samson, my best friend from grad school at the University of Virginia. My old roommate. For the first few minutes our conversation buoyed my spirits, volleying updates back and forth across the miles, but I began to feel tension. Something was building.

It came in her casual voice. "So maybe we could visit sometime." *We* meant her and her five-year-old daughter, Sabrina. Phyllis was a single mom.

Phyllis had never visited me before. Simon and I had visited her once while heading to Washington, D.C. Her daughter had been cute for the first ten minutes, and then she became the epitome of the terrible twos, whining for cookies and treating us to a lay-on-the-floor-screaming-and-kicking tantrum. I couldn't imagine having her in my house for an indefinite holiday, especially after all my efforts to convince Simon of the wonders of parenthood. But this was Phyllis. How could I say no? Maybe the spoiled baby had grown into a sweet five-year-old child.

"That would be terrific," I replied. "You know you're always welcome. When can I expect you?"

She became evasive. "Oh, I didn't mean anything definite. Just sometime."

"You'll need directions."

"I'll get them off the Internet. One of those mapping sites."

"Oh, sure." I gritted my teeth. I wasn't into surprises. I liked schedules. It's how I ran my life. Maybe Simon had rubbed off on me. Maybe it was from working hard, scrambling to get to the top, running a plant on a tight production schedule, arranging my life so I would be seen as a plant manager, not a woman. Maybe it was from years of measuring every week, every day, by temperatures and charts, injections and hormone levels, by doctor appointments and test results, because my body had forgotten I was woman. Whatever the reason, my life was planned out day by day, hour by hour. "Well, let me know so I can plan. I'll dust off the old Olivia Newton-John albums and uncork a bottle of chardonnay."

"You're a gem," she said.

"No, I'm a rock. You're scissors." *Scissors cut paper. Rock smashes scissors.* The old game had become our slogans.

She laughed, remembering. "That still leaves paper for Simon and Sabrina." *Paper covers rock.* How symbolic.

She hung up without saying good-bye. Phyllis hated good-byes.

My emotions plummeted again. Phyllis with no husband had a daughter she hadn't planned, hadn't wanted. And here

I was, married, settled, and begging for a child. The world was balanced by extremes, and I was on the wrong end of the teeter-totter.

Self-serving independence coursed through me. If a sperm donor would give me what I wanted, why shouldn't I go for it?

I couldn't stay inside thinking about it. I had to process the idea among people to see if the guilt of such a decision would swallow me. I had to pass the ultimate test—a visit to my mother.

Three

Our old family home was in a neighborhood that had gained prestige as newcomers bought up the old places and began calling them historical. As the home values steadily climbed, Mom became obsessed with the need to sell the old house. She was tired of keeping it up. She wanted to move to a small place without a yard, but Dad wouldn't hear of it. He had a shop out back for working on his cars. He never owned any new cars—always classics that he promised would make loads of money if he held on to them long enough. Their engines were holes that consumed his money faster than he could make it.

As much as Mom loved Dad, she couldn't sell his garage mess fast enough after his demise; his cars and motors had been a thorn in her side for forty years. Two of the cars were willed: the '73 Porsche 911 he left to me, and the '62 Chevy pickup he willed to Cousin Jim out in Iowa. In her haste to empty the yard, Mom heaped assorted parts in the back of the old truck so Jim could fix it as he went; never mind she had no idea what the parts were or if they belonged on a Chevy pickup. The remaining four cars, in various stages of repair, were disposed of in three days.

With the cars gone and the house cleared of all Dad's clutter, Mom sold the place in a week and retired to an apartment so new the paint and carpet kept her wheezing for a month.

At the apartment we became invited guests, no longer kids running in and out on a whim. I knocked. Mom came to the door, fluffing her perm and straightening her polyester blouse. Her three poodles bounced around her feet, yapping at me like they'd never seen me before. It made me think of Pigpen from the old Peanuts comic strip—Mom's own personal dust cloud of poodles. They bobbed around her everywhere she went.

"Come in, dear. What's the occasion?"

I had to have an *occasion.* "Nothing special. I just wanted to stop by."

She steered me toward the kitchen, the dogs moving in rapid steps alongside her shuffle. "I was getting out some pecan pie. Let me fix you some."

I didn't get my thinness from Mom. Pie, cookies, and cake sat on her hips like the overskirt of a Victorian gown. She'd probably intended to nibble away at her creation all evening.

The pie was too sweet, all corn syrupy. Years ago, I had offered Mom my secretary's recipe, which I preferred, but she continued to make this recipe, my sister's favorite. I swallowed each mouthful with a swish of water.

The poodles kept dancing around me. Why can't dogs be serene like cats? Even well-trained dogs seem to quiver with energy if you pay them the least bit of attention. Cats are so self-assured they don't need constant reaffirmation. I pushed away the most persistent of the three poodles, a black one named Nubs. Fluffy and Sugar, the two apricots, had learned better manners. They had been around longer and knew enough to keep their distance. Nubs bounced right back again and pawed at my knees. As soon as Mom turned her back for an instant, I pulled off a piece of crust and covertly tossed it into a corner for the three of them to fight over.

"Phyllis called today," I said.

"Phyllis Samson?"

"She's the only Phyllis I know."

Mom tilted her head at me. Ever since I was a little girl, the stance made me envision her physically putting on an invisible thinking cap. After a moment, she'd processed the notion as far as she could. "I believe you're right. She is the only Phyllis we know. No wonder. Who would ever give a baby such a horrible name?"

"I like it. It makes me think of her red hair."

"The name Phyllis has nothing to do with hair," she said.

"Poetically speaking, I mean. The way the syllables curl on my tongue. It sounds like her hair." I tried it out again for good measure. "Phyllis."

"One phone call with her, and you've dropped back into that weird, poetic, hippy mode she always put you in. I hope she's not coming here."

Mom was warming up for the ride down the "bad friends" path. She never liked Phyllis. Phyllis always had her head in the clouds and managed to stay in one scrape or another, leaving me to rescue her. Mom considered her a bad influence. I couldn't stomach that conversation. I took the half-truth maneuver. "Phyllis here? Wouldn't that be a surprise?"

A catalog lay on the counter within reach. I pulled it closer and flipped through the pages. I used to spend big bucks on clothing, but I'd quit buying new outfits ages ago. I kept hoping I would be pregnant and would need maternity clothes instead. Without thinking my mother might notice, I turned to the maternity section. A black skirt and coat appropriate for work caught my eye. I gazed at it, wondering if I would ever have a need for it.

Mom leaned toward me. "Are you?" The entire question hung in those words.

I debated how to answer. I could be optimistic and not let Mom know how badly things were eating at me. Or I could deflate like a balloon and admit that Simon and I were having problems because he was ready to give up completely on having a baby. I could even confide about the decision I was facing. But I didn't. Bravado rose up in me from the darkness pervading my attitude about life and marriage at that point. It was easier to take it out on my mother than on Simon. "If I were expecting, I'd tell you."

The snap in my voice brought a frown to her face. Maybe she understood what I was going through because she didn't reprimand me for biting her head off. She stepped back and stared at me a moment, then leaned on the counter. "Well, when you do get pregnant, you'll have a lot more choice in clothes than I had, that's for sure."

"I like this black one. It would be good for work."

"Sure. It's tailored and probably adjusts to last throughout your term. You should have seen what I had to wear. You wouldn't believe it."

"A tent, I expect."

"Worse."

"Worse? Than a tent?"

"Back then, the skirts had holes in them."

"Holes?"

She lifted her shirt and draped it around the aging bulge of her abdomen. "Like this. The skirt had a huge hole for a woman's pregnant belly to hang out. We wore long shirts over the hole."

I laughed. "You're kidding."

"Seriously." She started dancing around the room with her belly hanging out. "Can you believe it? Wobbling around like this all day." She jiggled her stomach for good measure.

I grinned, watching her frolic. "That would have been a sight to see."

"I wish I'd kept some to show you. I'd forgotten about them until I was packing up the old stuff from the house for Goodwill. I should have saved a couple." Her gaze became distant. I wondered if she was recounting her pregnancies and early times with Dad.

When she looked back at me, the laughter was gone from her face, and her voice was solemn. "I pray for you every night."

The thought of her saying prayers struck me deeply. She certainly wasn't an evangelizing Christian like Simon. In fact, she rarely mentioned God. I'd never imagined her saying bedtime prayers other than the ones she used to say with Babette and me as kids. We had been raised to be good and to believe in God, but prayers in our house were by rote, not heartfelt—at least not that I recalled. We never read Scriptures or discussed God or religion beyond the barest terms. It was understood that God was there, but he wasn't a notable part of life, unless something called him to mind, like death. Like losing my father.

I wondered if my mother had always had secret prayers and more faith than I'd credited her with, or if she'd discovered it during her recent years alone. The shock of her declaration dissipated, leaving me touched by her sweetness. Maybe she did have a soft spot for me after all. Nevertheless, the prayer, her belief in God, didn't sway my hardened heart. I almost told her to save her breath rather than waste it praying for me, but I changed my mind. Maybe it was just me God ignored. I concentrated on my plate and kept my thoughts to myself.

As I lifted the last bite of pie, the poodles erupted in a barking frenzy at a knock on the door. My sister didn't wait for Mom to answer. She burst through the door, kids in tow: Brooke, Bette, and Blake, all named with Bs in keeping with my sister and brother-in-law, Babette and Barry. Blake dragged his lean fifteen-year-old body in and flopped on the couch with one huge tennis shoe propped on the backrest. Mom would never have tolerated such an act from me in my youth.

"Oh, it's Baby," Mom exclaimed as she moved toward my younger sister.

"Hello, Babette." I say her name defensively. To everyone else, she has remained Baby, a name devised by me as a toddler and adopted by the world.

My mother loves nicknames but insists they must be earned. Apparently, I didn't rate one. I've been Carla forever, except during college. There, I tried to become Carley. The name rolled out of my mouth strange and foreign, a new me, a step above the beloved Babette—and for four years I trained myself to respond to my new title. In my mind's eye, I became a dark beauty with Hawaiian skin and flashing black eyes, instead of a disappointing mix of pale skin, pointed chin, and blonde hair too heavy and straight to be styled any way but as short as a man's.

After college, I landed a job in a bank that insisted I wear a nametag. I couldn't bring myself to proclaim Carley across my chest, where my mother would surely see it and make comment. So Babette is Baby, the cheerful, ever-in-the-right, can-do-no-wrong baby of the family, and I am Carla-the-plain. Only to Phyllis do I remain Carley.

Babette patted my back in greeting. I forced a noncommittal smile. "I didn't know you were coming." *If I'd known, I'd have gone to the mall instead.* I loved my sister, but I didn't need a parading example of motherhood right then.

Bette made a beeline for the refrigerator with Brooke skipping along behind. "What'cha got to eat, Grandma?"

Mom scratched her head and grinned. "What's round and flat and nuttier than a fruitcake?"

Brooke clapped her hands and jumped up and down. "Oh boy. Pecan pie! Can we have some?" Like my sister, Babette's kids shared Mom's food fetish and her waistline.

"Hey, Bette, bring some over here to me," Blake yelled from the couch.

The dogs bounced around while Mom hugged the lot of them and pulled dishes from the cabinet. I set my plate in the sink and fished around in the junk drawer for a pen so I could write down the Web address of the catalog. Hope sprang eternal that I might need the outfit.

My eyes fell upon a strange sight among the jumble in the drawer—a spark plug. I held it up. "What's this doing in here, Mom?"

She shrugged. "Something of your dad's. His lucky spark plug."

I fondled it. "And you kept it?"

She couldn't answer. She wouldn't become emotional with a gang of people around. She turned and busied herself with cups and napkins. I stood holding it a moment, wondering if she regretted getting rid of his other things so quickly. I held it to my cheek and thought of him. I could almost smell the oil on his hands and feel the scruff of his cheek on the afternoons I'd helped him work on his old clunkers. My dad had loved me so openly. The memory brought a lump to my throat. He taught me how to tear down a motor and rebuild it. He taught me to play football, how to ride a motorcycle, and how to build a tree fort. In my daddy's eyes, there was nothing I couldn't do. He taught me there were no genders in the world if I worked hard at what I wanted. He gave me the courage to forge through a master's degree in business and aim for the running of a plant instead of manning the secretarial desk.

To my mother, I was a girl. To my daddy, I was whatever I chose to be.

Maybe it was my independence that caused Mom to hold me at arm's length, or maybe through the years she resented the time I spent with Daddy instead of with her. Daddy took me everywhere. It was me he asked to accompany him to car races and me he took on escapades in search of additional junk cars for his collection. My mother certainly didn't have any interest in going with him, even for the sake of having time alone with him. Looking back, I think Daddy's and my joviality whenever we were together fed Mom's resentment of Daddy's cars in general—the expense, the mess, and the time he devoted to them versus whatever she had on her agenda. The older I got, the less I had in common with her, so I pretty much ignored her and Babette. They were like two peas in a pod, doing all the mother-daughter stuff together: shopping, cooking, sewing, and such.

Whatever the reason, Mom and I clashed, which made me miss Daddy all the more. When Daddy died, a part of me died too.

I shoved the spark plug back in the drawer and turned absently back to the others. Babette was pouring tall glasses of milk for the girls and herself.

"So how are you doing, little sister?" I asked.

"We're all great."

Blake chose that moment to entertain the room with a loud burp. Brooke gagged. "Oh, Blake, you're so nasty."

Mom guffawed, thankful for the opportunity to laugh away the nerve I'd struck. "If that was some kind of compliment, Blake, you certainly made it well heard. Glad you're enjoying that pie."

I rolled my eyes. Babette ignored the whole episode and continued talking. "We're just busy, you know? Brooke has ballet in an hour, and Bette has a piano recital this evening."

Mom piped in on cue. "I'm taking her to the recital."

Bette tossed me a ten-year-old, milk-mustached grin. Babette's family equated time with my mom as some kind of prize.

Brooke, with her blonde curls pulled into a ballet-looking bun and her baby fat squeezed into a pink tutu, spun in circles around me. I patted her head. She reminded me of Mom's poodles.

Babette continued. "And Blake has tae kwon do at seven."

The pause at the end was heavy, as if planned. They all stared at me, expectantly.

I looked back, puzzled, not comprehending their stares. Mom and Babette seemed to communicate without ever talking. They just *knew* each other's minds. I didn't. "What?" I asked.

As Babette smiled at me, I admired her. The fleshiness of her hips and breasts extended to her face, filling it out with a youthful, smooth, rosy complexion I envied. I wasn't wrinkled yet, but my thinness aged my features. My skin lay taut across my pronounced cheekbones, hard and angular; Babette sparkled with soft, inviting curves. Her face dimpled with pleasure as if she were doing me a favor. "Would you like to take Brooke to ballet?"

All my angst rose up and tempted me with the idea of poking her eyes out. They were tossing me a bone I didn't want. A week after my wedding, Babette had pulled me aside. "Now we can have babies together, cousins the same age." Back then, I had no interest in having a baby. I was still career oriented at that point. Nevertheless, two months after my wedding, Babette was getting the royal treatment over Baby Number Three. At the time, I didn't care, but later, when I started trying to get pregnant, she developed this idea of offering her children part time as a way of assuaging me. After all I had been through, she still thought offering me care of Brooke once in a while made up for not having my own child. I should have seen it for the love offering it was, but in my despair, I couldn't. I loved her children, but if she'd had a dozen, it wouldn't make up for me not having any.

"Sorry," I replied. "I have dinner plans with Simon. I only stopped in for a minute." Actually, I had nothing planned. I had thought of hanging out with Mom all evening, but I wouldn't admit it.

Mom quit picking at the pie plate. "Let me guess. Out to the club to hobnob with some of Simon's friends?"

Simon's manners were impeccable, which had always made Mom feel beneath him socially. It was an ego thing. My mother never tried to employ tact, let alone put on airs. Simon had traveled the world and rubbed shoulders with high-powered executives at the most formal of affairs. It showed. But he certainly never belittled my mother for her lack of social grace. It irked me that she dared cut him down in front of Babette, even if I was mad at him. So I lied to save face. "We're meeting some friends of mine from work. Believe it or not, I do have a few."

"Oh, certainly you do, but you don't spend enough time

with me or with Babette and her family. You ought to put family first."

I pictured Babette and Barry parked on our couch munching chips the way Aunt Marge and Uncle Dean had lounged around Mom and Dad's house. Then I added Babette's three kids devouring the contents of my kitchen. "I rather like my friends, Mom. They share our lifestyle and interests."

She patted my arm. "Ah, well, that may change when you have children."

Babette's face radiated a sweet innocence she managed to wear like a badge. Her eyes almost looked teary. "I suppose the news hasn't changed?"

The words bit into me. She knew what I was going through but remained convinced it was something I was doing wrong. Some months back, she and Mom had decided that I was suffering from a mental hang-up: *My aura was blocking my physical self from accepting a child.* Neither of them would let the idea go. That's what I got for seeking solace in my mother's house.

I didn't let the pain show in my face. After all, I was the strong one in the family. It wouldn't do to let them see me cry. "No. No change. There may never be any change."

Mom frowned. "Never say never. If you believe, anything is possible."

Believe myself straight to the sperm donor. I hid my feelings in sarcasm. I delivered it so well they didn't catch on. "Do you really think so? You think if I just wish hard enough, suck in my strength and do it, I'll really get pregnant?"

"You've certainly outdone everyone in the family up to this point: getting your MBA, doing a man's job of running that production plant, buying that mansion on the lake. Why should a small thing like having a baby be beyond you?"

Babette was wiping fingers and faces. "Because she can't use her smarts on this one, Mom. Any ol' dumb person like me can have a baby."

My mother nodded. "See there? Exactly what we said before. Your mental processes are blocking out the baby making. You remember the Whitakers, our old neighbors? You were too young to know about it, but Laura, Mrs. Whitaker, couldn't get pregnant, so she and her husband decided to adopt a child—that was David—and then when they quit worrying about conception, bingo, she ended up pregnant with Daniel. You're just thinking too hard about this whole pregnancy thing."

I looked at them as a whole—these two women and three children—my own living, breathing genetic pool. How could they ridicule me for my brains *and* for my lack of fertility? They didn't understand how much having a child meant to me or how the trial of infertility had eaten away at my marriage. They were full of platitudes but lacked real sympathy.

I looked at them stone cold. "If you were in my shoes and couldn't have a child, would you do whatever it took to have a baby? Does motherhood mean so much to you that you'd risk anything to obtain it?"

Babette hugged little Brooke to her. "Oh, definitely. It's worth whatever it takes."

Mom nodded. "Of course it's worth it."

That was the answer I'd come to hear. I could think of using an anonymous donor while looking them straight in the eye and not feel guilty. Having a baby would be worth the cost of being deceitful.

They continued to look at me with puppy-dog eyes. I used to think they were jealous of my success, but I was beginning to see they held themselves above me for never having reached toward worldly goals, for sticking to being house-wives instead. I could never measure up in their eyes. I lacked the final notch, the real proof of succeeding as a woman—motherhood.

I was determined to prove them wrong.

Four

The next morning, I had misgivings. I had tossed and turned all night at the thought of actually using an anonymous donor. In the throes of nightmares, I decided I had to discuss the issue with Simon once more, to make him understand what having a child meant to me.

He always rises an hour before me. He likes eating a big breakfast and watching the news before work. I'm the type who sleeps till the last minute, showers, sips some coffee, and runs out the door. This day, however, my nightmares had me poised for action. I woke early, and, as I had every other morning for the past year, I took my basal body temperature reading and charted it for referencing the midcycle plummet in temperature that would indicate ovulation. Then I lay there antsy, waiting for Simon to stir. As soon as he rolled out of bed and headed to the shower, I padded downstairs. I had his breakfast prepared when he entered the kitchen.

He took a seat on a stool at the counter, smiling as if I'd crowned him king. "Thank you. To what do I owe this treatment?"

"We need to talk."

His face stiffened over a mouthful of grits. He knew I meant the baby issue.

I persisted. "Why won't you discuss it?"

"You're turning this into a *blasted* science experiment."

I wanted to roll my eyes at his juvenile slang, the one tiny chink in his perfection. I'm sure it stems from his refusal to curse. He has to fill in the blanks with something meeting his mother's approval.

I kept my reply even. "It's not an experiment; it's medical advancement, no different from the medicines and injections."

"Taking a drug to make your body produce the right hormones or rhythm or whatever is one thing. When you plan to take my sperm from me and insert it artificially, you've taken away the natural progression of things. I want no part of it. If we're meant to have a child, one will come."

I fidgeted with my coffee cup and swallowed the words brewing in my mouth. I let his voice wash over me, past my ears, into the vacant, lifeless perfection of the family room.

I knew he was on a roll. Next, he would progress to God.

"If God intended for us to have test-tube babies and such, he wouldn't have given us the means to produce children within ourselves. You must put your faith in him, Carla. It is through him we are given the gift of life."

His speeches always drew my attention to his neck, long and skinny, like a chicken with a conspicuous Adam's apple. I used to think it made him look macho, an extremely visible sign of his masculinity; but as the days, months, and years of marriage passed, that bobbing speech ball became an irritant added to his condescending lectures. I tried to look away, to peer into the swirling coffee in my grip or even into the smutty gray of his irises, but I was locked into my own perverse aversion, bent on adding to the well of anger burgeoning in the pit of my stomach.

He continued, "We must trust God to bless us when he

sees fit. You've become obsessed with the notion of mother-hood. I wonder if you even think about the baby, or if it's just the first goal you've set for yourself that you haven't attained. You can't let go of it for a night, let alone a month. A baby isn't like one of your production schedules; you can't force it into being. If you would relax and let things be, and join me in prayer, you might get pregnant."

"You need to put down your Bible and study my infertil-ity manuals. God has nothing to do with it. This is medical science. It's just another life obstacle that I'll overcome. On my own."

He had a controlled trace of lines around his mouth as he counted to ten. Finally, his face relaxed and his eyes soft-ened, pleading as he spoke again, as if that would make a difference. "Jesus loves you, Carla. He wants to give you your heart's desire, but first you must lay your burden at his feet and open your heart to him."

My face took on the blankness of a wall.

He sighed and took a different tack. "How many times have you heard of couples adopting and then getting preg-nant immediately after? It's the pressure of trying that prevents pregnancy. You're ruining your chances—and our sex life."

Our eyes met and held. He sounded just like my mother. How could they dismiss my infertility so easily? My emotions were too raw to respond to his comment. I knew if I ever let my words out, there would be such a torrent, I wouldn't be able to stem them, and we would part ways, which I hadn't made up my mind to do … yet. I hadn't spent years in college and climbing the corporate ladder without learning a few life lessons. I had learned when to hold my tongue and when to let the chips fall. Words couldn't be taken back.

As for his argument, we had gone the natural route before embarking on more advanced measures. Nevertheless, he was right about our intimacy. Nothing was spontaneous anymore. I just didn't know what else to do. I wanted a baby. The need had grown and grown until I couldn't think of not succeeding. I had to be obsessed to force myself through all the procedures. Being lukewarm wouldn't get a woman to the end of it all. And at this point, I was determined I *would* get to the end with a baby in my arms. I had to.

If I accepted failure, I would fall apart.

The subject had apparently been exhausted. He spooned another mouthful of grits and focused on the television weatherman.

I left him sitting on the kitchen barstool eating his breakfast and padded barefoot across the cool white and green ceramic tiles, coffee mug burning my palms. I kept to the pattern of left foot on green, right foot on white, which made me totter back and forth inanely like a penguin until I reached the dim predawn hues of the dining room. My feet sank into the plush carpet, unwelcome warmth in a setting of ghost-white chairs and smoky gray table.

Simon had never, in all mornings past, joined me in the dining room for my morning quiet, which was fine because I didn't want him to, but it irritated me as well because it showed how little interest he had in me anymore.

I settled into my seat at the bay window and stared at the waking world. There, across from me, were my neighbors, their bodies filtered through the privacy window beside their bathroom Jacuzzi. Only their expressions were lost in the translation. Their every movement, every caress, was visible in the milky view. I knew immediately what I was witnessing. I should have turned away. I should have averted my eyes at least, but I, a dry-throated woman in a desert, drank in their passion.

The first time they came to our house, relief lit their expressions as they toured the layout. "Oh, the dining room," they exclaimed. "I'm so glad our bedrooms aren't end to end." No doubt they hadn't expected me to enjoy a morning repast in this formal room under their bathroom window.

I hadn't foreseen it either.

I hadn't foreseen my marital boredom.

Simon had wooed me well and lulled me with visions of bliss, an end to a stream of dating and second-guessing each date's intentions. Simon's courtship, like all his life, was purposeful. He traveled surefootedly down his path. I had joined him, rejoicing in his steadfast approach. Gradually, as we succumbed to the strictures of fertility treatments, the predictability of every aspect of our lives became tedious.

As I watched Sue and Al next door, I told myself they were probably just as predictable as we were after so many years of marriage; but they *seemed* romantic, set apart as I was, filling in words of my own invention, which I imagined fluttering out between sensual caresses. I sighed, left my coffee mug on the table, passed through the living room, and trudged up the front staircase to my empty, sterile bath to contemplate my course of action.

Five

Four appointments and ten days worth of injections later, I arrived at Dr. Freeman's office for blood work and a vaginal ultrasound. He declared that my follicles had reached seventeen millimeters, which was perfect.

"Rose will give you the hCG injection supplies. Projected time of ovulation is thirty-six hours later, and we want optimal conditions. So inject it tonight at eight o'clock, and we'll see you back here at eight o'clock Friday morning for insemination."

I felt giddy. I was actually going to be artificially inseminated. I grinned. If I'd examined my thoughts too closely, I probably would have vomited.

Dr. Freeman continued. "It's got to be in the hip, so you'll need help with this one. Don't try to do it yourself. Will your husband help you?"

"My mother will."

He nodded and left me with Rose for final instructions.

Mom had been a nurse's aide in another life, where she eyed a handsome soldier in bed who needed tender love and care and who proposed to her from the flat of his back. It was nearly impossible to imagine Mom filling that role of a sweet care-giving nurse, but Dad used to tell me the story with tears clouding his eyes. He had been bad off and needed years of bedside care, which accounted for my late arrival in their lives. Mom had stuck with him and learned as much as any full-fledged nurse. She definitely knew how to give injections. Much as I hated to ask her, I had no option because I hadn't told Simon I was still in treatment.

When I arrived at her house that evening, I got straight to the point. "I need you to do my hCG."

She knew what I meant. The agony was clear on her face. "Oh, Carla, I thought we agreed you just needed to relax about this whole fertility issue. I know I said children are worth extremes, but I hate to do this to you. Such pain ..."

"I don't even think about it anymore. Just do it." It wasn't the truth, but it would stop her fretting.

For the most part, I'd given myself all the earlier injections. They'd been in the thigh or arm. It took willpower, but I hadn't wanted to ask anyone else. At first, Simon had done them, but more and more often, I'd been left alone to handle them. So I did—twice a day for months. I wished I could inject this one as well, but I dared not do it wrong. I had to have help.

Mom followed me into the bathroom and glared over my shoulder.

"Let me mix it," she said.

"No, they showed me how."

"So now you know more about nursing than me, do you?"

"No, Mom."

"I worked for years, you know, in the regional hospital as an aide and then privately after that."

"I know. You've told me."

"You can't admit to me knowing more than you about anything, can you?"

I didn't answer. She'd done her nursing in another era. As

I handed her the needle, I worried that she had forgotten how to give a shot after so many years. I worried she wouldn't do it right. I might end up with air bubbles that would somehow make it to my brain and kill me.

I worried it would hurt so badly I would cry in front of her.

I tried to concentrate on the purpose. It would pop those ova right out of the follicles and prime everything for fertilization. With artificial insemination afterward, this one could be worth it. This one could really result in a baby.

I pulled down my pants and lay on the bed. I felt like I was sticking my fanny in her face. It's a degrading thing, even in front of one's mother.

Two of the poodles hopped up and snuffled around me. I batted at them with my hand. "Mom!"

She patted her side and walked to the bedroom door. "Come on, Nubs, Sugar. Out you go." She hustled them out of the room and shut the door behind them. They yapped on the other side and scratched at the doorframe.

Mom returned to my side and sighed loud enough to make her feelings known. A swab of alcohol, and then her hands touched my flesh, cold as a fish.

"Are you ready?" she asked.

I stared at her alarm clock ticking our lives away. "Yes. Do it. It's after eight already." I flinched at the prick and gritted my teeth through the pain as the drug burned a pathway through the muscle. As the discomfort subsided, I breathed again.

I sat up and took the empty syringe from her. "Thanks."

She looked defeated. I ignored her and cleaned up my stuff.

On Friday morning, I put on my good-luck brooch—a pretty

gold cat with ruby eyes. My daddy had given it to me in high school for being chosen as valedictorian.

I needed good luck. It was *the* day. The day of the insemination.

The procedure itself was no different from what I'd imagined, but Simon was right in one respect—I did feel like a science experiment. As the stranger's semen invaded my body, I became increasingly aware that all the cozy intimacy—the sensual, snuggling flush of procreation through lovemaking—was missing. I tried to tell myself the intent of having a baby was enough, but physically it wasn't. My heart pounded with worry. My mouth was dry. My throat constricted. I had to want this child more than anything in the world because in the end, if Simon found out, if my mother and sister found out, the child might be the only thing I had left.

The beauty of artificial insemination is that I was as fit as a fiddle afterward. No bed rest for two days like in-vitro patients. Anything goes. Live life to the fullest. I rested for thirty minutes after the procedure and then was sent on my way, first to put in eight hours at work and then home.

I felt like avoiding Simon by crawling into bed with feigned illness for the rest of the night. Foreign matter had invaded my body. I felt like a worm. I wished I were a worm, complete with my own male and female reproductive organs. But even worms must find mates.

As much as I wanted a baby, I didn't want this other man's sperm coursing its way through my most personal avenues. I had to do something to eradicate the feeling of being slime.

One thing I'd learned in life was to overcome the remorse of bad behavior by doing something worse. It made the first thing seem less important. So I did a worse thing than being artificially inseminated by a stranger ...

When Simon arrived home, I was sprawled on the couch in this little nothing of a black dress that he likes.

"Simon, I've been waiting for you." I rose at just the perfect angle for exposing my cleavage and showing as much leg as possible. I offered him a glass of wine.

He set a bag on the kitchen counter and his briefcase by the desk in the family room. "I stopped at the grocery store. I got some fresh grapefruit for your breakfast tomorrow."

Simon used to bring me flowers and chocolates; I had digressed to presents of grapefruit.

I wished he would loosen his tie like the heroes in movies, but that wasn't Simon's style. So I did it for him. I moved to his side, pulled the knot loose from around his neck, and slipped his suit coat from his shoulders.

Simon bent to pick it up.

"Leave it," I said in as husky a voice as I could muster.

"It's my good coat."

I kicked it away from him. He was supposed to be falling all over me by now. Instead, he peeled my hand off his tie, retrieved his coat, and shook it out. "Will taking the time to undress properly put us off schedule, do you think?" His sarcasm was obvious.

I sighed. "Forget the schedule for tonight. You're the one who said to give it up."

He kissed me and touched my cheek. "Well, then, let's go upstairs."

I sagged. No spontaneity.

He calmly climbed the stairs like a shepherd trudging home. And I, lamb that I'd become, followed the shepherd.

What he didn't know was that I was a wolf inside. The lamb was betraying him.

He shut the door as if someone else might wander down

the hall to look in at us, and then he retreated to the bathroom. When he returned, he came into my arms, his expression unreadable. His kisses were wet on my mouth. I sank into him, twisted his shirt buttons from their holes, and stripped him of his shirt. This, at least, he allowed me to toss to the floor as we fell together on the bed.

I relished the feeling of his flesh, warm and soft against me. His chest was as smooth as a child's and rippled with muscles from his constant workouts. The smell of his cologne and a day's body odor enveloped my senses; I gulped it in. He paused. His eyes regarded me placidly while I maintained my role of a wolf devouring its prey. I wanted to fill myself with him. I wanted to drink in whatever form of love he could give me. Resentment still rippled beneath the surface, but it only fed my desire and guided my hands.

We were both panting by the time I rolled off him. I tried to scrub from my mind the guilt of tricking him, of mingling his life-giving force with the stranger's alien sperm, but it wouldn't leave me. While we stared at the flat white of the ceiling, I pictured the two testosterone armies fighting their way into an ovum and wondered which, if either, would win. And if I became pregnant, would I ever seek to know the winner?

He broke the silence. "I ought to buy grapefruit more often."

I laughed but cringed inside.

He craned his neck to look at the clock, then pushed himself upright and stood just in front of me, glistening with perspiration. "I really hate to say this, but I ..."

"The club, right?"

"I promised to meet Jim."

He and Jim had been friends for years before he met me.

It wasn't unusual for them to spend Friday nights together at the club.

His eyes looked slightly misty. "I wish I hadn't made plans. I feel like you've returned to me."

His simplistic view of life stabbed at me. Did he really consider our marriage repaired with one act of lust?

He said, "If you want, I'll call and cancel."

"No. Go on. You'd be bored stiff sitting around here, and I want a short nap anyway."

He emerged from the bathroom after a quick shower and bestowed a light kiss on my lips.

"Why don't you join your mother for supper? Jim and I are playing against our meal—winner buys."

"That's fine, but I'll just eat here by myself. I would have to call Mom and warn her I was coming. She seems put off when I drop in unannounced, let alone show up for supper without an invitation."

"Nonsense. She's always saying she doesn't see enough of you. I expect she's lonely eating by herself most nights. I'm sure that's why she has us over every Sunday."

"I hadn't thought of that." The image of her eating supper alone struck me with a chord of melancholy.

"You go on to sleep. I'll call her for you on my cell phone on my way to the club." He kissed me tenderly. "Later then, Love."

He calls everyone Love. I wish I had known that when we were dating. I thought it was a special endearment until our wedding reception when I first met his mother and heard him call her the same thing. But this night, hearing it struck me with guilt. *Love.*

Out of habit, I stayed in bed to give the sperm time to find their mark without battling gravity. I pulled the white linen duvet over me and nestled into my pillow. I loved the smell of clean sheets, and this had been Abigail's cleaning day. With a sigh, I released my guilt to dreams.

It was almost seven-thirty when I awoke. Shadows were drawing across the bedroom. In the echoing silence of the house, I was struck by how alone I was. In my head, Simon's words resounded. He considered our marriage restored, repaired like a broken watch. He had such faith in God, he thought a word or gesture could patch up our problems. Were we so comfortably rejoined that he could take leave of our bed for a racquetball game? How little he understood the workings of a woman.

I was being a hypocrite, yet those thoughts remained paramount in my mind anyway. I also knew the truth. I had tricked him. Perhaps an inkling of renewed love, or maybe just lust, had returned during the game, but the act had been for my own means.

I took a quick shower and headed over to my mother's house.

The entourage of yapping poodles bounced around my ankles.

Mom was glad to see me. "Carla, come in, dear. Simon phoned to say you'd be along for supper. I was beginning to worry about you."

The cloying smell of grease hung in the air. Fried chicken. After four years of Simon's salads and light entrées, I couldn't face Mom's greasy food. Instead of heading to the kitchen, I collapsed on the couch.

"Aren't you going to eat?" she asked.

"I don't think so. My stomach is upset."

"That's the thanks I get for cooking a big meal and keeping your plate warm for hours."

"You go on and eat, Mom. I'll keep you company."

She huffed off to the kitchen. "I ate ages ago. I know better than to change my schedule for anyone else these days. I had enough of that raising you up." Her voice came in strained tenor notes from the reaches of the oven. "I'll just turn the oven off and put your plate in the fridge."

If my head wasn't already aching with the thought of warring sperm in my uterus, my mother had pushed enough buttons to start a headache spinning.

"I have an idea," I called out. "Why don't I take you out to Decoupage for that dessert you crave so much, their Chocolate Divine?"

Mom returned to the family room, her mouth twisted in the petulant way she had of showing displeasure when her words were going to say otherwise. "I suppose that would be all right."

If nothing else, Mom loved me for my ability to treat her. Babette never had a dime to spare.

The restaurant was crowded with young people dressed to impress, middle-aged couples in their finest casual apparel, and a few elderly men seated in the corner laughing over mugs of beer.

Henry Lee half-bowed to us in the foyer. "Hello, Miss Carla. You bring mother come see us. Very nice. Very please. Come. I have table."

"I just don't understand why he works here instead of in a Chinese restaurant," my mother hissed over my shoulder.

My mother kept everybody in their boxes, behind their lines. No wonder I'd had to break out and accomplish things in my life. Her mind-set was a prison.

Henry Lee led us between linen-covered tables toward a quiet corner. Eclectic photos of flower children from the seventies laughed down at us. He pulled out a chair and bowed with oriental grace. I slid into my seat and bestowed my most dazzling smile upon him. My mother harrumphed and seated herself.

With Mom settled into her layers of chocolate cake, syrup, and whipped cream, I ordered cold poached salmon and asparagus tips.

"I thought you weren't feeling well," Mom said between mouthfuls.

"The fresh air helped." Meaning the lack of grease-scum fog.

I was poised over my first forkful of salmon when Kevin Baxter sauntered up. "Carla, can it really be you?"

I looked up and caught my breath. Dark hair, masculine chiseled face, wide shoulders. He was even better looking than I remembered. "Kevin! How are you? It's been years. Have a seat."

Kevin had been my high school sweetheart. Graduation had been our last date. We'd agreed to go our separate ways after that because we had both set high goals for our lives and didn't want a mere romance to hinder us. Many a night I'd pined for him during my dateless phases in college. Many boring days before meeting Simon, I had sat at my desk and dwelt on where Kevin and I would be if we had followed our hearts instead of our heads.

"And, Mrs. Docker," he said, "what a surprise. I'd join you, but I can't. I'm with family tonight." He turned to me. "Maybe I can call you?"

"Sure, I'd like that."

In keeping with his old familiar ways, he gave my mother a slight hug and strode away.

My mother picked up her fork again. "Now there's the man you should have married. What a nice boy he is. No airs about him. I bet you would have had a dozen babies with him in your bed."

I stared after him. What could I say to that?

Six

After I deposited Mom back at her apartment, I watched an old rerun on the movie channel, then crawled into bed. Alone. Simon was still out.

There, in the wee hours of Saturday, I lay deep in a dreamworld where inklings of my old high school romance collided with the sperm still swarming in my uterus and created sleep-images of a baby whose face resembled Kevin's. How long I held that dream to my breast I can't recall, but the image developed like a Polaroid film slowly growing from a blur to clarity. The face of the baby, the feel of it in my arms, came to me in detail when Simon's weight fell on his side of the bed, shifted the mattress, and brought me to a confused consciousness. Which was real: Simon or the baby?

He turned on his pillow to face me and startled at my wide-open glaring eyes but recovered quickly enough to kiss me lightly. "I didn't mean to wake you."

He hadn't been drinking, or if he had, only mildly. I won't say he never drank, but since he'd gained religion two years earlier, he'd avoided it.

With Kevin fresh in my mind, offering me respite from my boring marriage, I began to wonder just how Simon could spend so much time with his buddies. Perhaps I was naive. Perhaps he had a friend I wasn't aware of—a female friend.

I'd been so fraught with timing our sex and producing a child, I hadn't contemplated the lure of a lithe, willing female body unhindered by schedules. In all my hours of dissatisfaction, I hadn't really considered infidelity for either of us.

I lay cloaked in the guilt of holding Kevin's dream-child and the medicinal infidelity of using the sperm donor. Yet I dared to think of Simon being equally culpable in his own sinful acts. I looked at him with new eyes. "Kiss me," I said.

"I just did."

"That wasn't a kiss. It was a peck."

He rolled over and mashed his lips into mine. I wrapped my arms around him and tried to keep him on me.

He pushed himself away. "What's gotten into you today?"

"Hormones."

"What, you're in treatment again?"

"I was being facetious. Don't you want to make love?"

"It's the middle of the night."

"So?"

He kissed me again, a heavy smack of dry lips against mine, and flopped back against his pillow. "I'm tired. Good night."

Doubt raised its spiteful head and chuckled at my disbelief. It was supposed to be *me* who didn't want *Simon*. I wondered when the shift had occurred.

I had to see if his kisses tasted different, or if he carried the scent of another woman on his flesh. I straddled his waist and nibbled at his mouth.

"You've forgotten your quota rule. More than once depletes the sperm count, remember?"

"It was so good this afternoon. Don't you want it again?"

"I told you, I'm tired."

I forced another kiss on him but sensed nothing other

than his aggravation. If there was a woman's scent left on him, he wasn't going to let me detect it. He smelled more like food than anything. Something spicy. Barbecue sauce.

In one sudden move, he rolled me over, lay on top of me, and kissed me fiercely. "You're making me crazy," he hissed. "You've left me cold for months, and now you attack me twice in one day. What game are you playing?"

"No game," I wheezed beneath his weight.

He regarded me in the dark of the room, the moonlight giving life to his shadowy features. His eyes pierced mine in search of what secrets lay within.

He grunted and rolled back to his pillow.

I stared at the ceiling and fell asleep waiting for his snores.

My mother called me Sunday morning at ten, whispering like a schoolgirl in a locker room full of eavesdroppers. "Has Simon left for church yet?"

"Yes. Thirty minutes ago. He attends Sunday school before the service. Why?"

"Guess who just called for you?"

"Publishers Clearing House, I hope."

"Ha! Like you need more money."

I paced through the front rooms, the cordless phone clutched to my ear. "Everyone needs more money."

"Which is why you ought to spread more of yours around."

"Let's not get into *that* again."

"Whatsoever you do for the least of my people—"

"The rich get richer."

"You act like you had no religion growing up. We might not have been big into Bible reading and whatnot, but we took you to church, didn't we? We taught you to do unto others."

"I don't need to hear this, Mom."

"I can't say a religious word to you, but you manage to sleep in the same bed as Simon, and he evangelizes every person he meets."

Mom's speech was not about religion, and she knew it. She had an irrational belief that the riches of the world should be spread equally among everyone, more specifically among her and Babette and whatever charities tickled her fancy, not ours.

Then a new idea occurred to me. I thought of her praying for me. Maybe she did have more faith in God than I gave her credit for. Maybe Simon's increasing faith had affected her more than me. How had she managed to reconcile with God, but I couldn't?

Simon's Christianity was understandable. It had built steadily over the past few years. When we first married, he seemed totally indifferent to God and righteousness, but he'd been in a car accident shortly after we married. Death had loomed with a new reality, and he had reconsidered the purpose of his life and the idea of salvation and heaven. The experience sparked an earnestness that had grown to the point of evangelization. He preached to me and everybody else about Jesus' love and compassion. I hadn't followed him down the path. God had done the unthinkable: he had taken my father from me. I had been closer to my father than to anyone on earth. When he died, I felt like a castoff, a sole survivor alone on the sea.

I hadn't thought much about God up to that point in my life, but people's platitudes after my daddy's death built up hatred inside of me. *He's better off where he is now*, they said. *He's in God's hands now.* Friends meant the words as comfort, but to me they were like darts hitting a black bull's-eye of emptiness, the center of my faithlessness. I tried praying a few times, to see if it helped, to see if God would answer in a burning bush or something, but the only answer I got was the ache in my broken heart. God didn't have time for me, and what little belief I'd been led to as a child frittered away to nothingness. I didn't want to hear about God and his love.

Maybe Daddy's death had the opposite effect on Mom. Maybe she felt vulnerable as a widow and had developed a closer relationship with Jesus than she'd expressed to me as a child. If she had, I didn't want her pushing it on me. "Simon respects how I feel about God. We agree to disagree. Besides, Simon has no qualms about us having money. He donates where he sees fit, but he doesn't think we ought to give everything away."

She snorted in my ear. I could imagine the twist of her lips. "I'm certainly not—oh!" I could hear frustration in her pause. "That's not why I called. Now you've ruined my whole mood. I was all excited about telling you that Kevin called."

My dream-child wavered before me. "Mom, I'm married. Kevin is just an old friend."

"He didn't have to be. If you'd listened to me, you'd be married to him instead of Simon." I absorbed my surroundings in the instant it took Mom to disparage my life, a glance that reaffirmed that everything was as it should be—home. A cardinal perched on the split-rail fence in the backyard, warily eyeing Simon's miniature gazebo birdfeeder. My roses, my comfort in life, splayed along the rails, the blossoms a celebration of my quest for a child. I could anticipate the smell of the perfect yellow and red blossoms, if I thought about them hard enough. The grass stood freshly cropped by the lawn crew. I thought of the statues standing regally at the entrances and the fountain that spouted a steady gurgle of

water by the front walk. I lived in an impressive home. I
loved it. Putting off marriage, going to college, those had been
good decisions.

"Oh, Mom, if I'd married Kevin, I'd be broke and living in
some little Twinkie of a house in Beaver Trails with three
snot-nosed kids pulling on me." Something twisted in me as I
said it. I would take three babies in any form I could get
them, but Mom's design for me would have had me following
Babette's path: married straight out of high school and pregnant in a year. Mom never appreciated what it took to get
where I was. As much as I wanted a child, at no point would
I have chosen to redo my life into Babette's.

"Don't be so quick to say that would be worse. I'm your
mother, Carla; I can read you like a book. The path you have
chosen has made you rich, but you aren't happy."

She didn't even pick up on my slight of Babette. Or maybe
she did but didn't say so. I tried to act as if I were above my
mother's spite, but inside I wasn't. Her words had been eating at me for years. She never seemed to have a good thing to
say about Simon. Lately I found myself echoing her words in
my thoughts, noticing all the things about him that bugged
me and none of the things I loved.

"I didn't mean Kevin's kids wouldn't be great." How could
they not? Hadn't I dream-rocked one the night before? "I
meant if we'd married, I wouldn't have gone to college, and
neither would he."

"I didn't go to college, and I can't recall you ever suffering
for anything."

Money. It always came back to money. I gave up. "So
what did Kevin want?"

"You, of course."

"And—"

"I told him you weren't here, that you throw perfectly good money away eating out every Sunday morning at Alonzo's Bagel House with that snooty Gina Adams."

I wanted to ask if she remembered that I'd thrown away perfectly good money taking her out for dessert on Friday, but I bit my tongue. "Couldn't you have just given him my phone number?"

"And chance having Simon answer the phone? What are you thinking?"

"He's nothing to me, Mom."

"Right. Tell me, does Simon know about him?"

I sighed. What was there for Simon to know?

The same thought coursed through my mind again when I stood in front of the bagel shop, my hand frozen momentarily on the door handle.

There's nothing to know came my internal response. If Kevin had notions in his head, they were all his. I certainly couldn't be held liable for a dream about him. That had been nothing more than conjurings from days of love-struck girlhood.

I swept into the bagel shop, my pumps clicking rhythmically against the red tile floor, slid into the booth farthest from the door, and opened a newspaper left there. The entire front of Alonzo's was glass, so I still had full view of the customers entering. I would see Kevin arriving if he came looking for me.

My friend Gina arrived a few minutes after me. No one in high school would ever have foreseen the two of us becoming friends. She's not my type at all. She's one of the country-club girls. I'm not. Back in high school she was a cheerleader. I was, well, smart. After four years of indifference to one another in high school, we were assigned to the same quad in our college dorm and became buddies simply as two girls from the same town facing the world on our own for the first time. Neither of us had changed. I'm still living with the basic boring looks I was born with. She still has legs fit for a stage and perfect L'Oreal red hair #77, which looks nice in the window of the travel agency where she plans out rich people's vacations.

She entered Alonzo's full of smiles and hugged two other friends before reaching my back table.

I nodded across the room at Nancy the Waitress, a big-breasted teenager who turned many a man's eye. She was a good waitress. Gina and I had been ordering the same thing for so long, Nancy never had to ask for our order anymore. A wave across the room, and breakfast was on its way.

"We're in hiding today, are we?" teased Gina as she leaned over and pressed her cheek to mine. Gina loves affectations.

I folded the newspaper and set it on the floor. "Alonzo doesn't have a table in here that could hide a mouse, let alone two women." It was true in terms of absent shadows in which to hide. Sunlight gleamed off the yellow counters and dappled the leaves of ferns that dangled from hanging brass pots. The light green walls caught sunbeams and cast them back at the tables and booths.

But two fresh-faced women easily blended in with the dozen other slim-waisted young people nibbling at platters of fresh fruits and bagels. In the corner, we were as unnoticeable as wallflowers.

"Then why are we sitting way back here? You must have some terrific secret to share. What is it?"

I laughed. "Me? Not a secret in the world. Just ask my mother. My life is so boring, she has to invent stories about me to tell her friends."

"That's true. With her trumpet, whatever the secret, it's bound to make the morning news."

It was one thing for me to think ill of my mother. I could profess that she got on my nerves and still know in my heart that I loved her. It was quite another thing for Gina to sit in front of me and insult her. I wouldn't stand for denigrating comments. "My mother is a lot of things, but she's not a gossip." Not in the sense of spreading ill words against anyone, at least.

My mother's reputation is a sore point between us. Every Wednesday, Mom plays Bingo with her old-fogy friends. Gina still holds it against her that one Wednesday night Mom inadvertently announced that Gina was engaged to Mister Executive himself, Dick Snyder. The mistake was innocent enough. Anyone listening to Gina would have concluded they were all but married. Unfortunately, one of Mom's old fogies was related to someone who was friends with Dick. When word got back to Dick, he dropped poor Gina.

She, in turn, dropped me for a bit after that, finding excuses to break our engagements. Then she caught sight of Simon's partner at the law firm, Greg. Personally, I think he's a big turnoff. He has a honker the size of my foot. He wears his hair long, pulled back in a ponytail at the office, but out in public he lets it swish around his face and shoulders, which is better because it distracts from his nose. Gina thinks he looks like a movie star. Go figure. Truth is, he has money, with potential to inherit millions from his daddy, and that's enough to make Gina forgive a few warts. Hopes of me fixing her up for dinner with Greg overrode any ill feelings she had toward Mom, or at least toward me.

I figured she would ask about him any minute. It had

been at least five days since she'd asked me to set them up. I was biding my time.

She pouted over mention of my mother. "Let's not talk about unpleasant things."

Granted, my mother could, at times, be numbered among unpleasant things, but if we scratched the whole list, what, I wondered, did that leave open for conversation?

Nancy padded over and set our plates before us. Decaffeinated coffee with a warm honey bagel for me and water with a small fruit platter for my friend, Miss Perfect Figure.

Gina had a topic prepared. "I talked to Betsy last night."

I could think of only one Betsy. "Betsy Marke Sable?" Betsy was not the type of person Gina associated with, even casually. Large, as in triple X, with an equally large blonde hairdo.

"Yes, her," Gina said. "Plans for our twenty-year class reunion are under way. She asked me to assist her on the committee."

Ah. Betsy wasn't popular, but she was too smart not to be included on the student council. The principal had insisted. So now she had the honor of organizing the reunion committee.

I swallowed a delectable bite of bagel. "I thought you said we were going to talk about something pleasant."

"I thought you'd be excited."

"About publicly announcing I've hit midlife?"

"There's more."

Kevin's image came to me. "I can't possibly guess what."

"Well, you know, it's the class president who's in charge of all this, right?"

"Of course."

"Well, he's here. In town."

My head throbbed. "You mean Kevin? I know. I saw him Friday night."

"So that's the secret! I bet your mother is having a field day."

"It's no secret. I took Mom out to Decoupage for dessert, and he was there."

"And what does Simon say?"

"Not a thing. I take Mom out all the time."

"Not funny. I meant about Kevin being here."

"I guess if he knew, he'd say it's a free world, and we'll share the oxygen."

Gina smirked. "So you didn't tell him. I think he ought to go pray over that Bible of his to ward off the Spirit of Christmas Past."

I admit, I should never have told even my closest friend what my best Christmas gift ever had been, but lonely young girls with too much champagne manage to divulge the secrets of their souls. In the wee hours of a cold February night, she and I sat with a fire casting the light of dancing flames around the quiet of a ski lodge. We reminisced about many things, but the conversation culminated with me confiding my most intimate Christmas gift—losing my virginity to Kevin in that very same ski lodge during Christmas break. I will never forget that night with him. In hindsight, I wish it had never happened, and moreover, I wish I hadn't told Gina about it. I was single when I told her. I hadn't foreseen a time when it would be a big deal. Now I've learned better, but it was too late to rescind the confidence. The best route with Gina was to act nonchalant.

I shrugged. "The past is the past."

"And the future is the future."

We chorused, "And today is God's present to you." It was Simon's favorite saying.

Immediately, I regretted making fun of my husband. Simon's intense faith irked me at times, but in my gut, even with my anger at God for taking my daddy, I envied Simon. He stood on the inside of some special realm of knowledge, and I was an outsider. I didn't share Simon's faith, but I really never intended to ridicule his beliefs. As in most things, I gained power by deriding what I didn't share. I felt crass for sharing such poor behavior with Gina. There was guilt enough coursing through me over the insemination without adding to the list. I owed it to Simon at least to maintain a respectable attitude toward him in public. It was no wonder Gina and my mother both figured I would jump ship and run straight into Kevin's arms. I was hardly behaving like an adoring wife.

I sobered and met Gina's eyes. They were twinkling like the sea on a summer day at the thought of Kevin and me.

Mom and Gina both suspected something rising between Kevin and me. She and Mom in agreement. What an oddity.

Were they seeing something I wasn't?

Seven

After eating, I left Gina with some friends at another table and headed to my car. I wondered why Kevin hadn't shown up. I hadn't wanted him to, but I'd expected it.

Outside in the parking lot, there he was, leaning against my shiny red Porsche.

"Not hard figuring out which car is yours," he called out to me. "You must've begged your old man for this hot rod every day since the day I met you. Glad to see he finally gave in."

"He didn't have much choice. He passed away, and he couldn't take it with him."

Kevin didn't laugh. He winced. "I'm sorry. I didn't know. He was a great guy."

I nodded as I approached. "I know."

"Can we go for a spin? I think I begged for it as much as you!"

I tensed. The car was my identity, singularly. Simon didn't even ride in it anymore. Actually, he didn't *want* to ride in it because it didn't have air-conditioning, and it always smelled slightly of oil and something foreign, which, of course, it was.

To take Kevin into my car would be an intimate act, a stepping back in time to when we were considered a couple.

Kevin wasn't in any hurry. He just leaned there, his hip

resting against the fender. Even while he was standing still, there was energy about him—the same as he'd had in high school—not a nervous tension but a physical essence of effortless motivation and pure confidence. He exuded the promise of a bright future, not exclusionary but encompassing, welcoming strangers to adhere to him.

Nostalgia welled in me. I walked to the passenger door, key in hand.

He placed his hands on my shoulders, his voice deep with meaning. "Carla."

My insides turned to jelly. I had forgotten the weight of my name on his lips, the way he could caress me with mere words, not just verbal, but written as well. We had exchanged letters from one campus to the other our freshman year, as friends straining to hold on to the web of our love, but exploring our new worlds, gloating over our successes until we crawled free of each other's web and set out independently. His prose lived forever in the archive of my mind.

"I've really missed you," he said, words that sounded too simple to convey the emotion caught in his throat and welling in his eyes.

"Now that's a man for you," I replied. "Leaves town for twenty years, then comes back and says he's missed his girl."

He dropped his hands. "Does sound canned, huh? I have missed you, though. Look." He pulled out his wallet and flipped it open to a worn photo. There we stood, arm in arm, grinning, me in an awful beige dress that made me look like a stick, and him in a rented tux, looking miserably uncomfortable.

"I can't believe you still have that picture in your wallet."

He shoved the wallet into his jeans' pocket. "You were something special."

"But Kevin—"

He laughed. "I'm kidding. I haven't really been carrying it around for twenty years. When I got to thinking about the reunion, I started going through my old scrapbooks and decided to bring it with me. Kind of encapsulates the whole reunion thing, huh?"

"A night of bad-looking clothes, a lot of toes getting stepped on, and worried parents watching clocks? Ugh. I hope it's not going to be that kind of night again."

"I don't know about the clothes or the toes, but I don't think our parents will care how late we're out."

I snickered. "Don't be too sure." Mom would have every detail ready for Bingo night. But he was right. I wasn't a teenager anymore. No one could tell me what to do.

I unlocked the passenger door for him, wondering where this mistake was leading me.

I settled behind the wheel and brought the engine roaring to life. With Kevin there, carrying me back to my teenage years, images of my daddy lit my heart at the sound. I sucked up the emotions and blinked away a stray tear.

I felt self-conscious with Kevin opposite me, thinking of Simon's superior attitude about handling a car. I had begun to think that all men judged a woman's driving ability. But Kevin was relaxed, one arm stretched out, hung on the back of my seat, his face filled with expectation.

I smiled as I shifted into gear. There's satisfaction in mastering such a compact machine. It responds to every pulse of fuel, every twist of steering, with acumen. Its power endows vigor.

In the early days, I thought my discomfort over Simon's presence in my car was merely new-love nerves, but later I realized he actually diminished the ecstasy of the ride by making me feel less capable than I was, so perfect was he. I invited him into my car less and less, until it became the norm for us to ride together in his, reserving mine for my personal, singular use.

Kevin wasn't at all like Simon. He became a soul mate. As we sped down the road, I could tell he rejoiced in my ability.

I headed toward our old high school, a nice, long drive to the far side of town.

"How is your family?" I asked.

"Fine. Mom and Dad are in their seventies now and slowing down, but both getting along. Dad still insists on planting that garden of his."

"He still owns that land out in Lincolnton?"

"Yup. You'd think he'd move out there, but no. Mom likes being in the city. Works for them, I guess. They've been married forty-five years. I can't argue with that."

What would Simon be like forty-one years from now? What would Kevin be like? "Wow. Forty-five years. I can't imagine."

"Me either. I only made it ten, and it seemed an eternity."

There it was, the burning question out in the open. "So you're not married now?"

"Divorced for three years."

I swallowed. Divorced the year after I had married. My proclamation to my mother thumped in my brain. "Any kids?"

"Two. A boy, eight, and a girl, five."

Two kids, not three. And most definitely they wouldn't be snot nosed.

"How about you?"

My heart raced with the engine. "Married. No kids."

What could he say: *Too bad? Wish you weren't married? Will you consider leaving your husband for me?*

"Tell me about him."

Summing up the enemy? "Simon is forty-two, tall, thin, smart. He's a tax attorney."

Kevin only nodded.

We'd pulled up to a red light. A huge truck equipped with tree-cutting equipment rattled to a standstill in the next lane. Across its black door, letters had been scrawled in white paint by some unsteady hand: *We cut trees.* People like those make me crazy. Why didn't they take the money from one job and make their truck look professional? I couldn't wait to get away from it. I rocked the car back and forth, playing with gas and clutch, willing the light to turn green.

"So tell me about your life," Kevin said.

Here it was, the reality of attending a reunion flaring in my face. Condensing twenty years of life into a sentence or two: *How do I define myself? With work?* "I live on Lake Norman, and I work a lot. I'm plant manager at Wymans' west facility." I knew without looking that the name wouldn't register. The company was fairly new. "We make boxes. You?"

"I'm kind of between things right now."

My glance at him was full of questions.

He continued. "I was in a pediatric practice in Richmond, but I had a conflict I couldn't resolve, so I'm thinking of joining a new practice in Virginia Beach."

I glanced at him and back at the twists in the road, savored the thrill of the curves, then tapped the gas pedal to send us shooting off in a straight stretch.

Kevin had never mentioned medical school in our youth. I looked at him again. He was wearing a Hard Rock Café shirt. He'd never had—and still didn't look to have—the puffed-up airs of many of the doctors in my social circle.

"So you're a pediatrician?"

"Yes." He chuckled. "I wouldn't have believed it myself. I just developed a love for biology in college, which led to med school. During my internship, I was so drawn to the pediatric ward that I kept on with it. I wanted to get into surgery, but Heidi ... well, I finally joined a practice."

I gathered that Heidi was the ex-wife. He must have loved her a lot to make such a drastic change from surgery to a practice. "I guess it wasn't enough," I said.

"What?"

I could have thrashed myself. Sometimes I speak before thinking how personal I'm getting. It was too late now. "Giving up the aim of surgery to join a pediatric practice. Since you divorced, I'm guessing it must not have been enough to satisfy her."

The color left his face. "No. There was more to it."

I felt like I'd kicked a wounded dog. "So why not reconsider and do what it takes to get into surgery now?"

Only the whirring of the engine filled the hollowness as I waited for his response, a response that he may have been pondering a while, yet hadn't admitted aloud. "Actually, I've been thinking about it."

I nodded. I'd said something he'd needed to hear. My face flushed with warmth. "Good."

"But for the next six months or so, I'll be here in Charlotte. My grandfather died and left me executor of his estate. I figure since I'm between things anyway, I may as well devote myself to it full time. And being here will make it easier to work on the reunion."

"Oh, not Grandpa Norris? I wish I'd known. I'd have attended his funeral. He was a great man. Made the best barbecue I've ever had."

"That's for sure."

It seemed ridiculous after I'd said it, but that's how people became cataloged in my mind, by the odd quirks or extravagances that made them stand out. Even now, if I knew a famous painter, I'd likely remember his taste in wine or the kind of shoes he wore instead of his paintings.

I'd spent little time in Grandpa Norris's presence, but a lot of time at his lakeshore home, swimming and skiing with Kevin. The Norris estate was more than a house. It was a ranch. I dwelt on images of the old man, a Carolina cowboy, seated on his chestnut quarterhorse with a genuine ten-gallon Stetson hat shading his long face. Grandpa Norris rode his gelding all over his ranch. He would come at a gallop down to the shore of the lake to check on the two of us. He had owned at least two hundred acres with cattle on much of it. It had been well outside of town back then. Now his ranch stood in the midst of magnificent subdivisions of million-dollar houses. A gold mine.

I thought of all the implications of having Kevin in town for six months, maybe longer, but pushed the ideas away. "So you're executor, huh? Remind me to give you one of Simon's business cards."

"I might need his help," Kevin replied.

I pulled into the school parking lot and stopped. The place was deserted except for two young boys playing basketball in the court some distance away. The thumping of their ball reached us out of sync with the action.

Kevin followed my gaze. "Sometimes I wish I was like them, still young with all of life ahead of me."

"If given the chance to live it over again, would you take a different path?"

He looked at me. "That would mean not having Ruby and Matt."

I correctly assumed they were his kids.

He turned to look straight ahead at the school. "I wouldn't change anything that would erase their existence. I would just do it better."

I revved up the car and jerked it into gear. I had said the same thing that morning, but it was difficult hearing it from him. Maybe I'd been wrong. Maybe now, with the reality of an alternate path, I would give anything to rewrite history, to live in that Twinkie house and make those two children my own. Ours.

And then I remembered the sperm, which had most certainly met with the ovum by now, and realized I had already done that, but with the future. I had chanced everything—my husband, my mother, my sister—to make up for earlier life decisions. I was rewriting the future with my own hand.

A few miles down the road, Kevin's voice cut into my thoughts. "I hope Simon will share you."

My eyes flashed a big *What?* at him.

"I can't handle this reunion all by myself. I was hoping you'd help me."

Meaning more time spent together. I left the sentence hanging there, my mind whirling as fast as the tires against the pavement.

Eight

I downplayed the whole reunion thing when I told Simon about it.

By the time I returned home, he had changed from his Sunday suit into shorts. He was standing at the kitchen counter with the television tuned into a golf game, while he cut up vegetables for salad. We habitually ate salad for lunch on Sunday to make up for whatever fattening supper Mom would force on us that evening at her house.

I propped myself on a barstool at the counter and sipped at a glass of grapefruit juice.

"What exciting news did Gina have this morning?"

He asked me that every week. Most Sundays I could honestly tell him we'd spent the entire hour talking about nothing of any significance. "Actually, she had some interesting news for a change. A committee is forming to plan our twenty-year high school reunion."

"Sounds like loads of fun."

"I've been asked to help."

"Of course you have. You've lived here forever. You know the comings and goings of everyone. And your mother has the nose for hounding out the most convicted wanderlust students of your class."

He sounded like Gina, making Mom sound like a snoop.

Just because my mother had friends all over town and always knew what was going on didn't make her a snoop.

"The meetings are Tuesday nights."

"Okay. You'll probably enjoy it. I'll be at the club anyway."

He was so pompous, he wouldn't even suspect a fling between Kevin and me.

Suspicions over his long evenings flashed fresh in my mind ... every Tuesday, sometimes Fridays, knowing I would never go with him. Maybe it was me who should be worried. Then a new thought crossed my mind. Just because he thought he had the upper hand on the fertility issue, did he think I also had to ask permission before I went somewhere? He certainly didn't ask my permission before making plans. I suddenly felt like an underdog who had to compromise with him. If only he knew ...

"I wasn't asking your permission. I was informing you."

He stopped chopping to evaluate my expression, then chopped again. "Okay. So you've informed me. I don't remember ever taking issue with anything you wanted to do. No big deal."

Short memory.

Supper at Mom's was the typical Southern fare of my youth, unaltered by the health awareness of modern America: meat-loaf, mashed potatoes creamed with mayonnaise, and a batch of collard greens. Meals without imagination. Mom never developed an awareness of dietary health despite Dad's death by heart attack. I figured it was guilt. If she had changed her diet after his demise, it would have pointed a finger at her cooking as the cause of death. On the other hand, not chang-ing her diet pretty much left the evidence on the table.

Simon took only a forkful of meatloaf from the platter and

ate his potatoes without butter. The collards had been cooked with fatback. He wouldn't touch them.

I grew up with Mom's cooking. It was thick with grease and far too heavy to suit me anymore, but today I wanted it. I succumbed to the unhealthiness of it because a part of me needed to come home, to turn the clock back to when I'd been an uncomplicated child.

My mouth was full of meatloaf doused in ketchup when Mom gave her irritating *I know something you don't know* tilt of her head and peered at Simon. "Isn't it exciting about Kevin being back in town?"

So much for her previous concern to keep it quiet. Maybe Gina and Simon were right about her gossipy nature.

Simon either ignored Mom's look or had never learned her brazen body language. He had his eyes and right hand trained on a glass of water and kept chewing his potatoes as if they were shoe leather. He didn't respond.

"You do know who Kevin is, don't you?" Mom continued.

Simon came to and swallowed. "Are you speaking to me? I'm sorry. No, I don't."

Mom switched to her cutesy look: eyes squinting and fake, pressed smile. "Why, Carla, you didn't tell your own beloved husband about your first love?"

I finished chewing and licked my lips. "Why on earth would he want to hear about childhood boyfriends?"

"Because Kevin was your true love."

"*Was.* Past tense."

"I would never have dreamed of keeping a secret like that from your father."

"You didn't have to. Dad was your only boyfriend."

She put her fork down. "You make that sound like an insult. Being true to one man was a virtue in my day."

"Times change."

Her lips pursed. She let my words settle.

I couldn't look at her face when she screwed it all up like that, so I looked at Simon. I could see him calculating how much effort it would take to finish off his potatoes. It filled me with momentary affection for him, knowing he suffered through this Sunday supper for my sake with little complaint. Mom's meals were like a hair shirt he wore for Christian penance—spending time with one's mother was the right thing to do, in his eyes. Since his mother lived hundreds of miles away, he made do with mine. I left him to his suffering and looked back at Mom.

I could have kept her anger broiling for another hour. I knew how to pull all the right strings. But it wouldn't be worth the effort of clearing the air later. Instead, I plucked a homemade biscuit from the covered basket in the middle of the table. "Chill, Mom. I'm not you. That's Babette's role. I'm the other daughter, the one full of faults."

She couldn't argue with self-denigration. She grumbled and took a biscuit for herself.

Simon had been paying more attention than I thought. Later that evening back home, when I carried a bowl of popcorn around the kitchen bar to the family-room sofa, where he sat staring at the previews on a rented video, he said, "So tell me about Kevin."

I felt like I'd been shot. My chest was suddenly hollow. I managed to set the popcorn on the table without spilling it and flopped on the couch facing him. "What about him?"

"Was he really your true love?"

"At the time."

"So what happened?"

Rain began spattering the deck. It turned torrential in the seconds that stretched between us. Were we making small talk here, or was he actually concerned there might be another man in my life, some pressing suitor to challenge his position? "We mutually agreed we both wanted to pursue college degrees."

"And that was it? You loved this guy, but you left for college without a backward glance?"

"We wrote letters and called, but you know how it is. Campus distractions, time goes by. We met other people. We didn't want to hinder our success by staying tied to each other. We were smarter than that."

He reached for the popcorn. "Smarter than that?"

"Come on, Simon. I certainly wasn't your first girlfriend."

"No." He crunched a mouthful and gauged my emotions with that steady gaze of his. "Just my last."

The words hung there. How could he always tell where my thoughts had been? Could Simon tell I'd been suspecting him of having a girlfriend? More likely, he was pressing guilt upon me to keep me in my place with Kevin.

"Oh, look, the movie's starting," I said and scooped out some popcorn. "I can't hear it over the rain. Turn it up."

The reunion meeting Tuesday night was held at Betsy's house in the suburbs, a little brick traditional on a quiet cul-de-sac. The front room was overdone in pink country furniture and white lace doilies. The air reverberated with chatter. Of the dozen or so people milling around, the men were dressed casually, except Peter Carter who had never, even in high school, worn anything but a suit, and John Howding, who appeared to be wearing the same overalls he'd worn to graduation. The women were laughable. One had dressed too youthfully, as if she had borrowed her outfit from her daughter's closet. Two others looked dowdier than Miss Sprain, the school librarian.

Gina wasn't surprised to see me arrive. She gave me her knowing little smirk. "I wonder who convinced you to help out."

"Civic duty," I replied.

"Now that's a laugh."

"Put me up there beside Betsy Ross and Mother Teresa."

"You're so quaint, Carla."

"Quaint? Weird, eccentric, unorthodox, strange, bizarre, different. But not quaint. This house is quaint, though."

"I'd never argue vocabulary with the valedictorian. You win."

"Chicken."

Betsy stepped up, the same double-chinned, round-faced girl she'd been in kindergarten. "No chicken, I'm afraid. I'm serving shrimp cocktail and wine. I thought everyone would have eaten supper before coming, Carla."

"Gina insisted you would have fried chicken," I said with a straight face.

Betsy is wonderful to pick on. She has never in all the years I've known her picked up on a joke.

"Oh my," she said, hand clutched to chest. "I must have something I can serve you. I'll order some chicken from the deli down the road."

"Okay," I said.

Gina caught Betsy's arm and gave me the evil eye. "She's kidding, Bets." Gina likes taking pity on people like Betsy. It makes her feel important.

Betsy forced a laugh and scuttled off to answer the door-bell. For all her weight, she moved like a lithe nymph. She teetered across the floor on her tiptoes, this huge woman, as if there were a ballerina hidden under the mounds of flesh.

Kevin was at the door. He entered, and the cluster of guests fell quiet.

"Oh goody, Kevin, you're here," chirped Betsy. "Can everyone find a seat?"

Seeing him in the doorway flooded me with a warm, dizzy feeling.

He came toward me, but I passed through the nearest doorway to hide in Betsy's cow-and-pig-decorated kitchen. After peering into three cabinets, I found glassware—something to keep my hands busy. I carried a tumbler of water back to the pink-flowered sofa and placed it carefully on a crocheted coaster. At least I hoped it was a coaster.

Kevin was already seated across from me in a pink armchair. "No wine?"

A reply leaped to my mind. *Can't drink wine. I might be carrying a stranger's baby.* I imagined Kevin's eyes popping out at the news. Would he ever speak to me again if he learned what I'd done? Instead, I said, "Gina has turned me into a health-food freak."

Betsy gave me an odd look. I guess she didn't think fried chicken fell into the health-food category.

We spent the next hour debating dates and sites for the big event. We finally settled on three possibilities, pending availability, and ended the meeting by reviewing the class list and narrowing the classmates with unknown whereabouts down to fifty-two. I copied their names and stuffed the paper in my purse. My mother would love the challenge.

Gina pressed a kiss to my cheek and left quickly. She had a date, she said. I wondered who it was that I hadn't heard about it. I was tempted to run after her to get details, but there was a greater temptation. I was ready, after watching him all evening, to speak with Kevin, alone.

I held back as everyone else was leaving. When Kevin approached me, I couldn't fight the flutter invading my body. I fumbled for an intelligent comment. "So you never did say. Where are you staying? At your parents'?"

"No. On the ranch. Everything I need is within reach that way."

"Sure."

We bid Betsy good-bye and stepped outside to the hushed lamp-lit dimness of the slumbering neighborhood. The other committee members faded out to their own cars.

"So what do you say to a cup of coffee?" he asked. "That wouldn't go against your health-food diet, would it?"

"Only if it's served in a doughnut shop."

"No doughnuts, I promise. Follow me?"

How could I resist? Simon was out with *his* friends. I could certainly go out, too. It was a chance to show Simon I still had some independence left in me. I still had rights as an individual.

After a few miles, I figured out where Kevin was leading me—to Grandpa Norris's ranch. If we'd been in the same car, I would have touched his arm and shook my head no. At least I think I would have. That's what kept pounding in my head. I wasn't ready to jump into a relationship with him. I was married. I was trying to get pregnant. I had things to sort out, and Kevin was complicating them. I only wanted coffee and a chat. But there he was, ahead of me in a different car. Short of flashing my lights, beeping my horn, swerving around him like some crazed television stuntman, all I could do was turn and head home or continue on to his destination.

I didn't head home.

I turned into the driveway—a long graveled lane thick with trees for the first twenty yards—and looked ahead at the house, lit up and waiting as if he had left earlier that evening with this decision firmly in his mind, this expectation of bringing me home.

Just as I pulled up behind him and turned off the car, my cell phone rang.

I almost ignored it. I expected it to be Simon, tuned in as he seemed to be on my mental processes, but I'm a victim of technology and a woman of the world. I answered it.

It was Phyllis. She was waiting at the house for me.

Nine

I gave my regrets to Kevin and asked for a rain check. I could hardly leave an out-of-town guest sitting on my doorstep.

When I got home, Phyllis's old blue Toyota Camry was in the driveway. I had imagined her driving something newer, sportier, but I should have known better. In finances, Phyllis was practical. She'd had to be. While I was still playacting maturity as chairman of French Club in junior high, she'd begun carrying the burden of family finances. Her mother was incapable, her father gone.

The car was the only sign of visitors. Phyllis and Sabrina were nowhere in sight. I unlocked the front door and walked through the house, flicking on lights and wondering if she could have entered somehow on her own. It wouldn't have surprised me. Phyllis was a myriad of personalities with untold secret talents.

The house appeared to be empty. I stepped onto the back deck. The spotlights cast light to the far reaches of the yard, down to the lake edge, where another light shone out over the dark black mass of water at the end of the pier.

There, at the water's edge, two lumps, one big, one tiny, sat huddled together. The big one turned and waved. I trudged down the steps and across the lawn toward them.

Phyllis didn't stand but remained settled in the grass with her daughter clinging to her side.

She whispered into the night. "It's so beautiful here. You never told me."

I never have figured out how to answer compliments like that, so I ignore them. "Come on inside. You must be thirsty after your trip."

"Oh, I just want to soak this up. The moon is shining on the lake like a spread of butter on burnt toast. Just look at the stillness of it. I wish the sun were rising. I can imagine the red glow creating pink clouds, birds rising into the wakening sky."

The light wasn't bright enough to chase the shadows off her face, but I knew without clarity of eyesight that she was haggard. I knew Phyllis well. Her words were trickling out in a dream-state, vocalized wishes pulled from deep inside.

"You'll see it in the morning," I said.

She didn't move. She just smiled at me, then back at the water.

I squatted down. "Are you hungry, Sabrina?"

Phyllis hugged Sabrina a bit tighter. "She's fine. Wonderful, aren't you, baby?"

Sabrina didn't look wonderful. Her pout glared through the dark. Still, it was better than a tantrum.

Phyllis said, "You've done well for yourself, Carley. I knew you would. You've always been so smart."

Warm shivers ran through me at hearing my college nickname. "Used up my smarts at UVA. Now I'm riding on my looks, so I'm about to hit dead-end."

Baiting Phyllis was useless. She never played the hook like Mom. Her attention remained on the scenery, staring at the dark shapes of trees hanging over the still water, houses looming up from the slope of yards, and toward the end of the inlet a stretch of wilderness, a tangled shore of undergrowth before an imposingly thick stand of pines. It had been a long while since I'd contemplated the beauty of it. I sat down facing more toward my guests than the water.

"I wonder how long it would take a person to swim to the other side," Phyllis said. "Look way over there, where all the trees are. I could imagine someone living there in a tent with all the world open around them." She took on a dreamy look. "Man and world woven of the same fabric, living together without boundaries of life. In death, they'd only blend further."

"Not me. I like boundaries. I like plumbing and hot showers, gas heat and electric lights. In fact, we have a whole guestroom just for you."

She laughed. "You're such a hoot. I didn't mean me, Carley. I just meant in a metaphorical sort of way."

Phyllis liked sounding lofty.

Her hair had gotten longer. She used to keep it short because it curled so much, little tiny pin-screws of red curls all over her head. Long as it was now, it looked unkempt. She wore dark stretch pants with a large, loose top hanging over, which added to her flyaway appearance. The artwork on the shirt was an intricate design, most likely hand painted. Many hours' work washed repeatedly into obscurity.

"You know me, Phyllis. I'm grounded in reality. Camping is cold, just like life."

She laughed again, a lilting laugh that rose from some deep spot within her, from a childhood that existed before the demons born of a trying adolescence. "Not bad. My metaphor was better, though." Her voice carried out on a wave of carefree abandon.

"Oh, I can do better than that." We used to have this contest of beating out each other's poetry. I know it doesn't sound like me, but Phyllis nurtured a different part of my psyche. She got me through Creative Writing at UVA. I cleared my throat and dropped it to an appropriately husky tone. "I stand still in life, so still I am but a reflection of the world. Like the waters at night, I glow in false light. But I am dark and full of meanings no one else fathoms. Even those who have dipped their oars know not my depth. Even those who have entered my waters know not the secrets I've hidden in the caverns of my abyss. I sparkle with brilliance in daylight that masks my dangers. I am outwardly beautiful. You need not know more."

I was speaking more of her than myself. She knew it. She turned to face me. The lights caught the well of tears spilling over. Phyllis and I weren't kindred spirits—the fabric of our lives was too different—but we'd been joined in life in some inseparable way.

She spoke. "I've got to leave, Carley."

I couldn't bring myself to face her current demon. "Don't take it so hard. Just because my poem was better doesn't mean you can't stay."

She tried to smile, but it never quite reached her face. She stood. Sabrina clung to her leg. She peeled Sabrina's hands off and heaved her up to her hip. "You're Mama's big girl, aren't you?"

Sabrina nodded, still pouting.

"You're not really leaving?" I asked.

She nodded slightly, but her eyes were still intent on Sabrina.

"I don't understand. You're not staying?"

Sabrina faced me. Her little-girl eyes were red and puffy, two narrow slits of darkness. Her mouth was clamped tight.

The next thing I knew, Phyllis had shoved her onto me. I staggered under the surprise. Two wiry arms encircled my neck. Two scrawny legs wrapped around my waist.

"Well—hello, Sabrina."

Phyllis ran up the slope.

"Where are you going?" I yelled.

Phyllis's voice came back to me threefold, echoing across the lake and back. "Take good care of her."

I jogged up the embankment after her, but the weight of Sabrina slowed me. Phyllis was cunning enough to have planned it just that way.

"Where are you going? Why are you leaving Sabrina here?"

At the top, she turned beneath the bright spotlight like an actress upon a stage. I saw tears streaming down her face. She yelled down to me, "I would have asked you outright, but I was afraid you'd say no."

A cramp shot through my side. I paused, panting. "When are you coming back?"

"Monday?" It was a question, not an answer. "I'll try to get back Monday. Take care of her, Carley. Please take good care of her." Her face softened then, a shifting in the brash rays of the spotlight. "I love you, Sabrina."

For a moment, I suppose, I was shocked, filled with indignation. How could she dump her kid on me and take off? But in my heart, I wasn't surprised. Phyllis had always been flighty. That was how she'd ended up with a child in the first place.

She turned and disappeared into the shadows around the corner of the house. By the time I reached the front yard, her car had pulled out and was disappearing down the road. There, sitting bleakly in the driveway, were two large suitcases.

I stomped closer with Sabrina still perched on my hip. No doubt, Phyllis was gone. I bore my eyes into the moon, looking for answers.

Phyllis and I first met at the University of Virginia. I majored in business, with a minor in economics. She started out in business, so we attended quite a few of the same classes and became study partners our freshman year. She switched to art her sophomore year. She had definite talent, but that wasn't the underlying reason. Business was a safe future. Art was flighty and daring in her eyes. Phyllis yearned for liberty. She was one of those teenagers who had always done the right thing, but she was drawn to crossing the lines to some invisible freedom she thought existed in the kids who partied all night and came to class with hangovers and bloodshot eyes. She couldn't bring herself to act like them, but she loved to live on their sidelines, rubbing elbows with them. Art was part of that life—deep discussions about philosophical ideologies, interpretations of modern works, and expressing all her inner turmoil.

She always came home to me, though. I was her anchor. Her flowery friends would sink her into mire, and I would pull her out, clean her up, and dry her tears. I wouldn't have stood for it year after year except that I had known the real Phyllis before her artsy friends came along. I always thought she would return to real life and be happy. And she did for long stretches, so I lasted out her storms. I kept her studying, shunned the bad crowd, and pulled her back when she got too close to the wrong guys.

Later, after graduation and my initial retreat to home and the banking job, Phyllis came through for me. She recommended me for a management entry position with a company where she'd been hired as a commercial artist in the marketing department. So I moved to Charlottesville and took the job. I figured the bad stuff was behind her. She was settled into real life. I moved in with her. We shared work, an apartment, and the care of her mother.

I'd known about her infirm mother, but I'd never helped her deal with the situation before. Immediately, I understood Phyllis. Daytime help was hired, but the burden of caring for an elderly mother was too great. I understood why Phyllis had felt suffocated, why she'd gravitated toward irresponsible kids. She'd dealt with her mother year after year alone. After just a few months, I was ready for my own place. I knew Phyllis couldn't cope with her on her own anymore. Together we found a nursing home that specialized in Alzheimer's.

Then the trend started again. Without me living with her, readily available to guide her along, Phyllis dipped into the wrong crowds more and more. Guys from downtown clubs. Not the nice clubs where the rest of us went for an after-work cocktail, but sleazy spots where smoke hung in a fog and drugs were passed in the alley. There, she met Ron, father to Sabrina.

Sabrina still hung latched to my side with tears of rage and fear contorting her face. Little Sabrina, so angry and feisty. I wondered what kind of life she'd lived in my absence, what Phyllis was like as a mother.

The night hung eerily around us. Tree frogs croaked. Cicadas squeaked in the trees. Cars rolled through the neighborhood.

"You don't even know who I am, do you?"

Her lips quivered.

"Oh, don't worry, it won't be so bad," I hoped aloud. How

hard could it be to watch a five-year-old for a few days? "I was with your mommy the day you were born. Did you know that?"

Her head tilted slightly, as if she intended to nod.

"You were the most beautiful baby I'd ever seen in my life." Not that I'd seen many at that point, but I had coached Phyllis through labor and watched Sabrina emerge all wet, red, and wrinkled. I'd never seen anything like it. During later years, while taking fertility drugs, I sometimes dreamed of her birth, confusing it as that of my own child, born and somehow lost to me. I would awaken and have to shake things back to reality, to being the observer, the childless, the barren. Now here she was, alone with me.

"Looks like we're having a pajama party. Let's get your luggage into the house."

I set her on the ground, her hand clasped in mine. I set the largest suitcase to the side of the driveway and carried the smaller one in. I left it by the door and took Sabrina to the couch, then retrieved the large one and heaved it in the door.

I stood there a moment, breathing deeply, trying to decide what to do. We had to start somewhere. I was stuck with her. I had to deal with it.

Since Phyllis's phone call three weeks earlier, I'd taken my last encounter with Sabrina and created an updated image of her in my mind: curly blonde hair, Phyllis's dimples, a healthy plumpness, and an engaging smile—a little darling to turn Babette's girls green with envy.

Reality was much different. Sabrina was nothing like my visions.

She looked awful in the lamplight. Pale, thin, sick with fear. Poor thing. Helpless, like the first time I'd seen her—at her birth—so new and fragile.

I observed as she moved to a window to stare out at the lake. No one would have a problem imagining her as my child. She stood there all arms and legs. Her blonde hair hung poker straight to her shoulders. The round baby fat had slimmed, sculpted into Phyllis's heart-shaped face. "Are you hungry?" I asked.

She looked at me with empty eyes, a shell of a child like a deflated balloon. She shook her head no.

"Thirsty?"

No again.

"Let's carry your bags up to the guestroom then, shall we?" I hauled the two bags up the stairs to the larger of the two spare rooms. She followed a few paces behind.

I loved the guestroom. It exuded tranquility and dignity. No old-fashioned, cheap particleboard furniture. No cast-off beds for guests in my house.

As I clicked on the light, I was surprised. The room seemed drab at night. I'd never noticed before. It was the front room, centered on the house under its own peak. By day, sunlight flooded through a huge arched window that had been added more as an outer architectural feature than for the benefit of the room. In the dark, the window was a gaping black eye. I pulled the blinds across, but the upper arch, uncovered, still winked with flecks of stars.

Several landscape prints hung on the ivory walls. A thick hunter-green comforter etched with ivory scrolls covered the mattress of the four-poster bed, which wasn't the dark mahogany of my grandparents' day, but light oak with tall, thin octagonal posts, and piled with pillows in shams. An open hope chest stood at its foot, with lace and blankets frothing over the sides, set up as if for a magazine photo shoot. The dresser on the near wall was narrow with an oblong mirror hung over it. It was serene even without the sunlight, but it was not a little girl's room.

Sabrina climbed onto the bed and laid her head on the mound of pillows.

I wished she would show some kind of emotion. Even a tantrum would prove she had some life in her. I decided she was totally exhausted. She was almost asleep where she lay by the time I unpacked her smaller case into the dresser, found her pajamas, changed her clothes, and tucked her into bed.

Back downstairs, I sat tapping the phone, trying to figure out whom I should phone for baby-sitting; after all, I still had to work the next day. I tried Mom first, being indirect, knowing ahead of time how the conversation would probably go.

"Hi, Mom. I thought I better let you know we'll be bringing an extra person with us for supper Sunday."

"Really? Who?"

"Sabrina."

"Who?"

"Phyllis's daughter. We're watching her for a few days."

"Without Phyllis?"

"Yes."

Silence stretched between us. "Do you know how to? I mean, you've never even watched Babette's kids for more than an hour."

"I'm sure I'll manage, Mom. I run a whole plant. One kid can't be that hard. I do need a favor, though."

"I know where this conversation is heading, and I understand your predicament, Carla, but I had my years of motherhood. I'm beyond all that now, so don't even ask."

"What?"

"If you volunteered to watch her, don't expect to hand her over to me."

I wasn't about to tell Mom that I hadn't volunteered. She would verbally shred Phyllis. "No, Mom, I wouldn't dare ask."

I hung up and was sitting there, tapping the phone again when Simon arrived.

"Hello, Love," he said. "What's up?"

While I collected my thoughts, I clasped the phone between my hands like a lifeline to normalcy. "We have a visitor."

He looked over his shoulder and back, searching. "We do?"

"Sabrina."

"Sabrina who?"

"Sabrina Samson. Phyllis's daughter."

"But she's a baby."

"She's five now."

"Where's Phyllis?" He looked around again, probably expecting her to step out of the bathroom or something.

"Not here."

He put his keys in a cubbyhole on the antique desk. "You mean you agreed to baby-sit her daughter?"

"No."

"I'm totally confused."

"So am I." I tapped the phone again, then stopped. If I told him exactly what had happened, he would go into one of Mom's routines, telling me what a horrible friend Phyllis was. "Phyllis showed up an hour ago. I thought she meant to visit. Next thing I knew, she was leaving without Sabrina."

"So she did ask you to take care of her?"

"Well, not in so many words. She just kind of handed her to me and said good-bye."

"My gosh, Carla, only you could be put upon so easily. Where is she?"

"I don't know."

"You don't know?"

"No. She didn't tell me where she was going."

He shook his head. "No, no, no. The child. What's her name ... where is she?"

"Sabrina. Upstairs asleep. Seemed exhausted. She fell asleep while I unpacked one of her suitcases."

"*One* of them? As in more than one suitcase? How long is she staying? Or did Phyllis not tell you that, either?"

I didn't want to tell him what my gut instinct was telling me—that Phyllis didn't know when she would return. In the back of my mind I kept picturing a single scene over and over again, from back when Sabrina was an infant. I'd made a promise. *I'd made a promise.* I shook the thought away. "Monday," I responded. "She said she would try to get back Monday."

"A whole week! What kind of mother dumps her daughter off for a whole week with strangers?"

"It's not a full week. And we're not strangers."

"Well, we're sure not family. She hasn't even seen you in three years. That's pretty much strangers in my book."

Simon wasn't helping. The images came again. Sabrina, three weeks old, dressed in a long gown with matching booties. Phyllis and I had taken her to the nursing home to meet Grandma, Phyllis's mother. What a mistake that had been.

Alzheimer's is a strange disorder. Phyllis's mother could tell us everything we wanted to know about 1949, but she couldn't remember anything about the present or why she was standing in the hall. She would head toward the bathroom and forget her destination halfway there.

Phyllis and I visited her often. She deteriorated to the

point that she was unable to recognize us from one visit to the next. Eventually she forgot our conversations from one minute to the next.

When Phyllis became pregnant, she didn't try to explain the situation to her mother. It was useless. She would've had to re-explain her condition on every visit. It wasn't worth the effort.

So nothing was said until the day we took baby Sabrina to see Mrs. Samson for the first time. Mrs. Samson was delighted at the sight of her. She told us repeatedly she had a baby girl, too. Phyllis nodded and explained that Sabrina was her granddaughter. Ten minutes later, Mrs. Samson asked us where the beautiful baby had come from and why we had her with us.

Phyllis had expected the visit to be hard, but not impossible. She left in tears. Back at her apartment, she sat me in a chair and placed Sabrina in my arms. "Carley," she said, "you understand that there is no one else on God's green earth I am connected to in any way, don't you?"

"Nonsense," I replied. "You have cousins in Maine."

"Step-second cousins twice removed or something ridiculous, who I've never laid eyes on, related through a father who died when I was seven."

"Okay, I give. You have no one but me and your mother."

"I don't have my mother. That's just it."

I sighed. She was right. There was no need to belabor the point.

Phyllis kneeled at my feet. "I'm making you guardian, Carley."

I stared down at baby Sabrina. "Ron might—"

"Ron washed his hands of her. Ron wanted her aborted. Forget Ron. He doesn't even know she's been born."

At the time, guardianship—possible motherhood—seemed preposterous. "What would I do with a baby?"

She took the baby out of my arms. "Nothing," she said. "You're just a backup in case I get hit by a bus."

"Struck by lightning, you mean."

"Huh?"

"You're always running out in thunderstorms."

"Nuh-uh."

She really did. I'd known a guy in junior high who had been struck by lightning on the football field. Because of that, storms scared me to death, and Phyllis knew it. She would go out for stupid errands in a storm just to get under my skin. I was a hard person to twist a knife in, and lightning was my Achilles' heel. When she wanted to hurt me, she knew running out in a storm was her best revenge.

"Yes, you do," I protested. "Promise me you'll never run out in another thunderstorm, and I'll be guardian."

She nodded. It was a done deal.

My father died two months later, and I, having realized how short life might be, moved back to Charlotte, to my roots, such as they were. I got a job as a production manager at Wymans, went house hunting, and met Simon.

It seemed a lifetime ago.

I set the phone down on the coffee table. "You just don't understand what Phyllis and I meant to each other. We were everything. More sisters than Babette and I have ever been." I stood. "Come on. You've got to see her."

We peeked into her room. The moonlight lay lightly across her face, a soft glow on a porcelain doll.

Simon tapped my shoulder and pulled the door closed. "She looks harmless enough. I guess we'll manage."

I followed him back down the stairs, thinking I needed

some of his faith. Her calm all evening hadn't been enough to erase my memories of her two-year-old tantrums.

And her presence had only escalated my inner pain. I wanted my own child all the more.

Ten

woke early the next morning, tense, remembering something had to be done. My brain was fuzzy with sleep. I felt dazed. Then two things came to me. I had to insert my progesterone suppository (twice a day for fourteen consecutive days to boost the lining of the uterus), and I had to deal with Phyllis's child asleep across the hall.

I hoped she was still asleep. I sure didn't want her to walk in on me.

Ten minutes later, task completed, I stepped across the hall in my nightgown and peeked at her. She was still sleeping. I gathered my clothes in the pale light. As Simon stepped out of the shower, I stepped in.

"Early bird, aren't you?" he said.

"I've got a chick in the nest." I stunned myself at the inference of my reply. I had meant Sabrina, but I had unintentionally referred also to the baby I hoped was implanting within me, the one Simon didn't know about.

"A blue jay," he said.

"Huh?"

"Blue jays lay their eggs in other birds' nests."

I stripped off my nightgown and tossed it into the hamper in the corner. The mirror reflected my naked belly, which was slightly swollen, but it had been that way for months from all the hormones I had taken. "A blue jay," I repeated, and stepped into the shower.

I dressed for work in navy slacks and a pale blue silk blouse. Nothing fancy, but professional enough. I had to go in for a while even if I didn't have a baby-sitter. I'd decided to take Sabrina with me and let my secretary keep an eye on he, while I held conference with my managers and checked out a few things on the production floor. Then I would take Sabrina out to lunch and the park or someplace fun. If I prepared my staff and simplified a few obstacles on the production schedule, I could hang around at home with Sabrina for a couple of days without too many problems arising.

I sifted through my meager jumble of jewelry for my watch and decided to wear my lucky cat brooch as well. I had a feeling that a little good fortune might be needed in facing Sabrina and Simon together today.

From the first moment, I knew I'd guessed right.

Sabrina was sitting on the family-room floor. Her placid eyes of yesterday now investigated me with a gleam of mischief. Unlike Phyllis's gratifyingly sincere expressions, Sabrina's smile flickered, bordering on a smirk. Phyllis, though flighty, had always been conscientious. This child, so docile the night before, now impressed me as an imp, a reproduction of Phyllis's reckless, dark side, with freckles and flashing eyes.

I'd learned from watching Babette's children through the years—I didn't reach out to Sabrina. I took a seat on the sofa across from her and sat quietly, waiting for her to make the first move. It didn't take long.

Her eyes were trained on me, appraising everything. Her gaze came to rest on my good-luck charm. The sleek gold cat with the ruby eyes glinted in the light. Its thin gold tail hung free. The sight of it drew her toward me, one finger extended in expectation.

"A cat," she said in a distinctive voice, husky for a little girl.

I nodded. "You can touch it. See? The tail moves."

She reached out and flicked the tail. "I had a cat afore," she said.

"Me, too."

"Mine ran away."

"Mine became very sick. My daddy had to take her away to the vet."

She sidled a bit closer. Her thin, stiff frame leaned against my leg. I breathed in her sweet little-girl breath as she spoke. "Was yours black?"

"No, but I bet yours was."

She nodded. "I miss her."

I could see her emotions shifting to the memory of a cat, a safe thing to cry over. I swallowed a response and laid my hand gently over hers. Her fingers were so tiny and warm.

She didn't pull away.

An idea coursed through me. "I think it's time we both had another cat. We could pick one out, and you could help me take care of it while you're here this week."

She tilted her head and spoke words quoted perhaps from Phyllis, clipped and overly adult. "You can't just replace living things. One won't never be the same as the other."

I nodded. Exactly the comment I would expect from Phyllis's daughter.

Her hand felt so tiny under mine. I wanted to hold her in my arms but stopped myself. I didn't want to force myself on her. "Let's not try to replace anything. But it would be nice to try to start up fresh and new. Somewhere out there is a kitten sitting all alone in a cage just hoping we'll pick her out and love her. I can hear her meowing in my heart."

I could see the image working on her. Despite her grown-up words, she was only five. A kitten was powerful medicine. She picked up a purple backpack from the floor. "Let's go. I want to leave right now."

I laughed. "I don't think they would give a kitten to some-one wearing pajamas. You need clothes on. And breakfast. Then we have to go to my office for a short bit. Then we'll have lunch and talk about the kitten, okay?"

"I'm not hungry."

"Let's start with your clothes and worry about food when we get to that point."

An hour later, I had her ready to go.

Abigail, our housecleaner, drove up in her rusty station wagon as we were leaving. She was a wiry teenager with huge eyes. Her jeans emphasized her bony hips and round bottom. I opened the front door for her.

"Good morning, Mrs. R."

"Good morning, Abigail. Simon left a list of extras on the desk, compensated, of course."

"Thank you, Mrs. R."

She sidled in past me and caught sight of Sabrina. "Oh. Hey there."

Sabrina clung to me.

"This is Sabrina. She's using the front guestroom. I haven't had a chance to unpack all her things yet. I think Simon included that on his list."

I could see the ideas floating around Abigail's mind. She thought I'd finally adopted a child. She loved telling me about the baby she'd had two years ago, at sixteen. She was one of many people who assumed we were childless by choice and felt it their duty to relay the joys of parenthood. I didn't grace her unasked questions with an answer.

I locked the front door and clasped Sabrina's warm palm in my large hand. We walked to the garage to a far slower beat than the racing pace of my heart. Not even Abigail could guess my emotional state. The wonder of Sabrina clasping my hand was remarkable.

Sabrina paused at the car. "Mama has a blue car."

"Do you like blue the best?"

"No. I like red."

I probably shone with pride.

She squeezed between the front seat and the doorframe to reach the back two narrow seats suitable for nothing more than someone her size.

I waved her up front. "You can't sit back there. There aren't any seat belts."

"I'm not allowed to sit in the front. Mama said."

"This car is different. It's very old. It doesn't have air bags."

"But the policeman will stop us."

"No, he won't. It's safer to be up front in this car, so you can buckle up. There aren't any buckles in the backseat." My Porsche is perfectly restored, but it's obviously not modern. No power windows. No air-conditioning. Everything is knobs, not buttons.

"I like new cars," she said as she slid into the front seat and buckled up.

She sounded like Simon. I revved up the engine, backed the car out, and sped down the road. Driving the Porsche never failed to stir my blood. "This car is a classic, which means it has more value because it's so special, very well built."

"Are you a classic too?"

I laughed. What else could I do? "Not quite, Sabrina. I'm not a car."

"Your name is. Car-la."

"That's true. Must have been my father's doing. He loved cars."

"So did mine."

That comment caught me off guard. Did she know who her father was? I assumed that Ron hadn't ever been included in the raising of Sabrina. In fact, I didn't think, after the last encounter I witnessed, that Phyllis would ever have let him into her life again. He'd been brutal to her. Had Phyllis forgiven him and allowed him to act as father to Sabrina? I wanted to ask, but I let it go. Better to keep things simple and ask Phyllis questions when she returned. We had plenty of time for working out the details of her life. For now, I had to keep things flowing. Take care of necessities. "I'll need you to sit in my office while I get some work done. Do you have something in that backpack to keep you occupied?"

"I thought we were going to get the kitten."

"In a while, after lunch, remember?"

"I want it right now," she exclaimed.

Her tone was rising. I could hear inklings of those early tantrums edging in. "Really, Sabrina. We can't go into a restaurant with a kitten. We'll go to my office, then eat, then get the kitten."

"We can go to a drive-through."

A week of hamburgers and fries rose up before me. I wasn't about to get started on that track. "Nonsense. We'll have lunch in a nice restaurant, and then we'll stop to get the kitten."

"I want my kitten now."

I didn't reply. I turned on the radio. It was set to classic rock, but I changed it to classical. I remember Babette saying it calmed everyone's nerves in the car. Sabrina started tapping her foot to it.

"Do you like it?"

"Sure. Bach's not bad, but I like Tchaikovsky lots better."

"Really?" I asked. I was shocked. She actually knew which composer it was? "What makes Tchaikovsky better?"

"It goes up and down more, hard and soft, with lots of instruments. Cymbals and everything. Mama calls it movement. Makes me want to dance."

"Ah. I bet you like *The Nutcracker*."

She nodded. "But the overture rules. The drums sound like a cannon. And big bells ring and all."

What a surprise she was turning out to be. I should have guessed that with Phyllis, though. Knowing music would be important to her. She'd studied it intently in college.

I wasn't sure what to expect from Sabrina next. Just before we reached the plant, I decided I had better coach her a bit on public protocol. "You need to mind your manners here, okay? My employees will expect you to be especially well behaved."

"Why?"

"Because I'm the plant manager. And because you should always attempt to make a good impression wherever you go."

"I know. Mama teached me that."

Her manners at the plant were perfect at first. I introduced her to Judy Spring, my secretary, a square-faced, efficient woman with wildly permed brunette hair and thick glasses that made her look rather domineering.

"Good morning, Miss Spring. I'm pleased to meet you," Sabrina stated with the matter-of-factness of a dignitary.

I smiled with pride. Judy raised her eyebrows at us and nodded. Approval from this mother of three was high praise.

An hour later Sabrina had tired of the few toys in her book bag. She fiddled with the knickknacks around the room, flipped the window blinds back and forth, dug in the dirt around the fig tree in the corner, and constantly whined. "Can't we go now? This place is boring."

"We can't go yet. I have a few things left to do. Come here, though. I'll show you something." I took her hand and led her through a maze of halls and offices to the production department where Hilda, an overweight, pasty girl, sat typing quality reports, and Dexter, a wiry man with shining opal skin, was checking stock quantities on a computer terminal. Across the end of the room was a plateglass window looking out on the production floor, a huge warehouse area with rows of machines clacking and whirring. Women in white hair caps paced up and down among the machines, working the lines. In the background, a brawny black man zipped along in a forklift, then paused and reversed, setting off a beeping warning as he backed up, loud even through the muffling barrier of the glass. The driver worked efficiently, moving pallets of stock in and out of the storage racks. I never tired of watching the whole production process. When everything was in sync, it was a reflection of me, parts of a whole all fitting together in place and on time, the way I liked my life to be. Perhaps that's why Simon's orderliness appealed to me at first. He synchronized my life.

"It looks dirty out there," Sabrina said.

"On the contrary, it's clean for a plant. It's kind of gray looking, though, isn't it? The machines, the cement floors. Not very colorful. Like black-and-white TV, eh?"

"I want to look at 'em closer."

"Can't do that. It's dangerous. And you're not insured. I just wanted you to see what a manufacturing process looked like."

"Mama's work is prettier. A big glass building. I got to go lots of times. I got to draw a lot."

Of course! "Come on," I said. I led her down the hall to the conference room and collected the easel and a handful of various markers and took them back to my office. That kept her content until lunch.

We weren't in the car two minutes before the attitude started again as I tried to convince her to eat somewhere other than McDonald's.

She made a face. "I don't eat *anything* that's green."

Nothing green. I sighed. I could imagine Babette smirking over the number of times I'd scolded her for not forcing vegetables on her children.

"How about spaghetti?" I asked, spotting an Italian restaurant in the distance.

"I hate spaghetti. It has noodles in it."

Well, duh. That cut out Italian. "Shrimp scampi."

"What's that?"

"You'll love it."

"I want a hamburger."

"Oh! A taco. All kids love tacos."

"I want a hamburger."

"Let's try Chinese. I see one up ahead."

"I want a hamburger."

Lucky for Sabrina, the China House had hamburgers. I was feeling defeated by this time, wondering how I would manage a whole week of caring for this odd little progeny of Phyllis's. I couldn't bear the thought of going home with her so early in the afternoon, so I took her to the park first, then to the toy store for a few things. That took most of the day. If I'd had the energy for another battle, I would have put the kitten off for another day, but I *had* promised.

Maybe if I hadn't been so tired, the pet shop wouldn't have seemed as trying. I kept my head about me and remembered this was a distraction to entertain Sabrina, even though it would become my pet after she left. I would have chosen the solid black kitten, but Sabrina had worn me down so much over the course of the day, I'd lost all my vigor. I tried to influence her. I leaned over and pointed out the attributes of the lively black one, its pointed ears and soft purrs, but Sabrina wouldn't be moved. She chose the pale tan one whimpering in the back of the cage. What did it matter what kitten we had as long as it gave her something to bond to?

We returned to the car, kitten in hand, facing the worst of the day: Simon. It was six, so he was sure to be home. I had to confront him with another newcomer in tow.

He was sitting in the family room, watching the evening news. He looked over at us as we entered but didn't say a word.

Sabrina walked right up to him, kitten in hand. "Hello. I'm Sabrina."

He seemed determined to put on his aggravated stance. He turned his eyes from her to me. "She brought a cat with her?"

Sabrina answered, "I just got her. Your girlfriend took me to the animal place. Do you like the name Taz?"

Simon looked back at her with his eyes sprung open. "My what?"

Sabrina cocked her head toward me. "Her."

"Carla is my wife, not my girlfriend."

"Oh. Mommy only has boyfriends. She says men are too hard to live with. What's your name?"

Her statement shocked the rigidity out of Simon's upright mind, and he mumbled, "Simon."

"I saw a cartoon once with a boy named Simon. He was stupid."

Simon, stunned as he was, only blinked.

I grimaced. "Come along, Sabrina. Let's put your new toys in your room and set up the kitty litter in the laundry room." I grasped the bag of toys and headed up the stairs.

"Your mother came by a while ago," Simon called out to us.

I wasn't sure of the significance of his comment until I opened the door to the guestroom. Worn toys from my childhood sat on cheap department-store plastic shelves. The dark green satin comforter had been replaced with one of those mail-flier-type comforters with some ugly-faced cartoon girl all over it. I shuddered and turned from it to face the toys: Barbies with their hair chopped off, ratty stuffed animals, a wooden choo choo, bunches of story-books. I knew Mom hadn't saved anything from the old house, which meant she'd ransacked Babette's store of goods. Babette had claimed every toy in Mom's attic during her first pregnancy. I couldn't imagine she'd released pos-session of them gracefully.

"Awesome," Sabrina said. She dropped the kitten on the floor, ran to the bed, and bounced on it.

"Sabrina, stop. We don't bounce on beds."

"Mommy said I can."

I braced myself. "This is my house, and the rules are different here, Sabrina. While you're here, you'll have to obey me."

She kept bouncing. "You're not the boss of me."

This child was nothing like my child would be. I wouldn't allow mine to become spoiled and difficult. I picked up the mewing kitten and stood in front of the bed. "Yes, dear, I *am* the boss of you. Now stop bouncing and take your kitten. She's crying."

"I'm tired of holding her." She bounced off the bed and looked at the shelf. "These toys look dumb. They're all old. I want my stuff."

I moved to the shelf and touched the nylon hair of my favorite dolly. "All these toys used to be mine. This was my old doll. Her name is Polly. I loved playing with her."

"She's ugly."

I closed my eyes. I had to remember that this little girl was venting frustrations. She'd been dumped off without warning and was probably missing her mother. Of course she wouldn't be in the most compliant mood. But it was hard. It wasn't fair. I wanted my own child, not this belligerent spoiled brat. *Be patient, Carla.* "Be patient, Sabrina."

Her demanding behavior continued throughout the evening. She didn't like anything Simon cooked. She didn't want to clean up after her kitten. She wanted cartoons on the television. I gave in. It was easier than warring with her all night. After all, she had so many adjustments to make. She sprawled on the floor, belly down, bare feet flapping in the air, chin on hands. For two hours she watched the flashing screen.

If Simon had even once said *I told you so*, I would have bitten his head off, but he sat in his recliner, covertly watching my struggles and smirking behind the newspaper.

Every time my patience felt stretched, I closed my eyes a moment and thought of Phyllis. And when I opened them, I saw again how small Sabrina was, how vulnerable and breakable despite her behavior.

Bedtime rose as another trial. She didn't collapse into bed the way she had the night before. After three trips up the stairs to tuck her back in, I finally lay down beside her until she fell asleep.

I looked at her slumbering figure. Pale eyelashes lay on perfect skin. The blush of day had faded in sleep. Her lips, tiny and perfect, smiled slightly. She shifted to her side and curled up.

When I descended the stairs at nine o'clock, I finally felt I'd returned to myself again, my own individuality without Sabrina's presence hung on me.

Simon was still reclined in his chair, reading the newspaper. The house seemed overly quiet after all the activity of the day. I put on one of Celine Dion's early CDs.

"Can you believe Sabrina knows the difference between Bach and Tchaikovsky?"

"Don't you?" he responded.

He missed the point completely.

"Did you get the mail?" I asked.

He looked up from the paper. "It's on the desk."

I leafed through it and stopped at a handwritten envelope. It was from Phyllis. A letter the day after she left? She must have written it ahead of time and mailed it right after leaving my house. I tore it open. It was pages thick, a short handwritten note with something legal-looking behind it. I felt faint. I forced myself across the room and sank to the sofa.

I could feel Simon's eyes boring into me as I read silently.

My dearest Carley,

All my life I've tried to be someone other than myself. You're the only one who ever loved me for who I really am, for my idiot self. Time and again you've picked me up and set me straight. I've lost my way again. But this time it's not just me. It's Sabrina. I can't pull her down with me.

You promised me long ago when she was new and innocent that you would be her guardian if I were run over by a bus. Well, there's a bus aimed at me, Carley.

You don't need to know what it is. You can't intervene this time. It's bigger than you or I. It's much more menacing. He won't let go.

Take my baby and raise her up to be like you, not like me.

I can't escape my problem, so I'm going to face it head-on and finish it completely. I promise this is my last request of you. You won't have to bail me out ever again.

Tell her I love her. Tell her I'll always love her.

All the legal documents are enclosed.

Phyllis

Tears welled. I knew what this meant. I didn't want to admit it, but I knew. She wasn't coming back.

The newspaper crackled as Simon folded it in his lap and laid it on the coffee table. He moved to my side and stretched his arm across my shoulder. "What is it, Love? Who's it from?"

"Phyllis." I stared at the papers in my lap. "She's, well, she doesn't say it exactly, but ..."

He straightened up. "But what?"

"I don't think she's coming back."

He took the papers from my grasp and flipped through them, stopping at the legalese. He was beside himself. "How could you be legal guardian of a child and not tell me?"

"Gee, it wasn't on my list of discussion topics for the first three dates. After that, I forgot."

"No one forgets being guardian of another person."

"I don't mean I forgot Sabrina; I just never thought to mention guardianship. I never thought it would matter. I haven't even seen Phyllis in three years. How was I to know she hadn't changed her will?"

"You've been sending that kid Christmas presents for five years and never thought to explain why?"

"I sent her presents because she was my best friend's daughter. I was there when she was born, for heaven's sake. I stood in the delivery room and coached Phyllis. That's not a relationship to be flippant about."

"Neither is guardianship."

I took a deep breath. I felt the heritage of my mother's habits coming to roost as my lip curled involuntarily. "It remains that Phyllis has left Sabrina here, and I am Sabrina's guardian."

"Not precisely. The courts have final approval. A will is only a written desire of the deceased."

"I can't believe you'd go against me. What would you have me do? Send her to foster care?"

"No. We need to find Phyllis and insist she take Sabrina back."

"Certainly. I'm not overjoyed at the thought of keeping

her. But I know Phyllis. If she took a mind to disappear, she'll be hard to find. In the meantime, she's asked me to love her child, and I will. I'll treat her as my own."

"You make it sound like a stray dog we just have to feed. She's a child, which requires a lot of time and attention. She's not yours. You can't pretend she is. The thought of ever raising a child of our own is overwhelming enough. I don't intend to raise someone else's."

Silence descended like the aftermath of an explosion.

He resented the very idea of a baby.

Had he never wanted a child? Had he hoped all along I wouldn't conceive? Agony filled me. I couldn't even speak. My mind twisted over all the past years, linking the signs together, putting his attitude into perspective. He'd told me too late. Too late on all accounts.

I knew I couldn't discuss this rationally with Simon. I yearned for Kevin's sympathetic arms.

Simon went to the phone and started dialing numbers. The call to Social Services' emergency number was abrupt. My mind was still on *us* when he hung up and faced me.

"They don't get involved in child-custody cases unless there's evidence of abuse. Phyllis is weird, but she's not abusive."

I could have spit at him.

He called the police station next. Again, he hung up with a frown. "They won't put out an APB for a missing person based on a letter. She's not really missing, in their opinion. The officer said they'd make note of it, but I doubt that means very much. I'll have to hire a private investigator."

I rolled my eyes. "Give it up, will you! Knowing Phyllis, she'll change her mind and come back next week. She's not irresponsible. She's not."

He put the phone back in the cradle. "Let's hope."

I couldn't look at him. Such turmoil stormed within me that I didn't know what to do about Phyllis abandoning Sabrina or Simon not wanting a child. I left him staring at the phone and ran up the stairs to our bedroom. I took out the progesterone suppositories and stared at them. I knew I still wanted a baby, even if he didn't, but my resolve wasn't quite the same as it had been. In the course of twenty-four hours, the idea of raising a child alone had become less appealing.

I undressed and sat naked on the bed, staring at the suppository, thinking of the path I had chosen. And then I pictured my mother kneeling at her bedside, praying that I'd conceive. "God's will or mine?" I asked the air. I inserted the suppository, pulled on my nightgown, and went to sleep.

Eleven

stayed home Thursday. I had advised my managers well enough to leave the running of the plant to their care for a few days. I wouldn't have been able to function at my desk, anyway. My heart raced with confusion. I needed to talk to someone, to someone who would listen with sympathy and understanding—to someone other than my husband.

As soon as I heard the garage door close behind Simon, I plumped up my bed pillows and called Kevin. "It's Carla. Did I wake you?"

"Shoot, no. Been out helping with the livestock. I just came in for breakfast. I wish you hadn't had to run off the other night. Is your friend still visiting?"

I explained what all had transpired since the phone call Tuesday night.

"So do you really think she's left Sabrina for good?" he asked.

"No. She spent all those years taking care of her mother when she could have left her in an institution and never visited her again. Sabrina is her daughter. And after just one day, I can tell they were very close. Things Sabrina says. I just can't believe Phyllis would abandon her."

"You're probably right."

"It's just left me in a quandary, though. I have to make

plans in case she doesn't come back. But I feel silly making plans when I really think she'll be here Monday."

"I understand." He paused. His tone changed, deeper, softer. "I really want to see you. Can you get away again?"

I thought of Simon rejecting Sabrina and the baby. Kevin wouldn't reject us. I needed his compassion. "I'll try. Give me a few days. I have to get all this straightened out, but I'll figure some way."

"I count the hours."

I laughed. "That ought to fill your days."

Sabrina poked her head in my bedroom door.

"I've got to go," I said and hung up. "Come on in, Sabrina."

Taz bounded around her, then slunk into the room as if on a hunt. Sabrina ignored her.

"Was that Mama on the phone?" she asked.

"No, it wasn't. Maybe she'll phone later."

She nodded. Her color had faded again. She stood as glum and pale as she had the night she arrived.

"I don't think we're ready to wake up yet." I flung back the sheets and patted the mattress. Taz jumped up, but I set her back on the floor as Sabrina crawled in beside me. We both snuggled into pillows and fell back asleep.

When I woke an hour later, she was still sleeping. I didn't dare insert the progesterone with her beside me. I carried one of the suppositories into the bathroom along with a pair of blue-jean shorts and a Hawaiian T-shirt. Today I planned to answer the beckoning of my roses. I needed some gardening time to work out my problems.

Sabrina was staring out the window when I emerged from the bathroom.

"What do you see?"

"Nothing."

I gazed out. "I do. A cardinal. See? He's eyeing the feeder, I bet."

She turned away.

"All right, then. Breakfast."

I spent hours in the garden. The earth was dry and crusty from the heat and my lack of watering. I preferred working when the dirt was damp, when the smell of it was strongest, like a powerful medicine to my senses. Still, the mechanical action of weeding relaxed me. My mind drifted over my problems. Everything seemed simpler in the sunlight. I still wanted a baby, even if Simon was opposed to one. I was obligated to Phyllis and Sabrina. Simon would have to adjust. We both needed time. Simon's motto flashed through my mind: *Have faith.* I would put that in Simon's face and tell him to have faith.

Sabrina ran around the yard for a while but eventually settled in beside me. For a few minutes, she poked at the hard dirt with a stick. Then she began watching what I was doing. She asked dozens of questions about the roots and stems and blossoms. After her display of music knowledge, I took the questions seriously and answered simply but accurately. I showed her how to pry up weeds with the trowel, loosening the roots so they wouldn't grow back as readily, and how to shake the soil off before tossing them into the weed bucket. She remained attentive for quite a while. By the time she was tired of it, I was too.

Sweat and grime coated us.

"Time for the pool," I declared. We changed into swimsuits. I drifted across the water on a float while she splashed about in some make-believe game. After lunch, I sat in the shade and read while she floated her doll around. By the end of the day, I felt much more in control.

Simon didn't. The whole thing had been weighing on his mind all day. "What will we do if Phyllis doesn't show up Monday?" he asked.

"I don't know. I guess we'll do what any couple would. We'll put her in day care till school starts in the fall." But I couldn't contemplate the thought seriously. Phyllis would come back. I *hoped* she would come back.

He grumbled and knocked shoulders as he pushed past me to stride outside.

He left me to struggle with Sabrina's behavior without helping one iota. I picked up the house constantly, but I couldn't seem to keep up with her flow of toys and games. I don't think Phyllis had ever made her clean up after herself. By nightfall, I quit asking her to help pick up her things. It was easier to clean up the mess by myself. She whined about everything.

During Simon's short passes through the family room, he frowned at the sight of the mess: a teddy bear on the couch, a ball on the floor, crayons and coloring books on the coffee table, the kitten in his chair. He stepped over her belongings without a word. He didn't have to speak. His expression said it all as he changed clothes and left.

Simon and I were fast becoming strangers under the same roof. I felt like a balloon ready to burst.

Sabrina and I were barely dressed the next morning when Mom bustled through the front door like the Queen of Sheba with my nieces and Babette hovering on her heels like hand-maidens. Her feet shuffled along at a frenzied pace as if she had forgotten she'd changed from slippers that were slightly too large into normal walking shoes. I think she spent too much time walking amid her poodles.

She stopped in the middle of my family room, five feet from Sabrina, who sat in a spread of Lego blocks snapping some contraption together. "So you're Sabrina." Hands went to hip, gift and all. "Well, that's a surprise. You don't have your mother's gorgeous red hair, do you?"

Sabrina finished snapping a piece in place, then took in my mother with a long look. "Neither do you, lady."

I chuckled.

I'd made the mistake of letting the news slip on the phone the evening before that Phyllis had sent guardianship papers. Mom's reaction was everything I expected—a thorough disparaging of Phyllis and a clucking over what I would possibly do with Sabrina. I figured she had come over to judge the situation first hand.

Bette and Brooke jumbled around Sabrina and helped themselves to her Legos. "Why'd your mama leave you?" asked Brooke.

Bette slapped Brooke's leg. "Mama told you not to say that." And to Sabrina, "Do you like it here?"

"I don't know."

Taz slunk into the room, crouched behind the end table, then pounced on the blocks.

"Oh, a kitty!" Bette exclaimed.

"It's mine," Sabrina said.

Mom wrinkled her nose. "I can't believe you would let her bring a cat into this house. All this beautiful furniture. It will all smell like cat within a week."

"A person could say that about dogs," I said.

Bette picked Taz up and cuddled her until the kitten's claws scratched her. She dropped the cat and turned her attention back to Sabrina. "Was your old house as big as Aunt Carla's?"

"I live in a apartment. A great big building."

Brooke piped up again. "You'd rather have your mama than a big house, huh?"

Sabrina shrugged.

I looked from the girls to my sister, imagining the conversation at Mom's that had spurred these comments from my nieces. Babette's judgments: my life in my house versus their life in their house. Babette curled up in Simon's recliner and put on her puppy-dog eyes to convey innocence. She didn't fool me.

My mother was still staring at Sabrina and shaking her head. "Heaven knows what you're going to do with her, Carla," she finally whispered to me.

There were so many insulting implications in my mother's words, I wondered whether she meant to degrade me or Sabrina. I plopped down on the couch. "I don't know, Mom. I suppose I'll have to muddle along with what little brains I have."

"At least you have your sister and me to lean on."

She hadn't even caught the sarcasm in my voice. "Now that's a load off my mind."

Mom crouched down eye-level to Sabrina as if she were a baby. "Sabrina, I brought you a present."

"Lucky you," Brooke said. "Grandma says we don't get one 'cause we've always been here."

"We get presents on our birthday, dummy. That's when we got here," Bette said.

Sabrina took the present and stared at it a moment before she began gently peeling off each piece of tape. I couldn't figure her out. The paper was purple with all different kinds of cars on it, not something appealing to a little girl at all. I figured it was left over from Blake's birthday. Sabrina couldn't be trying to preserve it. Phyllis hadn't been the careful-unwrapping kind. She'd torn into presents like a two-year-old.

Mom was getting teary eyed. "I'm so glad you like the paper. I bought it long ago for Carla's daddy. Never could bring myself to throw it away. But today it seemed appropriate."

That was a punch in the gut. Babette let out a mournful *ohhhh* and hugged Mom's shoulders. Sabrina continued to peel slowly. Bette went back to the Legos. Brooke started climbing on her mother's back for entertainment.

"Get down, Brooke. You're hurting my back," Babette said.

"I'm bored."

"Play with your sister."

"Why don't she rip it open?"

Babette sighed. "She's being careful."

Brooke rolled around and landed on Babette's lap. "I wanna see the present."

"She doesn't want to mess up the paper," I said.

Brooke scrambled onto the couch beside me. "She's like Uncle Simon, isn't she?"

I nodded and ruffled Brooke's curly blonde locks. "I guess she is."

The paper came off, was folded into a semblance of a square, and set on the coffee table.

Bette regained interest and half-crawled from the Legos to see what the treasure was. "Come on, Sabrina. Tear the box open."

Sabrina complied, tugging at the tape and flipping back the cardboard.

Inside the shirt box lay three items: bath salts, a small box of White Shoulders bath powder, and a yellow picture frame. Obviously not a five-year-old's present. Sabrina turned each item over and put them back in the box. She put the square of paper on top and lifted the whole thing up. "I'm putting them in my room."

Babette poked Mom. "See, I told you the powder was a good idea."

I rolled my eyes. Secondhand gifts. Mom had categorized Sabrina—not quite family, not good enough for a real gift, but important enough to be given something, like the mailman at Christmas and Mrs. Whitaker, who'd been her neighbor at the old homestead for twenty years.

I said, "If you don't like White Shoulders, why don't you tell Aunt Maggie instead of passing off her gifts to other people every year?"

"I thought she could put a picture of her mother in the frame. A girl should remember her mother."

I nodded. "Especially one with beautiful red hair. Anyway, she doesn't know about the letter yet. She thinks Phyllis will be back on Monday. Simon and I do, too. There's no way she won't come back."

Mom said, "Right. Miss Drugs and Harleys. I'm sure she'll be here at nine sharp."

"She never used drugs, Mom. She got arrested because she was *with* those guys."

Babette reclined the chair. "I didn't know you were putting the frame in there, Mom. I would have taken that."

Babette thought I didn't notice her eyes roving around the room, taking inventory. I ignored her and continued to stare Mom down. "By the way, thanks for the toys, but I'm sure Babette needs them back for her kids."

"Of course she needs them back. When I brought them over, we didn't expect her to be staying here permanently."

"We still don't," I replied.

* * *

That evening, Simon skipped his Friday club routine and stayed home. I wondered if he was trying to heal the distance between us, but I didn't ask. He'd rented a new video release. "Get her to bed so we can watch it," he said.

Easier said than done. Bedtime had become increasingly difficult. After her bath, I gave Sabrina permission to go down to the kitchen for a drink. "Be good," I whispered to her as we headed down the steps. "Simon is watching."

As she headed into the kitchen, I called after her. "Water." She returned with a glass of milk.

I took a deep breath. "Sabrina, I said water, and I've told you drinks must stay in the kitchen."

"Simon has his drink in here."

"Simon is an adult."

She proceeded toward the couch. I could feel Simon's eyes on us, watching us like actors on a stage, critiquing our lines to judge whether or not we performed correctly.

I let the milk part go. But Simon was watching. I had to save face. "Sabrina, go back to the kitchen."

"My mama lets me drink anywhere I want to."

"Sabrina, we've talked about that. We have different rules here. You must obey them."

She glared at me, kept walking, and tripped over a doll on the floor. The milk splashed out, across the coffee table, the magazines, the damask sofa, and the carpet.

"Sabrina! You are in major trouble now, do you understand me?" I shook a finger at her. "I can't believe you did this! You are a bad, bad girl." I'd wanted everything to go perfectly. Why hadn't she understood?

Instead of crying, her eyes spit fire at me.

"It's just a stupid old rug. Who cares?"

All the frustrations of the past three days rose in me. I gripped her arm. "You'll care when I'm done with you. You have to respect people's property."

Simon's voice cut through the air like ice, sharp but not raised. "Let her go, Carla, and go get a rag and carpet cleaner."

His voice brought me back. I released her, ashamed of my temper, but still seething. I didn't understand how she could be so sweet and then go into fits of obstinacy.

"Go," Simon said to me again.

I headed toward the kitchen, listening intently to what he would say.

"Carla told you not to drink milk and not to bring it in here. Do you understand that you broke two rules?"

She didn't reply. I stopped at the kitchen counter and watched them.

"I asked a question. Answer me." He was emphatic but soft spoken.

"I didn't want water."

"I didn't ask you what you wanted. I asked if you understood that you broke two rules."

I was impressed with the way he was handling it. His years as the big brother-*cum*-father figure had taught him well. He was separating the crime from emotions better than many a seasoned parent.

A bit of the flare died in her eyes. "Yes."

"Yes, sir," he prompted.

"Yes, sir."

"From now on you drink water before bed. If you drink anything else, you will be reduced to water the entire next day. No juice, no milk. Understood?"

"Yes."

"Excuse me?"

"Yes, sir."

"Fine. Up to bed."

She ran toward the steps.

"Sabrina," he called out.

She stopped and turned.

"Spilling the milk was not bad. Carrying it in here was. No one is convicted for an accident."

I doubt that she understood what he meant by *convicted*, but she nodded and plodded up the steps.

He didn't lecture me. He didn't even mention it. He put in the movie, waited for me to finish cleaning up the mess, then pushed *Play*.

I didn't want to sit with him. Guilt choked me. I shouldn't have let my anger get the better of me. My attitude had been as wrong as hers. I wanted to hold her and convince myself that I hadn't hurt her feelings. She had been bad, but I was the grown-up; she was the one who was feeling abandoned.

I needed something else, too. I needed some compassion. I needed caring arms wrapped around me. I needed to hear that I was doing okay at motherhood and that things would get better as we muddled along.

I put the cleaner and rag away and paused in the family room to stare at Simon. He wasn't going to give it to me. He couldn't tell me what I needed to hear.

He looked up from the television. "Are you ready? You're going to love this movie."

I didn't want to watch a movie. I wanted him to hold me. I wanted Sabrina cleaving to us. I wanted a family.

I walked past him and up the stairs to Sabrina's room.

She was almost asleep. I lay down beside her and stroked her silky head. She smelled like baby shampoo. I kissed her forehead. She mumbled something and flopped an arm across me. Tonight *I* needed *her*. I lay on top of the blankets and sighed. Why had the discipline mistakes seemed so blatant when I watched Babette? Being a mom was harder than I'd expected.

I woke in the black of night. Outside, the street was quiet, and Taz was curled on top of my legs, purring like a heater. Sabrina's body, so warm and angelic in slumber, rose and fell with quick childish breaths.

The door opened. A sliver of light cut across the room from the hallway. Sleep had cleansed me. I blinked and smiled at the light, knowing it was Simon. I was ready to make peace.

He stepped softly across the carpet and lifted the bunched-up covers back over Sabrina, then came to my side. His whisper hung like a dream around me. "Two hardheaded women. She's a lot like you, you know?" He kissed me softly, the way my daddy used to so long ago, a butterfly kiss that touched me deeply. I rose and joined him in bed.

The next day, I sat on the back deck watching Sabrina splash in the pool and called Mom on my cordless. The second reunion meeting had been moved up to that afternoon because half the committee members had high school-aged kids involved in the theater production opening Tuesday night. I had put off calling Mom all day, but I was getting desperate. It was almost time to get ready.

"Darling," she said in her you're-trying-my-patience tone, "I told you on Wednesday I will not baby-sit Sabrina. She's not our responsibility."

"But, Mom, I have to go to this meeting."

"I'd say it's time your husband helped with her."

"Right, Mom."

I hung up. How did my mother always know what was going on? The previous night had been his first real interaction with Sabrina—not something to build a relationship on.

I stared past Sabrina in the pool to the lake. A family of ducks, Mama with four fat ducklings behind, floated midway across our little bay. Two Jet Skis zoomed in, sped in a circle, and roared by, playing chase, which sent waves flapping across the surface. The ducks bobbed along over the rolling water. I felt like the ducks, bobbing along, close to being swamped by my problems.

I had to open communication with Simon and take a step in one direction or the other.

As if called by my thoughts, he came around the corner. Not a great surprise. He was a man of habit. He worked every Saturday morning, ate lunch at Franco's, bought groceries, then jogged for an hour, and followed it with a half-hour of laps in the pool.

He was singing quietly to himself. He often does when he's deep in thought. Most often it was contemporary Christian songs, but sometimes, like today, it was classic rock songs from the seventies and eighties, rooted in years of his life I hadn't been a part of, events he'd rarely revealed to me. The tune was familiar. A song by Chicago. I tried to remember it as I strained to hear the words—"Hard to Say I'm Sorry." I wondered if he was thinking of me or just singing on automatic, a melody left in his head from the radio in his car. He stopped singing as he approached the pool.

"Can you sit and talk?" I asked him.

His look was calm, indifferent. "Let me get wet first."

He dove into the water in perfect form and surfaced halfway down the pool. He struck out in a butterfly stroke, his figure gliding back and forth across the surface, his strength evident in the ripple of muscles across his back and arms. Fast, even-pumping strokes. His rhythm counted the passing seconds. Sabrina had paused in her play to watch and remained spellbound until he stopped.

"You sure do that good," she said.

"He does it well," I corrected her.

She made a face at me, then swished through the water toward him as he climbed the steps. "Can you teach me?"

"Of course he *can,* Sabrina. The question is, *will* he?"

He narrowed his eyes at me.

"I'm correcting her grammar, for heaven's sake, not insinuating anything."

He walked to the table and picked up a clean white towel he had left out before his jog, wiped his face, and toweled his hair before combing it.

I poured him some lemonade as he took a seat. "Simon, we have to resolve this. It's not her fault she got dumped here. You were so good with her last night, and now today you're giving her the cold shoulder again. Even if you're mad at me over this, give her a chance."

He didn't reply, but his gaze shifted to her and softened slightly. He sipped his lemonade.

I set my cup down. "Look, I have a problem. The reunion meeting was moved up from Tuesday to this afternoon at Gina's apartment. Mom won't baby-sit. Will you do it? I won't be gone very long. Please?"

"Hire someone."

"Simon, please. You ought to spend time with her. What if Phyllis doesn't show up Monday?" A voice in my head was telling me that his knowing this child would be the end of any chance of accepting her, but I was desperate to get away for a while.

"She'd better show up. But for now, the girl is your responsibility, not mine."

I actually moaned. "That doesn't mean I don't need a break! I've been with her around the clock for four days. I'm going insane." I realized Sabrina was looking at us, so I dropped my voice. "Please, Simon. You saw how she challenges everything I say. Give me a break. I'm worn out. And I need to go to this meeting."

"When?" he asked, in the same abrupt tone.

"I need to get ready now."

I could sense him holding his breath, controlling his emotions. His motto came to me: *Have faith.*

His answer seemed eons in coming. I was a child craning my neck to see the candy counter and waiting for my two-cent peppermint.

His words came out with all the air of his lungs. "All right. But don't be gone all evening."

I leaned over and kissed him. Without a word to Sabrina—I wasn't about to deal with an onset of tears over my departure—I dashed into the house, up the stairs to get ready.

Twelve

A half-hour later, dressed and ready for the reunion meeting, I paused in the upstairs hall. I could hear Simon's and Sabrina's voices rising above the splashing pool water, sporadic giggles ringing out. I stood on the upstairs balcony and spied on them.

"That's right," Simon said as Sabrina dog-paddled in circles around him. "Now you have to blow bubbles at the same time."

Guilt stabbed at me. How had I spent two afternoons by the pool with her, but never offered to teach her to swim?

I shook the thought away. I couldn't be responsible for everything. Besides, I didn't really like swimming. The chlorine made my skin itch and my hair brittle.

Below, in the water, Sabrina threw her arms around Simon. "I did it! I did it!"

Simon hesitated, then patted her back. "Yes, you did it."

A smile softened his eyes, and I gasped to see it. He didn't easily endow praise. My entire body relaxed from my heart outward as I stepped back through the door and hurried through the house, out to my Porsche.

The meeting was rather dull. After two days away from adults, I yearned for intelligent conversation, gripping news, controversial discussions, or something. The circles of inane conversation over trivial decisions gnawed at me. Compare this, weigh that, discuss it to death before deciding on any given issue.

Finally, it was my turn. Mom had done me proud by locating thirty-two of the missing addresses. The remaining names would involve more investigation.

"Oh," said Betsy as she took the typed list. "I found three. Let me see if you have them."

Right. Like Betsy could outdo my mother.

"Compliments of your mother, no doubt," said Gina, leaning over with a tray of carrots, broccoli, and fat-free dip. She always took advantage of her surroundings. In her apartment of gray carpet, charcoal gray leather furniture, smoky gray glass tables, she stood out in a white tank top and miniskirt. As many times as I had been to her apartment, I'd made the mistake of wearing—gray. At least my gray was a body-hugging knit sundress, but I felt like a sofa cushion.

She slunk over to Kevin—had I never noticed that self-assured gliding step she had?—and leaned over him with her cleavage hung in front of his face. "Care for any, Kevin?"

What an innuendo. The same thought must have flashed through every mind in the room. Kevin acted all innocent. "Not right now, thanks."

I repressed a groan. At the same time, it opened my eyes. Did Gina actually have designs on Kevin?

Bud Crawford stood up and cleared his throat, a habit that never resolved anything because he always sounded like a sick bullfrog. "That wraps it up then, huh? We all have our stuff to check on. Next meeting in two weeks at my place."

Everyone gathered belongings to leave. This time I was

right out the door with the rest of them. I figured I must have read more into Kevin's words on the phone than he'd meant. The way Gina's eyes were flashing, I had no intention of hanging around. I had enough problems without adding some weird Gina-Kevin-Carla triangle to my confusion.

Kevin had his own agenda. He squeezed between people and caught me at the curb. "Hey, look, I thought you were going to call me. We were going to spend some time together."

I blinked. "I thought maybe ..." No need to explain my observation. He was a man. He had to have noticed Gina. "I've got to get home." I unlocked my car door.

"Come on. You owe me a cup of coffee."

"I can't. I promised Simon I wouldn't leave him alone too long."

"Is there something wrong with him?"

I laughed. "No, nothing like that."

"Then what's your rush?"

The crowd had dispersed. It was only five-thirty. The sky was clear blue. An unexpected cool breeze was wafting across the lawns. Maybe a chat with a friend was just what I needed. Besides, Simon and I never ate before seven.

"It's complicated. He's watching Sabrina."

"Come on. He's a grown man, perfectly capable of watching a little girl for a bit. Give me an hour and tell me what's happening."

He looked so substantial standing there in front of me. Simon's body was well defined from his weight lifting, but he didn't have Kevin's bulk. Kevin was solid, thick. His face had softened with age but was still ruddy and handsome. Everything about him called out to my senses like an oasis. He wasn't holding any grudges against me like Simon was. I could talk to him.

I glanced at my watch again. "Forty-five minutes, max."

He took my hand and dragged me to his pickup. "You got it. Let's go."

I glanced back at my Porsche, but leaving it in Gina's parking lot was the most natural thing to do. Anyone who saw it would assume I had stayed behind to talk. I tried not to reflect on what Gina might think, especially if she had her heart set on catching the elusive Kevin. She wasn't above backstabbing.

His truck was cluttered. Papers lay strewn on the seat, old running shoes sat on the floorboard, and a couple of pens and loose change rolled around the dash. I was tempted to straighten the stack of papers. Instead, I relaxed beside him and listened to his country music.

He drove with one hand on the steering wheel and the other arm stretched across the seat behind me. "Tell me what's going on."

I explained about the letter and my guardianship.

"So Simon is taking care of her tonight? That's great. I remember the first night I had to take care of Matt alone. He was only eight weeks old. I was dressed for work, due for rounds in the hospital, and when I changed his diaper, he peed all over me."

Newborn stuff. It panged me to think I might never experience that. "I don't think Sabrina will pee on him. She's a bit old for that."

"Exactly. What could possibly go wrong? Five-year-olds practically take care of themselves."

"True, but she and Simon are both used to getting their own way. I'm not sure how they'll settle things."

"Have a little faith."

That sounded like Simon.

The park came into view. "Let's skip the coffee and go for a walk," I said.

We walked along the water's edge. We laughed about several people at the reunion meeting and how their lives had turned out so differently from what we'd expected. He slipped his hand into mine. My heart pounded. *We're just old friends*, I told myself. *Holding hands doesn't mean anything.* But I knew it wasn't so. We talked about our separate college days and career choices. Then he talked about us.

"I always thought we'd end up together, you know."

"Sure. That's why you married someone else."

He stopped and pulled me around to face him. "If I'd known there was any chance of having you back, I would have sought you out, but I figured you'd gone on with your life."

I pulled my hand free, turned, and kept walking. "That's exactly what I did, went on with my life."

Leaves crackled under our shoes. Squirrels scampered across the path. Geese plodded noisily out of the water, honking and hissing toward an elderly lady tossing hunks of bread.

"Are you happy, Carla?" he asked as he caught up.

I didn't answer right away. Was I happy? Would I veer from my course with Simon and cleave to something that used to exist with Kevin? "Happiness is relative."

"That's no answer."

"I've been happier. I've also been lonelier. I have too much going on right now to worry about it. I have a little girl at home who needs me and possibly a whole life to figure out for us."

He stopped me again. "I've been happier, too. I'm lonely. I miss you. Even when we went off to college, I had in my head that we were still together, just apart. Then I got caught up in life and married Heidi. Now, seeing you, knowing you're with someone else ..."

He didn't end the sentence. He leaned forward and kissed me. I don't think I was even surprised. I held back a second, then succumbed to it.

After all, it was only a kiss.

One kiss wouldn't change my marriage.

I couldn't let it change my marriage. I had a little girl waiting at home who needed me more than I needed Kevin.

Whatever my body was screaming, it couldn't be more than a kiss.

Thirteen

*K*evin and I didn't leave the park for hours. We walked up the hill and sat on the bench at the top, surveyed the park, and talked over all sorts of personal things: parents, siblings, the dogs we'd had in high school. Everything except The Now.

Then we went to supper at a quiet place with simple food on the outskirts of town where no one would recognize us. He suggested it, and I went along.

I couldn't let go of the moment. I didn't want to return to the present, to all my worries, to Simon's stern face and Sabrina's whining voice and all the battles I had to face to bring peace and order to my life.

I didn't mean to get home so late. I knew Simon would be furious being left with the bedtime routine on top of having to feed a child he didn't want. Sabrina was sure to have given him a fit over anything he offered her.

I trembled as I turned the key in the kitchen door.

The house was quiet.

I locked the door behind me and slipped off my pumps so they wouldn't clatter against the kitchen tiles, then sprinted across the family room and up the staircase.

Whispers pulled me to the end of the hall. I tiptoed,

slowly, straining to hear as I went, but Sabrina's pitch was too high; her words escaped me.

Simon's voice came to me as I neared the bedroom. It tickled my ears and alerted my senses.

"Yes, I do," he said. "Every night. And now when I say mine, I have something new to add."

"What?" She sounded so tiny after being away from her.

"God bless Sabrina," Simon said.

"Then I'll add you to mine."

"And Carla, too," Simon said.

"God bless Simon and Carla."

I peeked around the corner. She was seated cross-legged on the bed, hands folded, her eyes intent on Simon. Taz rubbed against Simon's leg, purring, and then jumped onto the bed and curled up in Sabrina's lap.

"Can I say God bless Mommy even if ..." She paused, and I wondered if she somehow knew about the letter. "... even when she's not here?" she asked.

"Yes, of course. Especially when she's not with you. Pray for her forever and ever. It's like reaching out your hand and touching her through God, wherever she is."

"God bless Mommy," she said with her eyes closed, then opened them again.

"I had fun today."

He nodded. "Me, too."

"I never had a daddy tuck me in afore."

He spoke very softly. "I'm not your daddy, Sabrina."

She screwed her face up at him. "You won't never be my daddy, will you?"

His head tilted toward the window for a long moment before he looked her in the eye. "We don't know what's going to happen with you, Sabrina. Carla and I will certainly take care of you for now, until everything is worked out. But no matter who you end up living with, no one will ever replace your real parents."

I couldn't believe it. He'd told her about Phyllis's letter.

Her famous whine returned. "I don't want to go nowhere. I like it here. I like you."

"Sabrina." His voice was stern, a reprimand for her tone. She didn't cower, but her expression sobered. There was a long pause. Her bottom lip quivered. He shifted a bit, wrestling with his qualms about being demonstrative. He'd spent too many years being the stern big brother. It had made him forget how to relax into being cuddly and soft. That had been his mother's role in the household. I hadn't thought of that in a while. I hadn't equated his reserve and reactions to what it must have been like raising siblings and having to act far beyond his age to keep things running orderly. He had grown up afraid to be too open with his emotions. He had repressed his affections for fear it would make him look soft, and he was slow to let go of those restraints.

He lifted his hand as if it were controlled by a marionette string—slow motion, stiff and forced—and laid it on her arm. "I'm glad you like it here. But we have a lot of legal red tape to wade through before anything can be settled. When your mother comes back, that will be all the better. I told you before, I'm sure she's going to come back just as soon as she can."

I bit my lip. What had happened in my absence? Was he really considering a permanent situation if Phyllis didn't return? Had his sense of responsibility opened to include her?

"Maybe if I call you Daddy, I'll get to stay here."

"I don't think that will help."

"Shirley Smith calls her parents Meemaw and Peepaw. Mommy said she was from some country place."

I was used to Sabrina's right turns in conversation. I held my breath waiting to see if Simon could follow her—and how he would react.

"People have different dialects and languages all over the world. In France they say *Maman* and *Papa*. Another place, I think in Brazil, in Portuguese, they say *Mãe* and *Pai*. Makes life fun, don't you think?"

She studied him closely, sucking in her lower lip. "I want to kiss you good night."

He sat very still for a minute but finally leaned forward. She scooted up on her knees, held his face between her tiny hands, and kissed him lightly on the cheek.

He sat back and smoothed her hair. I wished I had been able to see his expression, but his back was to me.

"Now, it's time to sleep," he said.

"Sleep with me like Carla does."

"No, you're a big girl. You know how to go to bed on your own. Get under those covers."

She slipped her feet under the blankets, displacing Taz, who flipped sideways and then resettled on the corner of Sabrina's pillow. Sabrina ignored the cat and pleaded with teary eyes, her voice edged with a whine. "But I don't like being alone in the dark. I have bad dreams."

He tucked the blanket around her and dropped Taz on the floor. "Nonsense. Think about all the things we talked over. Remember Jesus has his arms wrapped around you. No matter how alone you ever feel, he is with you—in the dark of night or the middle of a crowded playground. You can always close your eyes and feel him with you. He's there for the asking."

She closed her eyes. "I don't feel him."

"You're not being still enough. Be still in your mind. Feel his warmth surrounding you."

She peeked out one eye. "Are you gonna stay here?"

"No. I'm going to leave now so you can feel him in your heart all by yourself."

"Okay," she said and clamped her eyes shut. "Good night."

So docile! I couldn't believe the change in her.

I stepped out from behind the door and crossed the room. Simon glared at me, his opinion of my late arrival evident, but I focused on Sabrina. She squinted at me as I bent to give her a kiss on the forehead. Her breath rose up to meet me. The sweet smell of bubble-gum toothpaste filled my senses and I smiled. "Good night, Sabrina."

"Good night, Mäe."

Mäe! "Mother?" I prodded.

"Simon says I can only ever have one mama, but you can be my other one. Lots of kids at school have two. Now I will, too."

That took some of the glamour out of it, but I still hugged the name to myself. *Mäe.* It was a perfect moment in my life.

But perfect moments don't last.

I followed Simon to our bedroom and hummed as I undressed.

He came out of the bathroom in his boxers. "Long meeting."

"I'm sorry I'm so late. I guess I lost track of time."

"I'd say so," he said.

"Everything must have gone great with you two. I was listening at the door. She sounded so sweet."

"She's not sweet. She's willful and disobedient and spoiled. She's also hurting terribly and needs solidity in her life. I did what any responsible adult would do. I disciplined her when I had to and let her pour out her heartache when-ever the moment took her."

"Did you tell her Phyllis wasn't coming back?"

"Not in so many words. She kept asking if her mother had called. I said no. She kept asking when it would be Monday. I told her she couldn't count on her mother being here on Monday because things don't always go the way we plan. We have to grasp what we have in the here and now and be thankful for it."

His voice was cold, without the understanding tone he had used with Sabrina, but Simon tended to exude iciness when he was upset about anything. And he was upset, for sure. So was I. His words hit home. Sabrina was my here and now. She might not be on Monday, but she was today. Nothing else seemed solid. Not Simon, not Kevin, and cer-tainly not a baby after years of failure.

I just wanted to be held and loved. I wanted soothing words and tender caresses.

I crawled into bed, naked.

He knew my intentions. He stopped two feet short of the bed.

"Not tonight, Carla. Not this on top of everything else."

"What do you mean?"

"I could start with you staying out all afternoon and evening, then coming home as if nothing is wrong, but it's more than that. For all these months I've performed on your schedule—when you need it, when it's right for fertilization. You know what I want? I want to seduce you for a change. I want to actually just have the urge and be the one in charge, saying I want it. It's like you've become the man of the house, and I've become some sex servant."

I couldn't help myself. I laughed. "If your colleagues

could hear that complaint!"

He nodded, but didn't laugh. "I know it sounds stupid. And it's not that I don't want us to be equal partners. In fact, that is what I want. Equality. Not you dominating me or vice versa. If we've quit with the scheduled sex, then give me a break here. Let me lead. I want to come to bed with my own urges for a change. I want to seduce you."

"So come seduce me."

He pulled a T-shirt from his dresser drawer and left the room.

A few minutes later, music drifted up from the family room. A sappy love song. I wondered whom my husband was dreaming about.

I touched my lips and thought of Kevin.

I slept fitfully, rising once to find Simon asleep on the couch, one arm hanging to the floor, his feet perched over the end. Never mind that we had a whole spare room upstairs. He was making a point.

I went back to bed and stared at the ceiling. I thought of his words to Sabrina about Jesus holding her. After all her nights of crying and turmoil, she had settled into bed easily for Simon. I wanted to be glad he'd done so well, but jealousy rose in me and burned like a fire.

I shoved away my resentment. I hadn't the energy for it. I wanted sleep. I wanted peace. I thought of his words to Sabrina and closed my eyes. I tried to picture Jesus sitting beside me. All I saw was the inside of my eyelids.

The sun edged up my bed in long streaks of light shining between the slats of the blinds. I winced as I glanced at the clock and realized it was time for Simon to leave for church.

He would expect me to be in the family room with Sabrina, not upstairs in bed, especially after my escapade the evening before. I heaved myself out of bed so he wouldn't berate me for making him late.

I rarely left my room before dressing in the morning, but I didn't have any time left. I pulled on my long pink satin robe, thinking it looked the most motherly of the lot, like a film-star mother from the forties, except my hair was poking out here and there where I'd slept on it. I shrugged at my disheveled image and headed downstairs.

Two minutes more and I would have missed them. They were at the kitchen door, Simon squatting on the floor and buckling Sabrina's sandals. Sabrina looked like an angel, decked out in a pale blue dress with a puffy underskirt and lace trim, something I hadn't seen before. Had he taken her shopping the day before? Her hair had been pulled into a ponytail, not quite smooth on top, but impressive considering that Simon had never fixed any child's hair that I knew of. Then again, maybe he had styled his little sister's hair every morning before school. I pictured him standing in the bathroom—a skinny kid of ten, then twelve and fifteen—creating pigtails and braids, and later helping his sister with curlers and a curling iron.

He wasn't a man of words; he was a man of actions.

"What's going on?" I asked.

Simon stood up. "We're going to church, of course."

This was different from bedtime prayers and little Bible stories. He was trying to exert some power. "You're taking Sabrina?"

He reached over, opened the door to the garage, and waved Sabrina through. "Go get in the car, Love."

Always the lawyer, he set precedence right then. He

initiated us as parents who would argue only in private.

With Sabrina out of earshot, he said, "I thought you were set on us assuming the role of parents, at least temporarily."

"Yes, I am. What other choice do we have? My best friend trusted me to care for her daughter. And we want a child. I don't understand why you're fighting me on this."

"I'm not fighting you. I'm taking her to church."

"But Phyllis isn't Christian. She wouldn't want that for Sabrina."

"She made you guardian. You made me husband. That makes me the father figure and responsible for her upbringing."

"Upbringing according to what her mother would want."

"No. Upbringing according to the best of our abilities. If you want us to assume this role, we are responsible for her, body and soul. We will dress her the best we can. We will feed her and educate her and teach her to ride a bike the best we can. And I will take her to church, because that is what a father does. A Christian father, anyway."

"What if she doesn't want to go?"

Blankness settled on his face. All the tension fell out of it, emptied the fire from his eyes and the anger from his thin, set lips. He had gone beyond exasperation and was trying to reach his *point of peace* as he called it. "We are all brought to Christ in our own way, Carla. I can't force my faith on you. I know that. But a child must be taken by the hand and taught. If I am to act even temporarily as her father, she will be treated no differently than a child from your womb. While she's here, I will work toward her salvation as I would my own child's."

I raged at the thought of him taking control, and yet I also rejoiced. He was taking an interest in Sabrina. If it took the power of the Bible held between them to accomplish the feat, I had to bow to it. As I backed off and observed them, I wondered if I, too, would bow to the power of God's Word before all was said and done.

Nevertheless, I let him go out the door and considered it a victory. I had no idea what had transpired in my absence, but my heart leaped with gratification. He seemed to have come to terms with Sabrina in his own way, at least for the short term.

Unfortunately, he was still holding a grudge against me for staying gone so long, for not telling him about Sabrina up front, for ruining our sex life, and for draining our marriage.

And he didn't even know about the insemination ... yet.

I could safely say Sabrina had finally settled into the house, at least until Phyllis returned.

The question was whether or not Simon and I would stay together.

Fourteen

ince Simon had carried Sabrina off to church, I decided to follow tradition and head out to the bagel shop.

Gina wasn't there, but I took a seat at the closest table and waited. Two lean male bodies walked past, sat at the end booth, and bent their tawny heads forward in conversation. A perfect brick-house Barbie showed up and slipped onto a stool at the front of the shop to flirt with Tony, the owner and cook. One of the tawny heads poked up to gaze at her, then fell forward to murmur again.

Minutes later as Nancy, ever efficient, set my food in front of me, Kevin walked in the door and slid into my booth. "Your mother was telling the truth. You do eat brunch here every Sunday."

All the ambience of the night before was gone. I could hardly look at him. My mind was still confused over Simon and Sabrina. "My mother always tells the truth. It seems to keep me in trouble."

He half-stood at that comment. "Do you want me to leave?"

"No, sit. I need company. Looks like Gina isn't showing up." No big surprise there. She had probably seen Kevin dropping me off at my Porsche after nightfall. If she actually had her eye on him, she would be rather peeved at me.

Nancy sauntered up, took his order with only half a smile, and left. To Nancy, Kevin was just a middle-aged guy with nothing special going for him. In this healthy-body dining spot, she saw major hunks every day. If she had known how loaded Kevin was, she might have batted her eyelashes a bit more, but I don't think Kevin would have noticed. His attention was locked on me.

I lifted my eyes and closely appraised him in the morning light. He reeked of manhood. His hair was still damp from showering. He hadn't shaved yet. I liked the shadowed scruff of his chin. I wanted to reach across the table and run my hand over his cheeks and jaw. He had a deep green polo shirt on, with the three little buttons left undone. The fringe of his hairy chest drew my eyes.

His voice yawned with the morning. "How did Simon get along with ... what's her name?"

He asked his question with such innocence. His eyes became wide and round. His mouth fell into a soft smile. The moment transcended all the years, back to when he had used his wiles on teachers and unsuspecting friends to get the goods on local happenings. What he was really looking for was trouble between Simon and me, a weak spot to crawl further into my life. I didn't plan to let him find the rift just yet. "Her name's Sabrina. Simon handled it fine."

"Not sore at you for missing supper?"

"He never mentioned it, actually."

"I bet. If I had a woman like you coming home, I wouldn't waste time talking either."

If only he knew.

I leaned back in my seat. Simon flitted through my mind, but only momentarily. Here was a man willing to listen to me, intent upon my words, and ready to share my heartache as Simon had ages ago. The difference was that throughout our relationship, Kevin had never lost his intense interest in my life and had showed me the same importance each time we met. Simon, on the other hand, didn't want to talk. Simon didn't even want to look at me, let alone touch me. He'd made that plain by his night on the couch.

As Kevin gazed at me, powerful memories of being admired and touched tingled up my spine. My ego craved being regarded as a woman, completely. Simon wouldn't talk to me. I yearned for a man's compliments and attention. "You and I spent many an afternoon talking."

His face remained calm, but his eyes gleamed. "Give me your afternoon, and we'll talk up a storm."

I knew what he meant. I was tempted, so very tempted, but an image of Sabrina in her puffy blue dress rose before me. The curse of responsibility and propriety bled into my brain. I blamed it on the hand of God giving me a flare of conscience.

I shook my head at him. "I have plans already." I didn't really, but I couldn't have Sabrina and Simon starting up some kind of family-tradition thing while I played footsie in the park with an old beau. I wanted it all, and I just couldn't figure out exactly how I could blend both my desires into one.

Gina chose that moment to show up looking like some ethereal princess of the sunrise. Her skin was so flawless, her hair so glossy, and her clothes hugged her oh-so-perfect curves; all my good feelings evaporated. I felt frumpy. Kevin noticed her, too. His eyes lingered on her a second too long. I swear she must have expected him to join us.

Her voice was as crisp and perky as her skimpy blue jumper. "Good morning, Kevin. I'm so delighted we have some male company this morning."

I sipped my orange juice and said nothing as she shimmied in beside him and faced me. Hers was a game of cat and mouse, and I wasn't playing.

She signaled to Nancy for food, then laid her hand lightly on Kevin's arm. "You two must have had quite a night to still be together this morning."

Right. Like she hadn't seen him drop me off at my Porsche and drive off. If she wanted to insinuate we'd spent the night together, I wasn't going to deny her the pleasure. No need to let her know how miserable things were between Simon and me or how platonic I remained with Kevin. She would only use it to her advantage. And she already had enough advantages. I was, after all, only human. "Fantastic night, actually," I replied.

Kevin raised his eyebrows, but let my comment pass. "That was a great meeting, Gina. You have a nice apartment," he said.

Gina lifted her arm away from his as Nancy laid their plates down. I suspected, more than saw, her hand drop to his leg. "You're welcome to come over anytime, Kevin. I love entertaining."

She left a word off there. What she meant was she loved entertaining *men*. She didn't give a flip about doing the society scene. She attended everything in town but was usually too lazy to offer any dinners in return. She used her single status as an excuse to everyone.

"In that case," he said, "how about escorting me to the mall and then fixing lunch for me? I was trying to convince Carla to come with me, but she's already busy."

The only thing Gina loved more than the male species was the mall. Her dawning expression put the Cheshire cat to shame. "I'd love to!"

There I was, the third wheel. I had gone years without giving Kevin a thought. But now, watching Gina weave her little web around him made me want to sprout claws from my fingertips. My marriage became a separate thing, set aside from who I was. I was filled with a stronger desire for Kevin than I had ever experienced in high school. I wanted it all. I wanted my marriage and my old beau, which made no sense at all. Irrational jealousy. But why not? Simon had rejected me straight out, not even tempted by the sight of me naked in bed, and Kevin had plainly expressed his desire. I was a woman. I needed to be loved. Kevin belonged to me, not Gina.

My stomach twisted as I left them to their afternoon delight and headed home. I tried not to think of how they would spend the hours or how they would end the day together. I tried to convince myself that it didn't bother me. Instead, I thought of the insemination, the eternal hope of having a baby. I hugged my secret inside, wondering if this time it would come true.

Fifteen

Back home, I sat at the kitchen table and counted days on my pocket calendar. I had three more days to go before my pregnancy test.

I laid a hand on my stomach. Had anything been different? With all the hormones I'd been on, I wasn't sure I would recognize a change.

I pulled a crystal goblet from the cabinet and drank a full twelve ounces of ice water. If my period was coming, I didn't want to get bloated. There was no reason to think this month would end any differently than all the months and years that had already ticked by. I had been on this roller-coaster ride too long. I felt depressed, and I hadn't even heard the bad news yet, the negative result. It had become bad luck to be too hopeful. I had decided that if I expected the test to be negative this time, maybe it would come back positive.

Sabrina and Simon came into the house singing.

"*I love Jesus, and Jesus loves me. When I get to heaven, it's Jesus I will see ...*"

Simon stopped when he saw me, but his smile lingered, fading away gradually as he sobered.

"My," I said, "sounds like you learned a new song, Sabrina."

"Yup." She skipped off through the house, her music floating behind her.

Simon met my eyes, a strange, foreign look I couldn't define. He walked toward me, then stopped to yell, "Sabrina, set your dress on the bed to be hung up, please." He came closer and laid his hands on my shoulders, kissed me gently, formally, then dropped his arms and walked toward the stairs.

I followed him toward the singing imp. "I'll help her with it. Let's take the boat out and eat at the Lakeside Restaurant."

"I didn't know you had plans for us. I scheduled a golf game with Rick."

I trudged up the steps, facing another day on my own.

Sabrina was well behaved all day. The Taylor kids were home from vacation and came over to meet her.

"Can I play with them?" she begged.

I looked at Melissa, the twelve-year-old with lipstick and eye shadow, and the two boys wrestling, punching, and sneering at each other behind Melissa. I wondered why they would call on a five-year-old.

"We're going down to the lake, Mrs. Rochwell," Melissa said. "We'll watch her, we promise."

Not hardly.

Sabrina, wide eyed at the sight of them, pulled on my shirt. "Please can I? I never got to swim in the lake."

"We have the pool."

"But there's fish in a lake."

Exactly.

She continued to plead.

With my last objection being safety, Melissa ran home and returned with a child's lifejacket. I followed them down to the dock and sat with my feet dangling in the cool water while the four of them jumped in and splashed, climbed out, and jumped in again. The noise was deafening, but I hoped the exercise and fresh air would mean an easy bedtime that evening.

I was wrong. Sabrina started begging me to sleep with her before her pajamas were completely over her head.

"No, Sabrina. You went to bed just fine for Simon last night. You must do it again tonight."

"But I'm scared tonight."

"Well, do what he said to do."

"Huh?"

I mentally pried my mouth open and forced the words out. "You know, think about Jesus or whatever holding you."

I didn't fool her. "Why didn't you go to church with us? Don't you like to sing?"

"Something like that."

"Pai said people who don't go to church don't know how much Jesus loves them."

"Some people love Jesus even if they don't go to church."

"Do you?"

I had walked right into that one. "I try to love everyone. Isn't that what Jesus asks you to do?"

"Yes. That's what the teacher said in Sunday school. She said when we get to loving Jesus, we start loving everybody more, even ourselves."

Mom thought I loved myself too much already. "Sounds like a good plan."

"I talked to Pai about it on the way home. He said when we learn to like ourselves, it's easier to love God. And when we love God, we like ourselves better. It's a circle."

"Simon is very philosophical."

"What's 'sofical mean?"

"It means he likes circles."

For the sake of peace, I lay down beside her and rubbed her back as she fell asleep. I had stuff to think about anyway, like Jesus wrapping his arms around us both and why exactly I was opposed to trusting in him.

My father's face came to me, and I moaned. I had loved my father dearly. Wasn't it God's fault he died? Wasn't God supposed to have his hand on all the world? How could I trust God when he had taken my father?

I could see my father shaking his head and smiling peacefully toward me. Others went on without resenting God for the death of loved ones. How?

After my father's death, I had railed against God in anger. And then I ignored his existence, sure that if he existed he would make himself known. And then, in desperation for a child, I had turned my eyes heavenward and asked God for his mercy. He hadn't heard me. He hadn't answered. "All in God's time," Simon assured me. I ignored him. *Let him wait on God's time,* I had thought; I would control my own destiny.

Lying beside Sabrina, I became aware of the truth. Even in my sardonic realism I knew God existed. I had known it even when I insisted for my own peace of mind that there was no God. What I hadn't done was what Simon had told me time and again: I hadn't subjugated myself before God, laid my woes at his feet, and left my life to his will.

I still couldn't bring myself to leap from that edge. My daddy had taught me to be self-sufficient, and I was. I could shoulder the world all by myself. To let go and allow someone else to take control would be to admit defeat. I wasn't one to lose at anything. I went after what I wanted, and I usually got it.

My problem was that I didn't know what I wanted anymore. Should I try to work things out with Simon, or give up and go for Kevin?

Sixteen

stayed home all day Monday. I didn't want to risk a chance of missing Phyllis's arrival.

Sabrina wore a path from the family room to the living-room window.

Phyllis never came.

At ten till five, I called Phyllis's office in Virginia. I had worked there with her for several years. The number came to me as if it had only been a week since I left. The same receptionist answered, a young girl who spent her life drifting from one ski partner to the next. "Hello, Evelyn. It's Carla." I tacked on my maiden name. "Carla Docker."

"Hello. It's been ages! How are you?"

"Fine, fine. I was wondering if Phyllis is in today."

"Goodness, no. Haven't you two kept in touch? She quit last year. I heard she moved away, not even in the area since January."

"Oh my. That's right. What am I thinking? I forgot she gave me that new number. Take care."

I stared at the phone and thought of the letter. She'd moved and not told me. She really was on the run. What was she running from? I hadn't a clue. Except that she had said *he* in the letter. A man. She must have gotten mixed up with the wrong sort of man ... again. I rubbed my temple and wondered how I could reach her, how I could help her. How I could save her once more.

Simon walked in with the question on his face.

I shook my head.

He didn't scold or reiterate his feelings. He kept his voice low. "I'll call a private investigator tomorrow. We can't just wait indefinitely." He pulled a bag out of his briefcase and a storybook out of the bag, then motioned Sabrina to sit with him in his chair.

I couldn't take it. I walked down to the lake and cried.

On Tuesday, I saw Kevin in passing at the grocery store, a chance meeting with Sabrina in tow. He couldn't have known my schedule. The luck of our passing made it all the sweeter. The sight of him made my breath catch.

He made a point of speaking to Sabrina. "I've heard about you."

Sabrina frowned and pulled on my arm. She was in a pensive mood. She knew Monday had come and gone. "I'm hungry."

I had learned that children were always hungry between mealtimes, but rarely hungry when the food was put in front of them. The cycle drained me. Why couldn't she say something nice to Kevin and not just stand there, demanding to be fed?

Apparently Kevin didn't find her reply the least bit out of line.

"I bet you are hungry," he said to her and looked back at me. "My kids are always hungry. Let's go get a greasy hamburger."

Ugh. Just what I didn't want. But Kevin didn't have fast food in mind. He piled us into his truck and carried us through town to the little Mom and Pop's Diner where we'd bought burgers, fries, and thick shakes in high school.

"So Phyllis didn't show," he said.

"No."

"And?"

"And Simon is hiring an investigator today to find her."

On Wednesday we saw Kevin again. This time at the drugstore checkout. He waved a candy bar at the cashier to ring up, then passed it on to Sabrina without comment.

With my finger poked in her side, she thanked him.

Lunch was my treat that day, a nice place with lobster and Alaskan king crab. Shellfish can make me ill, but I love it so much that sometimes I risk it. I'd been thinking of oysters all day.

Kevin seemed unaffected by the posh surroundings. He leaned his elbows on the table and stared into my eyes. "I haven't seen nearly enough of you. When are we going to have some time alone?"

"When am *I* going to have some time alone? Does that happen after kids?"

He laughed. "You need a baby-sitter."

On Thursday morning, I woke up dizzy and nauseated. The oysters.

When I wasn't up by nine, Sabrina peeked into my room. "I'm hungry."

"Sorry, hon. I don't feel well. Can you eat a banana?"

"You have the flu?"

"No. The oysters from yesterday. They make me sick sometimes."

"Then why'd you eat 'em?"

"Stupidity."

She had edged into the room and stood at the foot of the bed.

"You can come close. You're not going to catch any germs. It's just my body telling me not to eat oysters anymore."

She came to my side and laid her hand on my forehead.

I smiled wanly. "Do I feel okay?"

"I guess. Mama always did that when I got sick."

I noted the past tense but withheld comment. "She was checking your temperature. Your body heats up when it's fighting off germs." I patted the bed. "Want to get in with me?"

She crawled into bed, and we slept together until ten o'clock. I woke up feeling refreshed and gladdened by her little body in my bed. "Oh my! We have to get ready, quickly. I have a doctor's appointment in an hour."

I noticed my neighbor Sue Taylor at home and begged her to watch Sabrina for an hour while I ran to the clinic to have the blood sample drawn.

I returned right on time and towed a reluctant Sabrina out of the Taylor house.

The results weren't ready till hours later. I called the nurse at three.

"The test was inconclusive," she said. "Your hCG count isn't high enough to confirm anything."

My brain froze. "What does that mean?"

"It means we don't know anything. You need to come back in tomorrow."

If anyone had touched me right then, I would have shattered. I was strung miles up in the air on a high wire, the thinnest line of hope I'd had yet. Hoping and yet not daring to hope. I felt like I was holding my breath. I couldn't take a wrong step. There might be a baby inside of me, and if I took a wrong step, said the wrong thing, it would disappear.

I couldn't keep still. I washed dishes, rearranged books on the shelf, snapped at Sabrina for turning on the awful noise of cartoons. I had to get out of the house.

We went to visit Mom. Sabrina sat happily in the kitchen and pigged out on chocolate cake and vanilla ice cream. Mom urged me into the family room.

"I'm hearing lots of interesting tidbits about you this week," she said.

I could only think of the baby, but Mom wouldn't know about that yet. She couldn't. But her cronies must have found something to gossip about. "Let me guess," I said. "Your buddies have caught wind of Sabrina's presence, and they think she's some child I had in college or what?"

"Now, that's a thought. But no, I'd told them about her already."

"Figures. So what's the buzz about?"

"That you've been seen out with Kevin, of course. The word is you're getting back together."

I froze. If others knew I'd been seeing Kevin, what might Simon know? But I couldn't let Mom catch me off guard. "The woman is always the last to know. I hope you pointed out to them that I'm married?"

"That's why it's hot news. Everyone's waiting to see what comes of it. Simon was never right for you."

So much for her Christianity. But I wasn't touching *that* subject. "Mom, I'm not going to do anything stupid. I'm married, *and* I have a child to care for. Phyllis didn't come back Monday."

"What? You're thinking of that girl as family now?"

It choked me to say the words aloud that had been echoing around in my head like passage to an alien dimension. "It appears Phyllis may not be coming back."

Sabrina entered the room. "You go watch TV, dear," Mom said to her as she motioned me into the kitchen. "But surely you'll find Phyllis and give her back?"

"We're trying, Mom. But the police said if she doesn't want to be found, she won't be. They said a dead body is easier to find than a live one. Our last resort is a private detective."

"So hire one."

"We have. He hasn't found anything yet."

She gathered dirty dishes and clanked them together in the sink just loud enough to punctuate her hostility.

I said nothing.

She just couldn't accept it. "You can't mean you want to be stuck with her?"

Here it came. Another box. Sabrina's would be labeled *Burden*.

"You're not thinking straight, Mom. I would have thought that you and Simon would both have chosen the word *blessed*. Don't all things come from God?"

I meant to stun her, but nothing fazed my mother. She changed tactics. "She's so skinny. I don't think Phyllis fed her."

"She's eating plenty with us."

She rinsed the dishes and set them to dry. She shrugged stiffly. "Well, I hope your marriage can withstand the pressure of raising someone else's child. Simon's not exactly the easygoing type."

"Simon and Sabrina seem to really like each other."

My mother looked at me skeptically.

"Mom! Why do you dislike Simon so much? You should see him. He is really good with her."

The words settled around us. I defended Simon so vehemently to my mother that I wondered why. Simon did seem dry to outsiders, but he was a good, hardworking man. I had shared my life with him for four years. He was conscientious, industrious, and even loving in his own quiet way. But why was I defending him? He was stubborn and willful and despicable when it came to the whole insemination issue.

But I knew why I was defending him. He had shown great affection for Sabrina, teaching her to swim, buying her clothes, and talking with her. I had never expected that.

Two plates smacked together in the water. Mom held them up to examine them as if they were something valuable, as if they held more importance than my marriage. I was on the edge and knew better than to let my words fly. I skipped further small talk and got straight to the point of my visit. "I thought maybe I would try once more and ask if you would babysit. Friday?"

"Who are you going out with?"

"Does it matter?"

She regarded me for a moment. "I'll do it."

I don't know what made her give in, and I didn't ask. I just wanted a night off to be by myself with time to think.

That night, I lay in bed beside Simon and thought of Kevin. Were my mother and her cronies right? Was I on the verge of giving in to my desire? Was my marriage going to last, or was I flirting with disaster?

I turned toward Simon. His breathing was heavy, deep in slumber. I knew in my head our marriage was the right choice, but I had to have the reassurance of his touch. I had to know he really did care about me. My head was full of Mom's words. My eyes were full of Kevin. My heart was racing with uncertainty.

I propped myself up on one elbow and ran my hand up Simon's chest to wake him up.

His eyes opened. He didn't speak. He just lay there and stared at me with hard eyes.

"Come on, Simon, it's been days. You mean you don't want me to take the initiative at all? I need you, Simon."

"Do you need me? Or do you just need sex?"

I sat up and crossed my arms. Inside, I was crying with the need to express my love, but those words didn't come out. All the endearments and passion were sucked back inside. The flutters of tenderness were whisked into oblivion, replaced with scorn. "You want me to become some submissive little wife. I can't. I'm independent. If I feel excited, I want to do something about it."

He closed his eyes. Praying, I supposed. Finding that center of his. I was poised for a battle.

He opened his eyes and spoke. "Do you remember when we used to share our fantasies?"

His words squelched my resentment. I nodded. I wasn't the only one thinking of our beginnings.

He sat up and put on the silky blue robe my mother had bought him for Christmas. He had laughed at the gift, at my mother's notion of him, but used it all the same. He went to the bathroom, then headed out the bedroom door, waving me to follow. "Come on," he said.

My interest was piqued—Simon up in the middle of the night! I followed him down the stairs and stopped at the bottom. Moonlight dimly lit the room through the back patio doors. Simon didn't turn on a light. Instead, he went to the mantel, struck a match, and lit the five candles on display there. Flames danced as he moved toward the stereo. Music fluttered into the room, the same sappy soft love song I'd heard him playing Saturday night after I'd stayed out so late and he'd slept on the couch. He hadn't been thinking of another woman. He'd been thinking of me. Tears trickled down my cheeks.

He pulled me to the center of the room. "My tough lady isn't crying, is she?"

"I'm not tough."

"Only on the outside. Like an M&M's candy. Soft and sweet on the inside."

I smiled through my tears. I had forgotten his funny analogies. It had been a while since he'd used one. It had been a while since we'd even talked about anything that wasn't an argument.

"Now, let me lead," he said.

I understood.

I sank into his arms, head on his shoulder, and danced with him, small shuffling steps not meant to do anything but keep our bodies melded in rhythm. His hands started on my waist but soon wandered up the back of my shirt, lightly scratching my skin, teasing my flesh with his tender caresses.

I turned my mouth to his, and we kissed—really kissed—tasted each other with all the emotion of our first kisses, all the promise of the future.

Morning came all too quickly, with little sleep behind us. Simon had left at dawn without my even stirring.

I felt woozy all morning.

I was afraid to even think of my sick stomach being anything other than flu or the oysters. To think it might bring bad luck, might tease the fates and snatch any trace of fetus out of me.

I had planned to go into the plant but changed my mind.

I couldn't go to work. I couldn't begin to act nonchalant. Only one thought raced through my mind, and I had to be at home when I found out.

Seventeen

I dialed the plant to speak to my production manager. "Max, I am so sorry. My friend still hasn't shown up. I'm going to register Sabrina for day care or something, so I'll be in next week, but in the meantime, I'm leaving you in charge for the rest of the week." We covered some touchy areas that needed watching and rescheduled two meetings. Max was capable of doing my job and was glad to have the chance to prove it. It wasn't often I stayed away from the office for long stretches.

We had a long weekend coming up for Independence Day, so, counting the weekend, I had through the following Tuesday with Sabrina before going back to work full time. Odd that I had wished the days by at first. Now there seemed to be a hundred things to get done. Clothes to buy. A visit to the park. She had asked to plant a pot of flowers for the front step, as the Taylor girl had done next door.

I felt miserable from lack of sleep, but in my bones I thought miserable must be good. Miserable could mean good news.

As I showered and changed, my hands lingered over my naked body, looking for a bulge in my abdomen that didn't exist yet, seeking a sign in my breasts, but finding none.

*   *   *

I dressed Sabrina and packed a picnic lunch for the park.

First, we stopped at the Women's Fertility Center. I left Sabrina in a special kiddie waiting room complete with television and puzzles and adult supervision.

Rose, Dr. Freeman's nurse, was the kind of assistant who remembered names and history. She took the time to know her patients and remember the details. She raised her eyes as I walked by with Sabrina. I explained it all to her while we waited for the doctor.

She patted my arm. "If your friend has that much faith in you, it's all for the best, especially with you wanting a child so badly. God works in strange ways. The way I see it, God gave you blessings twice over."

I didn't reply. She sounded like Simon.

Dr. Freeman stopped when he saw me in the lab and laughed at me. "Rose told me the story. Now, with your luck, not only will your hCG count be up, you'll end up having triplets."

I felt the blood drain from my face.

He laughed again and patted my arm. "Calm down. We won't even know if the test is positive for a few hours yet. We've kept you on a stringent schedule of hormones. As long as you adhered to the dosage, we won't expect more than one."

I nodded, speechless.

At the park, the morning sun lay like a warm hand upon us, cutting through the chill left from the June night. We walked across the grass to a sunny spot. I planned to bask there for hours, listening to Sabrina chatter while ducks squawked a ways away, down at the pond.

It was tough waiting hours and hours to have the doctor's confirmation. It made me wish I had chosen a smaller clinic where my lab work would have been processed immediately. Still, it was a sweet agony holding a secret from the entire world.

I kept my eyes averted from the bench where I'd sat kissing Kevin. I couldn't add that scene to the tensions of the moment.

Sabrina had remembered a blanket. She made it her job to spread it on the grass and then unpacked all our food while I lay flat on my back, pondering life. A unicorn-shaped cloud floated overhead. An elderly man with clothes hanging on him like a thin scarecrow nodded as he shuffled by with a trash bag. Birds twittered in the trees.

"Mäe, the nurse said that was a baby-making place."

I rolled over and chuckled at her. "I guess you could call it that."

"Did you order a new baby there?"

"It's not a matter of ordering one. The doctor gave me medicine to help me conceive, to have a baby. Later today we'll see if it worked."

Sabrina had smoothed out the blanket and set out two plates with sandwiches and carrot sticks. A terrific job for a five-year-old. "Have you done this before?"

"'Course. Mama and I used to go listen to music in the park." She sank to her knees.

"Sounds like fun." I thought of her analysis of the composers. "What kind of music?"

"Different kinds. I like music. I like to dance to it."

"You like to dance? Why didn't you tell me?"

"I did. I told you I wanted to play some CDs, and you said I couldn't 'cause they were Pai's."

Her use of our new titles delighted me. Would the baby call us by those names?

"Oh, Sabrina, I'm sorry. Simon is very particular about his things. Maybe we can get a small stereo for your room."

"Pai already let me use his. I danced a bunch for him. He's just like my daddy. Daddy likes to watch me dance too."

I wasn't sure what to say. This was the second time she had mentioned her father, a man I was led to believe would never know of Sabrina's existence. "Do you know where your daddy is?"

"At the park. I always saw him at the park. Mama said he could only meet us there. Not at home. He kept on asking, but Mama said not to tell him."

She flopped back on the blanket and chewed on a sandwich.

"Sit up, Sabrina. You're going to choke."

Ron's image whirled in my mind. I imagined that he and Phyllis had reunited for a brief sexual encounter. Perhaps Phyllis, in her inevitable belief in human goodness, had confessed Sabrina's parentage. What a mistake.

The sun became hot and draining as I contemplated what Ron's knowledge of Sabrina could mean.

Nothing, I decided. He hadn't done anything in five years to claim her. He wouldn't now.

I sat up, determined to get on with the day. "Pass me one of those sandwiches, and eat your crusts."

"No, the crusts are for the ducks, silly."

Silly. Had that word ever been used to describe me? I had a lot to learn about being Mäe.

While we were running our errands, I sidetracked to a small, white building downtown. It was time to start acting like Sabrina was a permanent part of the family. I couldn't live from day to day wondering anymore. "This stop is for you, Fancy Feet."

"I'm not Fancy Feet."

"Maybe not yet, but this place will take care of that."

We walked into the dance studio, empty this time of day except for an office worker. "I'd like to register this young lady," I explained.

"Has she ever had ballet before?"

"No."

Sabrina spoke up. "Have too. I'm not a baby, you know."

The lady and I both looked alarmed. Me, because Sabrina hadn't told me. The lady because she must have wondered why I didn't know of my daughter's activities.

"Excuse me, Miss Jenkins," I said to the lady's nametag. "I stand corrected."

We were given a form to fill out. "There is a summer class in progress. It just started last week. She can come Saturday at three o'clock, if you'd like her to start right away."

Sabrina nodded excitedly.

I debated. I was tempted to ask for the Tuesday evening class, to see Sabrina outdance Brooke. I reconsidered. Better to let Sabrina practice first, so I nodded. "Sure. Three o'clock Saturday."

As we got into the car, I patted her rump. "Better hurry it up there. We just added shopping for dancewear to our list of chores."

Sabrina yahooed and clicked her seat belt into place.

At two, I pulled through a drive-thru and ordered Sabrina a milkshake. As she slurped on it, I called the fertility center and asked for Rose.

"The count looks great. It's right up there now. We'll need to confirm it with a vaginal ultrasound in two weeks, so let's schedule that. If it all goes well, you'll switch over to your regular obstetrician for the ten-week exam."

"You mean ... I mean ..." I couldn't get the words out of my mouth. They were stuck in my head and in my gut. "It's positive?"

"Yes, ma'am. A strong indication. As I said, the ultrasound will verify it."

"It really worked. I'm having a baby."

She laughed. "Yes, it looks that way."

"Oh, thank you. Thank you."

I sat with the cell phone in my lap and stared out the window. I felt like I was going to explode. Nothing seemed real. After so many failures, so many negative results, I couldn't trust the news to be true. I couldn't believe it to be true.

"The medicine worked, huh?" Sabrina said.

Sabrina had heard it, too. Proof positive.

She made it sound so simple. To her, being here for a week of it, it must seem simple. I cried and nodded, amazed at being able to declare it. "Yes, it worked. We're going to have a baby."

"That's why Pai doesn't want me. He musta known you ordered one."

I reached across the seat and hugged her. "I love you, Sabrina. You're not going anywhere until your mother shows up."

I shouldn't have said it. Her lips quivered, and she turned away from me.

"She'll be back. I know she will. She loves you, Sabrina. She said so, remember?"

"Now it's all goofed up."

"What's goofed up?"

She wouldn't speak or even look at me. The new wondrous light of my baby clouded over. Already my emotions were being divided, my attention torn, and the baby had barely been announced.

During all the years of trying to conceive, I had dreamed a dozen ways of telling Simon the news, but none seemed appropriate now. Not with problems still strung between us. Not with Sabrina in the house. Not with the possibility of it not being Simon's child.

I decided to leave Sabrina with Mom for the evening as arranged and insist Simon spend time with me. I would wait and tell him when we were alone. We would forgive each other all our shortcomings, and our marriage would become solid again.

Things didn't work out as planned.

I didn't get Sabrina off to Mom's soon enough. We were still home when Simon returned from work. I was upstairs putting on a touch of lipstick. As I came down the stairs, I heard them talking in the kitchen.

He looked at me with raised eyebrows when I entered. "You had a doctor's appointment today?"

"Yes, I did." I reached for a glass. I needed water before my throat closed up on me.

"I thought we were done with all that."

Sabrina chirped in. "Mäe took some medicine. Now she's going to have a baby. But I don't have to leave."

"Carla's been taking medicine for a long time," Simon said. "It doesn't mean she's going to have a baby."

I should have thought it through, but I didn't. I blurted my words out in defense. "Yes, this time it does. I'm pregnant."

I'm not sure if it was surprise, anxiety, dread, or disbelief

I witnessed, but his face became deathly still, paled to the bone, his eyes wide and unmoving.

I took Sabrina's hand. "Mom's waiting for Sabrina. Let me take her, and I'll come back. We'll talk."

Sabrina charged through Mom's door and burst the news to Mom. "Mäe is having a baby."

"*My is having a baby?* What kind of grammar is that?"

"Oh, Nanny, don't you know that Mäe is Poor-Geese talk for Mommy?"

I chuckled. I was a goose in her mind! Mother Goose? "She means in Portuguese."

The rest of Sabrina's sentence took a second to sink in. Mom went from bewildered to astounded. She looked from Sabrina to me. "You're what?"

"Gotta go, Mom. If I don't get back by ten, plan to keep her for the night. Here's her stuff." I dropped her new overnight bag by the door and departed.

I wish I had anticipated Simon's thought process in my absence. I should have foreseen it, but it wasn't at all what I had anticipated.

He was seated in the family room, listening to Bach and sipping wine. Normal, controlled Simon. His color had returned, but life hadn't. He looked at me without emotion, his face a wall.

I sat on the coffee table in front of him. First things first. Get it said aloud. "We're having a baby."

It was as if my words didn't sink in. His mind was somewhere else. "Are you leaving with him?"

I had no idea what he meant. "Leaving with the baby?"

His face turned red. His eyes, white rimmed, narrowed

at me. "Yes, with the baby. It's his, isn't it?"

Mom's gossip collected in my head, but still ... "What are you talking about?"

"Come off it, Carla. I'm not stupid. Everyone in town knows you're sleeping with him."

"With whom?"

He stood up, his voice rising with his body. "That jerk—Kevin Baxter!"

I kept my voice low. "I am *not* sleeping with Kevin. How could you think such a thing?"

"I know you're seeing him. Sabrina told me about your lunches together. Did you think she wouldn't?"

"He's a friend. We shared lunch fully clothed. Unlike you, I don't go to a club twice a week with half-naked women poised all around for the taking."

He gritted his teeth. "Don't turn this around, Carla."

I waited. I wouldn't let him bait me.

"Look at the facts, Carla. You try everything under the sun to get pregnant for a couple of years, and suddenly Kevin Baxter comes into town, and—boom—you're pregnant. I've thought the dates out, and he arrived exactly on your fertile day—that Friday when I was safely out for the night. There's only one explanation in my mind."

I looked at it from his viewpoint. And then from mine.

"You think he came into town and we jumped into bed together? You think I hold that little respect for our marriage?"

"It hasn't been much of a marriage of late, has it?"

I should have thrown in his face how tempted I'd been to sleep with Kevin, but I was too off balance by his insinuations. Half of what had held me in check was Simon's lofty expectations, his code of honor. Did he think he was sole proprietor of morals because he went to church?

"It is not Kevin's baby. I haven't slept with him." *Not since high school.*

"It's the only thing that adds up."

He'd backed me into a corner. If I wanted to set things right between us, I didn't have a choice anymore. I glared at him, challenging him with my declaration. "I used a sperm donor."

He shook his head. "I thought maybe you were going to say that, and I don't buy it. Seems to me, you didn't talk about artificial insemination until just prior to him arriving on the scene. You must have known he was coming back to town."

"That's ridiculous. How would I have known he was returning? You ought to know why I used a donor. I asked you repeatedly about insemination. You wouldn't even discuss it."

"I discussed every livid thing about your infertility until I was sick to death of it."

"You're right, but that's all you did. Talked! You never tried to help me with any of this."

He was still stretched out on the sofa. He turned from me and stared up at the ceiling. "I couldn't."

"Why not? The idea of a baby was too overwhelming to you?"

"No." He turned to face me, pain etched in every line of his face. "It's because I'm physically unable to provide you with a baby, Carla. That's why I know it's not mine."

I sat down, stunned.

"And that's how I know you cheated on me."

I shook my head. "I didn't sleep with Kevin." I hardly even cared whether or not he believed me. All I could think about was the gravity of his confession and its monumental implication.

I looked at him as if studying a stranger. He closed his eyes, took a deep breath, and exhaled slowly. One tear rolled out of the corner of his eye. I had never seen him cry. He had been upset many times, but he'd always covered it up or shoved it away.

He sat up, bent over, and buried his face in his hands. I could hear his raspy breaths as he tried to gain control. I didn't rush him. After a few minutes, he wiped his face on his shirttail and looked up at me.

"You know I had testicular cancer when I was twenty-four."

"Yes, but you said you were fine now."

"Everything is fine as far as the cancer. What I didn't tell you was that I was engaged at the time."

I didn't want to hear his story, but it was better than hearing his accusations.

"Her name was Francesca. We'd been dating two years. We were saving up for a deposit on a house. We wanted everything to be perfect. We were young, but we had our whole future planned out: the house, the kids, a dog in the yard. Then I noticed the lump in my right testicle. It overwhelmed me at first. There had been nothing to predict it. I still don't know if it was inherited from my father's family or what, but it was like being run down by a train at midnight. Francesca stayed with me through it all—the initial surgery, then the lymph nodes and all. In the end, the cancer was the lesser of my life problems."

"What do you mean? What problems?"

"Before surgery, they recommended banking some sperm just in case."

"Just in case of what?"

"Well, sometimes the surgery can cause nerve damage

that results in retrograde ejaculation, meaning the sperm travels into the bladder instead of out the urethra, rendering the man infertile. Or radiation treatments can cause at least temporary sterility. Francesca was afraid of that happening. All she ever talked about was having children. When they analyzed my sperm, they found out I was infertile *before* surgery or radiation. It wasn't caused by the cancer. It was just a double dose of bad luck."

I was trying to absorb what he was saying, but my thoughts were following two different paths: Francesca and his cancer. I couldn't concentrate on one without the other. I stared at him like an idiot for a full minute before the news struck me like a tomahawk to the head. This was more than him not really wanting a baby. This was an inability to have one. "You're sterile?"

"Not completely, but very, very low count. And there's nothing that can be done for it. My condition wasn't caused by a drug or bicycling or anything else they warn about and correct nowadays."

"You let me suffer all this time. I can't believe you didn't tell me before now. How could you not tell me?"

He put his hands on my shoulder. "Before we got married, you told me yourself you didn't want children. You were a career woman. Remember? I'm a career man. I spent my youth raising my brother and sister. Having children never mattered to me. I'd practically spent my entire life being a father already. So I took your attitude toward children at face value. I couldn't chance bringing the subject up."

He was right. I had been career oriented when we met. It wasn't until we had been married a couple of years that I had been struck by the passion to have a child. He had put up a bit of argument against it, but he'd gone along with me. He had even produced a semen sample. "But the specimen you took to the doctor—he said it was low, but still within range."

He turned away from me. His voice dropped to a whisper. "I cheated. I paid a guy a hundred bucks to produce a sample. I had no idea he'd have anything but a normal count. He had two kids illegitimately."

I was stunned. All the procedures I had tolerated, all the anxiety of waiting month after month. My eyes felt like they were bugging out of my head. My ears felt like they were on fire, and my heart was pounding. "I can't believe all this stuff I've gone through and you never said a thing ..."

He leaned closer and tried to hold me, but I pushed him backward and stood up. He stood, too, his arms hanging at his sides. "I knew right off I loved you, and I wanted you so badly. I didn't want to take the chance of losing you. My father ran out on me. And Francesca ran out on me. I couldn't stand the thought of losing you, too. I thought you would reconcile yourself to life without kids the way I have. Besides, there was always a slight chance; I'm not totally sterile, and that whole thing with Abraham ... I thought if we had faith ... I thought if it made you happy, it was worth it. If it didn't work, I figured you would eventually give up and realize we were happy, just the two of us."

"But you knew before we got married!"

"Did you marry me to have children? Or did you marry me because you loved me and wanted to spend the rest of your life with me?"

How could he be so obtuse? I wanted so badly to punch him right in the face. Instead, I reached down to the coffee table and picked up the Orafor figure—a smooth crystal sculpture of an elephant given to Simon by a Swedish client—intending to hurl it across the room. He anticipated my actions. "Violence solves nothing, Carla." His eyes flashed, reprimanding me like a schoolteacher.

Whatever sympathy I may have drummed up for his side of the matter fled. He was always so in control, it made me irate. I let loose. "You're right. Violence doesn't solve anything and neither does screaming, but they sure help me release my anger!" I yelled into his face, then lowered my voice. "I may not be in control of my emotions like you are, but I haven't lied. What do you suppose God has to say about that?"

I dropped the Orafor at his feet, grabbed my pocketbook, and left.

Eighteen

It didn't take much thought to decide where I would go.

Simon hadn't believed me about the sperm donor. Instead he'd accused me of sleeping with Kevin; I figured I might as well commit the crime.

I didn't worry about Kevin not being home. I was led there by some gravitational pull and knew he would be waiting.

Grandpa Norris's ranch house wasn't nearly as magnificent as the houses in the new neighborhoods bordering the land. It was brick and sprawled over an impressive 5,000 square feet, but I remembered the layout was rather dated even back in my teenage eyes. The windows were old and unimpressive, the carpet dull and dark. The best room in the house was on the front. It was intended to be a living room, but Grandpa Norris had covered the walls in white oak paneling and bookshelves. He'd used the space as an office for running the ranch. I remembered the house room by room as I drove toward it. Happy times. Laughter. Back then, forever had stretched in front of me, full of grand possibilities.

The gravel of the driveway crunched loudly beneath my tires as I pulled around the circle, up to the front door. I imagined Kevin in that front room, bent over papers at the huge antique desk.

Apparently, he'd heard the car or seen my headlights. As

I stepped from the car, he opened the front door and stepped out to greet me. The door half closed behind him.

I bounded up the steps, into his arms. "I'm so glad you're home. I really need to talk," I said. I swept past him into the house, my emotions rampant, my antenna high. I was in that strange frenzied state of running on adrenaline, absorbing every detail, yet feeling above myself, floating on energy waves.

I ignored the front rooms and moved down the hall. The kitchen and family room lay across the back of the house, with a sliding glass door leading out to a cement patio and pool. The clear pool water dimly lit, the blue hue glowing upward in the dark of night, created an amorous atmosphere. It drew me toward the glass doors, until the movement of a person in the family room stalled me. I turned. I couldn't believe my eyes. Gina.

"What are you doing here?" I asked. As if I couldn't guess.

Kevin picked up a chic little black satin pocketbook from the wet bar and handed it to her. "She was just leaving."

Gina pouted. "But Kevin!"

"Carla's upset. She needs to talk."

"Well, I'm her friend, too, you know."

"Please, Gina," I said. "I'll call you about it later."

She batted her eyelashes at me, all innocent. Kevin whispered something to her. She chuckled and squeezed his arm. I didn't care; I just wanted her gone. She kissed him on the cheek and strode by me. As Kevin ushered her to the front door, my eyes focused on the pool again, glowing in the night, and I stepped outside to the patio. I stared at it, mesmerized, knowing that its depth and clarity somehow held the secret of life and love.

"Grandpa Norris never used it anymore," Kevin said as he

joined me, "but he had it filled every summer to attract the great-grandchildren to his house."

Beyond the pool, bushes bordered a small stretch of grass reserved for family recreation. The bushes were impenetrable now, ten feet tall and almost as thick, but I remembered from years earlier. Beyond the hedge, the barn and cows stood within sight.

"It's peaceful out here," I said.

"You're right about that." He stepped up behind me and touched my back. "Total privacy."

I thought briefly of Gina. She could be such a shameless hussy. I knew she was throwing herself at him. Kevin had always been such a pushover; I doubted his ability to turn her away. He was easy prey for a girl like Gina.

I turned to face him, thinking we were of a like mind. I wanted him fiercely. I expected him to kiss me.

He was still talking. "Personally, I love the isolation, but it's going to drive my kids crazy. They're used to a neighborhood with other kids running in and out all day long."

"Your kids are coming?"

"Sure are. Thought I told you. Since I'm here in the house, working on settling this estate, I decided it was time to claim some of their childhood. They're on summer vacation for six more weeks. It's perfect timing."

I thought of how much time Sabrina took. "But how will you get any work done with children underfoot?"

He shrugged. "If it takes eight months, what's the difference?"

"You said you wanted to get back into surgery."

His eyes took on a faraway starry look, like the night around us. "I spent a lot of years running around to the tick of a clock. Right now I don't have to."

The light must have shifted right then. He suddenly

looked older, settled. Maybe his face wasn't quite as energetic as it had been in high school. My first impression in the parking lot two weeks earlier must have been an illusion of memory. His lack of ambition unsettled me. It must have shown.

He continued. "I take it you're not planning to stay home with Sabrina."

"No, definitely not."

"You must love your job," he said.

I nodded, admitting only to myself how easily I had shifted priorities lately.

"Is that why you don't have children?"

"One's not dependent on the other."

My response must have been too ambivalent for him. He walked to the edge of the pool and stared into its depth.

Seeing him on the edge of the water was too tempting. I had too many conflicting emotions welling inside. I wanted to go back to the carefree days of high school. I wanted to laugh. I needed to laugh. I walked up behind him and pushed him in. He landed with a splash that showered the patio.

He came up coughing. "What'd you do that for?"

I kicked off my shoes and unbuttoned my shirt. "To give myself an excuse to join you." I slipped off my pants and dove in, slicing through the water with barely a ripple.

Kevin pulled himself to the side to watch me swim the length and back again. I rested my hands on the side and laughed at him. "Aren't you coming back in?"

He took off his shirt and kicked his wet pants aside. His body startled me. I'd wanted him to be the same as I remembered, without the aging, but it was there, no longer neatly tucked into a shirt and waistband. His stomach hung loose.

He slid into the water and waded toward me, chest deep. "I can't figure you out," he said.

"Don't try."

My hands slid over him. Such a different feel. He was hairy where Simon was smooth. Soft where Simon was hard.

I'd gotten used to Simon. The difference was exciting, yet disconcerting. I knew this man so well on a level I had never known Simon, with all the secrets of formative years. At the same time, he was also a stranger. I knew nothing of the modern workings of his mind.

He bent his head and kissed me, the pool water slick between us.

I wanted to be carried back to being a young girl, to the innocent splendor of our first sexual intimacy. I felt wanton and rejoiced in it. I wanted to abuse Simon for lying to me. I wanted to betray him for betraying me.

His hands touched my flesh, but my body didn't respond. Pleasure didn't tingle up my spine or throb within me. I tried to make wanting it enough, but I felt like a rubber doll, forcing my motions. Why couldn't I do this?

Emotions raged, not toward Kevin, but toward Simon. Simon's lie cut into me and shredded my desire. Tears spilled forth again. My shoulders shook with sobs.

"What's wrong?"

My voice caught. "It's not you. It's me. It's Simon."

Kevin pulled me into an embrace. My skin chilled in the water and added to my shaking. I couldn't look him in the eye. Instead, I stared at how the thick hair on his arms lay slicked down by the water, darker and more visible.

He put his arm around my shoulder and led me from the pool. "Come on. You're in no shape for this. I'm such a dolt, thinking ... Oh, forget it."

We stepped dripping from the pool, slumped slightly in our awkwardness, goose bumps pricking up my legs as he guided me into the family room, leaving a trail of soaked carpet behind us. "Wait here."

He returned with towels, a T-shirt, and a blanket and proceeded to slip my wet things off, towel me, and wrap me in a blanket. Lust still played beneath the surface, but his eyes softened with compassion.

"Sit. I'm changing. Then I'll make coffee."

I sat stiffly on the couch, a bundle of nerves, until his stirrings through the house brought the hum of pipes, the thump of drawers and doors, the clank of pots. I relaxed in the familiarity of homey noises and sprawled out across the cushions.

I was dozing when he returned carrying a tray of steaming mugs and slices of refrigerated cake.

I sipped at the hot brew, stared at the cake, and allowed him to gradually cajole the predicament from me, his hands smoothing my hair, rubbing my back, touching my cheeks with tender gestures. Hands on my body, not searching for sex, but offering comfort. That's what I had craved. It broke the lock on my heart. I became putty and revealed the whole awful truth of my marriage and the insemination.

When my words sputtered to an end, he tilted my face up and kissed me. The kiss was so different, so tender. It was a caress, an expression of all we wished could pass between us.

"I've wanted you like that since the moment I saw you in the restaurant," he said. "If things were different, I wouldn't let you leave, but you have a lot to sort out. Too much. When I make love to you, I want you thinking of me, not him."

I gathered my strength with a long breath. "I want to be with you."

His expression drooped. "I know a part of you does, but

you have two children involved. I've seen first hand how hard this is on children."

"Neither child is his." I said it without emotion this time.

"Not genetically."

I sighed. "What should I do? He lied to me. Our whole marriage is based on a lie. How can I even go back and talk to him?"

The battle in his heart played across his face. He shifted from lover to friend, the friend he'd been long ago in school before the age of discovering our sexuality. He smoothed my hair again and took my hands into his. "Because I know you well enough to know your marriage was based on a lot more than this issue."

Simon's words came back to me. *Did you marry me to have children? Or did you marry me because you loved me and wanted to spend the rest of your life with me?* "I've always wanted children," I insisted.

He looked straight into my eyes. "Are you sure?"

I had forgotten how well he knew me. He knew where my priorities had always been: material success and personal gratification in a career. "Okay, so my priorities changed. I'm successful. I'm well off. What's wrong with wanting children now?"

"There's nothing wrong with it, but you can't change horses midstream without including your spouse. It's not fair." Tears glistened in his eyes. I knew this was a personal remark, a conclusion of his own life, his own failed marriage.

He continued, "You owe it to Simon to talk this out. And you owe it to us. I want you totally, completely, not with a part of you remaining behind. He's got to have a chance to make amends, and you've got to attempt to do the same."

"Me?"

He nodded. "Your deception wasn't any less than his. A child is a forever life-decision, not to be taken lightly. You took responsibility for laying this unborn child on Simon without his permission."

"Well, he doesn't have to stick around for it. I'm totally capable—"

He patted my shoulders. "Calm down. I know all that. But see it from his point of view. He's had it in his head that he would never have children, and now in the span of a couple weeks he has at least two. That's a big adjustment. If it had been a mutual decision, neither of you would be so upset."

He was right. I had to talk to Simon.

I dreaded it, but I had to do it. I had to set my life on one course or the other.

He kissed me again, lightly. "I'm not going anywhere. If it's over with him, I'll be here."

Nineteen

I didn't pick up Sabrina. She was better off spending the night at Mom's. She didn't need to hear whatever went on between Simon and me. Part of it would be about her, no doubt.

I expected him to be gone—off to visit his friends at the club—but the lights were on. From the garage, I heard the piano. He was playing, pounding out songs I'd heard him play with true expertise on many occasions. He hadn't played anything in quite a while. He had never before pounded at it like a beast. As I came in the door, the music stopped. He was striding across the family room, a bottle of bourbon in his hand. He sprawled on the couch and glared at me. My mouth hung open. Bourbon was a thing of the past, something from our dating days, before he had become a churchgoer.

He took a gulp. His expression glazed over with detachment. "I figured you'd be back."

"I forgot my toothbrush."

He stared at the ceiling. "Let me guess. He didn't want the kid."

What Simon meant was that Kevin didn't want the kid, *either*.

My keys clanked down on the coffee table. "Don't put your opinion on someone else."

"I don't know, putting an opinion on someone isn't as bad as putting someone's kid on them."

"I've told you. It's not his child."

His eyes narrowed at me. "I've been thinking about that for the past few hours. I decided I'd rather it be Kevin's. Please tell me it is Kevin's. Otherwise, I have to think about this stranger, some pervert that gets off selling buckets of himself to some clinic. Then I have to think about how you let him invade our house and our life and your body."

He made it sound so crass, I hunched down and shrank into myself. "They don't take any old jerk off the street. I had pages of information to choose the donor from. Eye color, hair color, education, interests, IQ."

He said, "At least Kevin is a decent-looking guy. Smart."

I stood up. "You're right, he is. And the donor thing doesn't turn him off. He told me to give you a chance, to talk this out with you, to give you time to come to terms with all this, but I can't talk to you anymore. You're so hung up on listing all the ways you've been put out that you can't grasp the idea of having these kids to love, to give us something to grow old on. Sabrina might be tough, but that's also her strength. And this baby might be from some stranger, but it's half mine, too. It won't be a stranger. It'll be my child, raised by me."

"You've had a hard enough time caring for Sabrina. How do you think you'll handle two kids alone?"

"That's the point. I won't be alone."

"So why don't you leave? Just go to him."

I took a few steps toward the door, then stopped. I was seething. Why did he always make me feel like he had the upper hand? I turned around and sneered at him. "You make me sick. I've been trying to get pregnant for two years! You were sitting here smugly knowing you were infertile, yet I'm supposed to pamper you to help you adjust to the idea? Who made you king of our lives? You knew my intent. It's me who's been wronged here. It's you who didn't tell me we couldn't have a baby. If you had been honest in the beginning, maybe I would have accepted our marriage on those terms. I didn't marry you to have a baby, but the notion was there as part of the package."

His face altered like the turn of a kaleidoscope. His expression became pained. His eyes pleaded for me to believe. "Anything's possible with enough faith. Maybe God would have given us a child if you'd been patient."

"He did give us a child. Two children."

"No, you stole those kids. And look at their fathers. One is a known rapist, and who knows about the other. He could be some strung-out drug addict."

My back went rigid. "Are you implying these kids are beneath you? Maybe they're a threat to your status or something?"

"Criminal tendencies are inherited."

I glared at him with all the contempt I felt inside. "You *worship* a guy who was executed as a *criminal*."

That gave him pause. I don't think he had ever quite thought of Jesus in those terms.

He answered, "Jesus is not some *guy*; he's God's Son. His only crime was preaching and healing. His crucifixion was a human suffering he endured for our sake, for the forgiveness of our sins. Symbolic."

"Really? Symbolic of what, my dear Simon?"

His churning mind didn't catch up with his reply until it was out. "Symbolic of his love of all people, which is why he was born in a stable, to show us that his kingdom is heavenly, not earthly, and we should love the poor and—"

"And criminal," I finished for him. I let it sit there a moment, then continued. "I don't by any means consider Sabrina criminal, but even if she were or if this baby were, your faith ought to bridge that gap. Put your actions where your Bible is, Simon. Reach out for a change and open up. Take a chance on someone outside your carefully contrived niche."

His brow furrowed and his eyes narrowed. I could see his religion clashing with his careful life. He said nothing. His gaze turned upward to the ceiling. The silence stretched on.

"Why won't you talk! I'm doing everything I can to keep us together, and all you do is lie there and stare at the ceiling! I want us to be a family. You and me and Sabrina and this baby. Who cares how they came into our lives? They're here." Then the nurse's words came to me. "We're twice blessed."

He cut his eyes at me, as shocked as I at my reference to anything holy.

My cell phone rang. Once, twice. I would have ignored it, but I had this sensation—intuition? It was Mom.

Her voice sounded panicked. "Carla, you've got to come over right now. There's a car out in the parking lot. Sabrina saw it from the balcony. She says it's her daddy. She's crying, 'I didn't tell him the address, I promise,' over and over. I don't understand any of this."

"Oh no! Lock the doors and keep her away from the window. I'll be right there."

"What is it?" Simon asked.

I grabbed my pocketbook from under the coffee table. "What do you care?"

"Just because I don't want kids doesn't mean I don't care about what happens to Sabrina."

I hesitated. "She's in danger. Ron is stalking Mom's apartment."

"Ron?"

"Her father."

He sat up and came to his feet. "Her father? I thought you told me Phyllis was raped."

"She was. By an old boyfriend. Ron isn't supposed to know about Sabrina. Phyllis said he was out of the picture for good."

"A living father. This changes everything."

He didn't grasp the urgency. I swung my pocketbook over my shoulder. "Are you coming or not? I'll explain on the way."

He detoured to turn off the stereo, then followed me in long self-assured strides to the car. Simon is at his best when he has a mission.

I got into the Porsche without thinking about driving with him along, and he got in without comment. I backed out and squealed away from the driveway. It wasn't until halfway down the road I got that uncomfortable feeling of my *driving being judged*, but I shrugged it aside. There were more important things at hand. The roads were quiet. The darkness seemed enveloping. I could drive without thinking.

"Phyllis met Ron in a bar," I explained. "He was baby-faced, cute. Looked real innocent. All sweetness and romance. They dated a couple of months, all steamy sex. She loved relaying all the details to me. That was Phyllis for you. Then she got sick. She'd had endometriosis for quite a while, and it got to the point she couldn't stand it anymore, she was hurting so badly. She had to have a cyst removed from her uterus. Four weeks after surgery, she still didn't want to sleep with him. She'd developed this fear of sex. She'd had increasingly severe pain prior to the surgery, and it had built up in her head. Ron didn't seem to care at first. He slept around nightly and came back to her. She was so wrapped up in him, she didn't care who he slept with as long as he came back to be with her. But one night he said he'd had enough. He was determined to have her. When she refused him again, he went nuts. He beat her, then raped her."

Simon went rigid in his seat. "Sabrina."

I understood all the emotions he was putting into her name as he considered the danger she was in, the agony suffered by her mother, and her parentage. The same thoughts were racing through my mind. The pain of admitting that Sabrina may have inherited Ron's violent temperament was unsettling. The thought lay between us, stretched out over a mile, unspoken. Sabrina was fathered by an abusive dopehead, an idiot, just like Simon's image of my unborn baby.

I was calmer now, fired by reality instead of anger. I had to defend both children. "People are more than heritage. They are environment. It's been proved again and again."

"I've seen that anger in her."

I ran a red light without a twinge and returned to his base—God. "You, with all your faith in God, can't overcome genetics? You preach life and love and forgiveness, and you're going to say Sabrina isn't worthy of your time now because she has a jerk for a father?"

"You're not asking for my time. You're asking for my life, taking her in permanently and setting her whole future on my shoulders."

"I thought that was Jesus' intent. Didn't he take us wholly upon his shoulders? Isn't that the example he expects us to follow?"

Simon didn't answer.

"Simon, I won't ask for even a minute of your precious

time. This is Phyllis's child. I made a vow to her before I made my vow to you. And this is so much more than a vow. This is a child's whole life. Sabrina is helpless. Unless we find Phyllis, Sabrina needs me to take care of her. I might not be the best parent in the world, but right now I'm all she has. If you don't want to help, when we get back to the house you're free to go. I can't keep debating this. What's here is here. She's not going away. The baby's not going away."

His chin rose a notch. He hated being cornered. "I didn't say I wanted to be free."

Was he saying he would stick with us?

The last mile was spinning away beneath us. He lowered his voice. "If this Ron really is her daddy, it may only be prayers that keep Sabrina in our house."

"Why?"

"The law sides with blood relationships. If he challenges your guardianship, she'll be given over to him."

"To an abusive pervert?"

"Do you have proof?"

I pounded the steering wheel and shook my head.

"Even if you did, the harm was to her mother, not her. That's not grounds enough to deny him custody."

"You can't be serious."

"There's one advantage on your side," he said.

"What?"

"You have a solid marriage of four years, which offers Sabrina a stable home environment."

The irony kicked me right in the stomach.

Twenty

I pulled the car into Mom's apartment complex and looked Simon in the eye. Same stern-faced Simon he'd been all night, but also resolute, dependable—the traits I had fallen in love with so long ago. I never would have pinned him as a hero, but there he was, rising to a charitable deed, stepping out to save the life of a child he didn't want. He would hold our marriage up as solid if it meant protecting Sabrina. He would do this in the name of doing right, but seemingly not for love of me. Did he really have a Christian need to be good, or did he rejoice in the afterglow of egotism? I couldn't have chosen at that moment. I couldn't understand how he could be willing to protect Sabrina, yet not accept her.

"A solid marriage," I echoed.

His eyes moved beyond me to a car at the edge of the parking lot. "Is that him?"

Most of my knowledge of Ron was through phone calls and luncheon gossip between Phyllis and me. I had met Ron in person only a few times. But I hadn't forgotten his face. I squinted at the navy sedan. The driver's door had been rammed ages ago. The dent was rusted. Inside, a man with short black hair was peering at Mom's apartment windows. I concentrated on him until I could be sure. He turned slightly, and I saw the wide nose and narrow chin. "Yes, that's him."

I reached for my door latch, but Simon grabbed my arm. "He'll know he has the right place if he sees you get out."

"I can't help that."

"Yes, you can. Leave me here. I'll call the cops to send him off."

"Are you crazy? You think I can leave her now?"

"Quit thinking about yourself. Leave for her sake. He's unsure what to do right now, or he wouldn't just be sitting there. Seeing you might spur him to action."

I nodded. "Okay. I'll pull into the Quick Mart and watch from there."

He squeezed my hand. "I'll take care of her."

Did he mean *for now* or *forever?*

I waited until he reached Mom's door before pulling slowly out of the apartment complex to park at the corner store. Ten minutes later, a cop drove by me and pulled into the apartments. No lights flashing. No fanfare. Just a routine loitering call to them. Shortly thereafter, Ron's car left with the cop car tailing him.

I returned to the apartment and banged impatiently. "It's me. Let me in."

Mom yanked the door open. "What on earth kind of person was Phyllis? My land! You've put my life in danger."

"Relax. He's gone, now. Besides, he's not after you, Mom. He wants Sabrina." I pushed past her to take Sabrina in my arms. She started sobbing. "I'm sorry, Mäe. I'm sorry."

"You're all right, sweetie. You didn't tell him where you were. You didn't do anything wrong."

I pulled her against me and stroked her head as I looked up at Simon. "Did you tell the cops—"

"Yes," he finished for me, "they'll patrol the area all night."

Mom huffed. "That's well and good for you. You won't be here pacing the floor all night alone."

Simon and I exchanged a look regarding the obvious question. He nodded.

"Pack an overnight case, Mom. We'll take you back to our house."

Just what we didn't need.

"There isn't room for two decent-sized people in your car. Where do you expect to put four of us?"

She was right. Neither she nor Simon could fit comfortably in the tiny backseat. And she wouldn't consider driving her car at night.

"I'll drive you in your car," Simon said. "That way you'll have it to drive back in daylight."

Smart man.

It took an hour to get Mom packed and to our house. I led her to the back guestroom.

"Sure seems strange spending the night at your house."

"I guess it must. It's definitely a first, isn't it? Here you go, the guestroom."

Mom stood in the doorway and stared at her surroundings. "They sure don't waste square footage on bedrooms nowadays, do they?"

The third bedroom was smaller than the other rooms, closed in compared to the large farmhouse bedroom I had grown up in, but right on par with the guestroom in her apartment. I figured she would like the room. We'd used more of an antique theme: a battered-board look to accommodate an old picture of ships in harbor that Dad had given me. I never really liked the picture; it was too rustic, too brown, and not well done. But it reminded me of Dad and the stories he had told me as a kid about hanging around fishing docks and helping shrimpers in the summers as a teen. I liked having things that re-created memories. Otherwise, I might forget. I might forget the smell of his aftershave or how warm his hands were in the middle of the winter. Right then, I remembered everything about him without looking at the picture. His love washed over me like a warm breeze off the lake. Mom always reminded me I was a girl, but to Daddy I could be anything I chose. He lived outside Mom's boxes and rules. He made me pickle sandwiches and gave me ice-cream cones for breakfast; he taught me to fish with a bamboo pole and to make a clubhouse with tin and old boards. He set me in my own boat upon the ocean of life and told me I could be whatever I wanted to be if watched, listened, and learned.

Mom glanced at the picture without comment and sat on the very edge of the bed like a kid with her feet dangling off.

"This room's not used that often, Mom. Sabrina needs the bigger room for play area."

"What happened to that nice quilt you used to keep on this bed? Isn't this green coverlet the one that used to be in Sabrina's room?" Her voice sang out, high pitched with tension.

"I like this green one."

"It's so quiet in here without my dogs. We should have brought them along."

"I don't think so, Mom. Dogs prefer their own territory. I'm sure they're fast asleep at home already."

"Did you change the mattress, too? It feels stiff."

Sabrina appeared in the doorway. "Nanny, my mattress is soft. Why don't you come sleep with me?"

"Back in bed, Sabrina," I ordered for the tenth time.

Mom looked from me to Sabrina. "I believe I will sleep with you, Sabrina. You're probably scared still, aren't you?"

They shuffled down the hall together like two old buddies. Who would have guessed that my mother was scared of boogey men?

I thought of the big empty farmhouse and then of the apartment with no porch or operable windows, no opening but the one main door.

No wonder she needed yappy dogs. Dad had been her best friend, too.

Twenty-one

Simon didn't come up to bed until the hall was dark and the night was heavy with slumber. I was already in bed, reading a book and trying to calm myself.

I looked over the edge of the book. "Tell me what has to be done to protect Sabrina from him."

He crossed his arms. "Depends on his intent. If Phyllis has truly disappeared and he decides to challenge the documents she left, our first step is to file a complaint for custody. The courts will assign a mediator to attempt settlement with both parties. If that doesn't get rid of him, we go to a formal hearing. Since he hasn't filed for custody, I have to wonder about his motive. Worst case is he nabs her without confronting us."

I gasped. I wouldn't let Ron get hold of her. If I'd never seen her, I would have fought him. But now, knowing her, loving her, I would die to keep him from laying a hand on her.

"What will it take to win?" I asked.

"A good lawyer."

"You're a good lawyer. You can do it."

"Tax law isn't anywhere close to child custody, Love."

My heart softened at the endearment. I know he didn't mean it as such, but it was the ease with which he used it. He didn't have his guard up against me anymore.

When he emerged from the bathroom in his silk boxers, all fresh and good smelling, he perched on the side of the bed. His expression had turned stern again.

My ire rose. I thought I could read the whole insemination thing glaring at me in his face, again. I expected him to return to the discussion full force. My body tensed.

My expectations were wrong.

"This thing with Ron ..." He let the sentence die and took a deep breath. "We have to decide some things, Carla."

I gazed at him and waited. I was sure *my things* weren't the same as what he had on his list.

"What do you want from me, Carla?"

To the point. I laid the book on my chest and bit my lip, thinking. What did I want? Could it be this simple? If I could wave a magic wand, what would my life look like? Kevin flashed to mind for a moment, but I had Sabrina to think about.

I wanted Kevin. I couldn't deny that. But he knew me as well as I knew myself. I had to work it through with Simon far enough that my decision to leave would be objective and not an act of angry rebellion. I would forgive Simon for his deceit long enough to see the future more clearly. I could step back and rationalize the whole thing. I'd needed the fertility treatments for myself, anyway. If he'd told me outright about his infertility, I would never have taken the treatments, would never have had the insemination, and would never have gotten pregnant.

If he were willing to accept the child, could I put aside his deceit about being infertile and be happy? Would I stay? I focused on a vision of us. "I want us to be a family. You and me and this baby. And if Phyllis never comes back, I want to adopt Sabrina as our daughter. I want to let Sabrina run through the house, making noise and dropping toys without worrying if it's going to bring a tirade of *Why do we have her here* comments from you. I want you to touch my stomach and dream about this baby and rejoice in it because it's *ours*, even if it isn't yours. And I want us to love each other like we used to."

"We can never love each other the way we used to with all of this between us. Can't you see that? It won't be *us* anymore."

I saw the problem then. It flashed like a neon sign: *Change.* "But life evolves. We'd stagnate without moving forward. We have to keep reaching, climbing the next step. When I get to the top of the mountain, I won't be asking the guru for the meaning of life. I'm going to spread my arms out and say, 'Look, buddy, I've had it all. I know what life is about, 'cause I lived it.'"

"I guess that depends on what you wanted out of life. I was happy in our quiet routine."

I sighed heavily in frustration. "We'll still be *us*; it will just be an expanded *us*."

"Expanded all right. Doubled in a month."

He didn't know about the possibility of multiple fetuses. "When we got Mom's call tonight, and you knew Sabrina was in danger, didn't you ache inside? Can you imagine life without her now?"

"Much as I've come to care about her, yes." He ran a finger down my leg. "I can imagine life alone without children between us or that schedule you had us on. I can imagine all sorts of things."

I had to show him I would be here, that children would enhance our lives, not diminish them. I leaned forward, shifted up on my knees, and nibbled his neck. "A family won't diminish my imagination."

The strap of my nightgown slipped from my shoulder. He reached up and caressed my cool skin. I turned my lips up to him, kissing him with the lightest kisses I could manage—a string of enticements to reel him in.

He came to me hook, line, and sinker.

We still hadn't resolved a thing.

Even in the light of day, Mom wouldn't return to her house alone. Sabrina stood in the dining room staring out the window, her usual routine, while Simon and I playacted as if there was nothing wrong between us. He set to work in the kitchen and prepared a healthy breakfast for Mom: fresh cantaloupe and whole-wheat pancakes with low-fat syrup.

Sabrina joined us and poked at her food.

Mom ate her fill. "It's nice to have you cook for me for a change," she said. Taz rubbed against her feet. "Let's go check on my precious babies. They'll need their walk."

Simon was still eating his portion. I was scrubbing the pan. "Mom, your car is here. You can leave whenever you want to."

"You think I'd go back there alone with that man—" She caught Sabrina looking at her and dropped the end.

"I'll tell Daddy he can only come to the park, like afore. He likes to watch me dance at the park where the band plays music. I have dance class today, Nanny. Ballet. Mäe bought me leotards and ballet shoes. Will you come watch?"

Mom and Simon both gaped at me. I smiled and shrugged, then went back to washing the mixing bowl.

"Is it time to go yet, Mäe?"

"Not till three, Fancy Feet. That's way after lunch. Eat up your breakfast or you'll fall over your feet from starvation."

"Can you come, Nanny?"

"Not this time. I'll put it on my calendar for next weekend, though."

Mom with her social calendar.

"There, Simon, you're done. I'll just get my things, and you can follow me home to make sure everything is the way we left it."

He was too much of a gentleman to refuse her. "Sure. I'm on my way to the office anyway."

Which just happened to be in the opposite direction.

I thought of my job looming on Wednesday. It seemed to be in the opposite direction, too—opposite from my new life. How in the course of a week had a position I had worked so many years to obtain faded into the background?

Sabrina and I read a few books and then settled down to color some pictures. There in the quiet that stretched between us, I decided it was time to find out what had transpired between Phyllis and Ron, at least to the extent that Sabrina could relay the story. "I'm sorry you were scared last night."

She didn't respond.

"Tell me about your daddy's visits in the park. Did you like seeing him there?"

"He made up funny words to the music. It made Mommy laugh."

"Did it make you laugh, too?"

"Yes. But sometimes I wished he didn't come with us. The times he smelled yucky."

"You didn't like the way he smelled?"

She shook her head. "Sometimes when he smelled yucky, he laughed a lot. But sometimes ..."

"What?"

"... he made Mommy cry. He pushed her to the ground and messed up her pretty clothes."

"Did you see him very often?"

"Used to, no."

"But then you started seeing him more often?"

She stopped coloring. Her face paled. "Mommy told me not to never tell him where we lived and not to never go anywhere with him unless she was there."

"I know. It wasn't your fault he found Nanny's house."

Her eyes glazed over, and she seemed to shrink into herself. "He tricked me."

I could see the terror take over her. She started shaking. I eased my body around hers and pulled her into my lap. "When, Sabrina? How did he trick you?"

"One day he came to my day care. He said Mommy was hurt, and he was taking me home to her. Mommy screamed at me. She said why didn't I ask him our special word? You know, the secret word. I'm not supposed to get in anybody's car unless they know the secret word. She was mad that I didn't remember. I didn't mean to be bad."

"Your mommy knows that. She was just upset. She was worried about you." I ran my hand down her arm. "Did he visit you a lot after that?"

She nodded. "At first he was nice to Mommy. He bought her things, and they sang silly songs together."

"So she liked having him there."

"She painted a picture of him without any clothes on."

That sounded like Phyllis, but not Ron. I was trying to envision a new and improved Ron. It didn't hold true for me. I had to ask Sabrina outright what was on my mind. "Did he ever hit your mommy?"

She stared at the floor. "When he smelled funny. She locked the doors, but that made him madder."

"Did he hurt you?"

"He spanked me and pinched me sometimes. But it only hurt really bad the time he hit my head."

I fought hard to control my reaction and kissed her head lightly. "Poor baby. I bet that made your mommy mad."

"She made me stay in my room. I had to be real quiet so he'd forget I was there."

I cradled her tightly against me. "That was very smart of you."

When I eased my grip, she clung to my chest and became very still and serious. "One day Mommy was sick. She took some medicine and went to sleep. He came in my room and told me I had to take a bath with him. When Mommy found us in the bathtub together, she got the maddest I ever seen her. She grabbed me out of the water. We got to sleep in a hotel that night. I thought it was gonna be fun, 'cept Mommy kept crying. Then Mommy took me to a new day care, and she went back and got all our stuff. She said we had to have a new house."

"But he found you again?"

"It wasn't my fault. I promise. Mommy said he followed her from work. We went lots of places after that. She worked at restaurants and little stores and stuff. Sometimes I went with her. I had to sit in little rooms and hide. I got to sit up all night eating doughnuts and cake. But he kept finding us. That's when Mommy said we had to come here. I'm glad I got to come here. Simon doesn't hit you."

"No, darling, he doesn't."

"Mommy said I would be safe here. She said I had to be brave and not cry. She said it would be lots of fun, like a special secret vacation. I wish he didn't find Nanny's house."

"He found Nanny's house, but he didn't find you, did he? He's probably gone now."

She'd quit shaking. Telling the story calmed her. It was me who sat shaking at that point. "I'm glad you came here, Sabrina. We'll keep you safe. And before you know it, your mommy will be back for you."

She snuggled further into me, and we sat there a while gaining comfort from each other. Until the doorbell rang.

We both jumped. But it was only the Taylor kids. "We're playing hide-and-seek. Can Sabrina come play?"

Sabrina scrambled between my legs and out to the front patio before I could respond.

"Good morning, M'issa," Sabrina said, hugging her new friend.

Melissa patted her head like a puppy dog. "Get your shoes on, Sabrina, so you can play with me."

I couldn't argue with such affection. I carried a lawn chair and my book out to the front and settled in the sun. Within an hour, there were more kids in my yard than I'd ever known lived in the neighborhood. Two freckle-faced sisters with long ponytails rode up on matching bikes. A carrot-topped boy and twins in matching jumpers ran up behind them. Three teenage boys dressed like Babette's son, Blake, with their jeans hanging around their hips to reveal their underwear, sauntered up and looked around as if they weren't sure how they'd ended up there or if they wanted to stay. I stared at the waistbands of their boxer shorts and tried to determine what they were trying to say with this fashion statement. *Nothing is private, including my underwear? I want sex so badly, I start out the day with my clothes half off? If you think our clothes are ugly, you ought to see our underwear—so here's a peek?* I laughed and went back to reading. A few minutes later I noticed they had lost their "cool" stance and were hiding and running like all the other kids. Later, a black boy and his little sister, both dressed in tailored short sets, joined the game. A group of giggling girls wearing dabs of makeup arrived to eye the Underwear Boys. Personalities clashed again and again, but inevitably they were all kids. They ran and hollered and solved their differences. Sabrina kept up with the best of them. And surprisingly, the Underwear Boys seemed to take her under their wing and helped her into good hiding places. Wonders never cease.

Sue Taylor came out her front door at ten with a stack of paper cups and a huge pitcher of lemonade. The early-morning Seductress transformed into the Kool-Aid Mom. Maybe I would manage motherhood after all.

At eleven, I heard the phone ring inside. I cursed myself for not having the foresight to carry out the cordless—another lesson learned as Mäe.

I grabbed the kitchen phone on the fifth ring. It was Mom.

"I just tracked down the last of your classmates. Sheila Hill. She's in California now, can you believe it? That mousy girl is a model. Obviously not a very good one, or we'd have heard of her. But then, I'm surprised she became anything at all."

"They do a lot with makeup."

"They must. But those glaring lights. Don't they show just every imperfection in a person?"

"Sabrina is outside."

"What? Of course. She's a child. Fresh air. Good thinking."

"I mean I need to get back outside with her."

"For goodness' sake, don't let me keep you. Just because I've been on the phone long distance for the past two hours, don't feel you owe me anything like a decent conversation."

"Sorry, Mom. I'll pay for the phone calls. Send me the

bill when it comes. I just don't want to leave her out there alone."

"Alone? She doesn't have any friends yet? She told me about a Melissa."

"There are twenty kids in my yard. She has lots of friends."

"You said *alone*."

"I meant without me watching, in case Ron shows up."

"He's not watching your house; he's watching mine. That's why I've stayed on the phone—to keep myself busy. And now you've made me think about him again."

I could hear the kids hollering. Someone was laughing heartily. "Bake a pie," I said. "That will take your mind off of him."

"I can't bake a pie. I have to take Brooke shopping for some new church shoes."

I sighed. Did she take me in circles on purpose?

She said, "I don't suppose Sabrina needs church shoes?"

Was this another attack on the lack of religion in my life? Why couldn't she and Simon understand my lack of faith? Sure, I had finally admitted his existence, but what had God ever done for me that I should dedicate myself to him? I'd had to fight and scrape for everything I'd ever achieved. I didn't see his hand in anything except taking my daddy from me. My daddy was the one who had set me on the road of life, not God. Daddy had taught me to be independent. I wasn't about to give up the power I had over my own destiny to a God who took my daddy away from me.

I could almost feel God stroking me, asking me to look to him, but I couldn't do it. I couldn't give in. I had control over my life, not him.

The mere insinuation from my mother's lips made me

resolute. No one was going to force God or Sunday worship on me. I wasn't a child anymore. I gripped the phone tightly. "No, Mom. Sabrina doesn't need shoes."

"You mean Simon isn't taking her to church?"

Outside, the voices rose to a higher pitch.

"No, Mom. I mean she has new shoes. Got to go. Good-bye."

I slammed down the phone and ran back outside. The kids were milling around the black boy and the oldest Underwear Boy.

"You cheated, ferret face," said Underwear Boy.

"I tagged her fair and square," replied the black boy in a cool voice. He stood so straight and tall, so level headed, it was hard not to believe him, but I had become endeared to Underwear Boy for helping Sabrina hide.

Sabrina! I looked around frantically. I didn't see her little blonde head. I ran up to the group, right between the two quarreling boys. "Where's Sabrina?"

"I don't know," said Underwear Boy.

"But you were helping her. I had to answer the phone. Oh no." I turned in circles. "Where is she?"

I spotted Melissa. "Do you know where she is, Melissa?"

"No, ma'am. She was here a minute ago."

Dread cut through me. "You didn't see an old blue car pull up, did you? Any of you?"

The kids were chattering among themselves. They weren't listening. "Shut up and listen to me! This could be life or death! Did any of you see a navy blue car pull up? Did someone take Sabrina away?"

Carrot Top shrugged. "There's lots o' cars."

"This car is navy blue with a dented front door. Oh, please, didn't any of you notice?"

Melissa said, "I didn't see a car like that."

The black boy waved his arms. "Let's all look for her. Come on, gang."

My heart pounded in my chest. My ears throbbed. Should I call the cops? Should I call Simon? Or just look?

I had to look first. I couldn't take time to call someone if she were right here, wandering around the yard where I couldn't see her.

Then I almost vomited. The pool. The lake.

I took off at a run, unlatched the gate, and rushed to the side of the pool. Nothing. It was still, sparkling in the high-noon sunlight. No body.

I rushed down the brick walkway to the lake edge. The water was clear along the edge of the bank but quickly became murky brown toward the end of the dock. I didn't know what to do. Should I dive in and start looking? What if she hadn't come near the water at all? If Ron had gotten her, I would be wasting precious time on the wrong lead.

My head ached with confusion. "SABRINA!"

In the ensuing seconds, I envisioned my mother and screamed at her, blaming her for her inane phone call. I blamed Underwear Boy for stopping to fight when he should have been playing with Sabrina. In my head, I screamed at Melissa for even knocking on my door that morning. I envisioned Simon berating me for my lack of ability as a mother, for being stupid enough to think I could care for a single five-year-old, let alone a newborn or two besides. I imagined Phyllis accusing me of killing her only child after putting so much trust in me.

And the minutes ticked by with me standing there staring at the water.

I pulled off my shoes and was about to peel off my shirt when I heard Carrot Top's squeaky shout go up.

"I found her! I found her!"

I left my shoes and ran up the slope, forcing my feet to forget how tender they were from years spent in shoes without barefoot summers to keep them tough. I cut through the gate and looked around. Where had the voice come from?

"Where are you?" I yelled.

"Over here," came six voices gathered around one of the big boxwoods at the front of the house.

Sabrina smiled up at me like a true winner. "I'm the best one, Mäe. Nobody could find me for a long time, and I did just what Jerry said. I didn't tell nobody where I was."

Jerry. Head-honcho Underwear Boy. I smiled weakly at him and ruffled Sabrina's hair. I sensed this was not a time to get mushy, not in front of her throng of new friends. I knew something about having an obtuse mother. I sniffed up the tears threatening to spill. "Good show, Fancy Feet. We all declare you the official winner."

She said her good-byes, and we retreated indoors for lunch and recuperation from my heart failure.

I paused in making her a peanut butter sandwich and stooped down. "I'm so glad you're here, Sabrina, safe with me."

In the back of my mind, Ron still loomed, and I wondered how I could live day to day always worrying about finding him around the next corner. I had to take action.

Twenty-two

When Simon arrived home from work, I didn't tell him about Sabrina giving me a panic attack. Sabrina told him her version, though, which was enough to raise his eyebrows. "Exactly how many kids are a kazillion?" he wanted to know.

"About twenty, I guess. They had a ball. I'm exhausted just from watching."

He eyed the family room and peeked into the bathroom for signs of juvenile invasion, then picked up his grocery list and set to work taking stock of the cabinets and refrigerator.

"Add paper cups and lemonade, would you?" I asked.

His pencil paused.

"Sue Taylor played Kool-Aid Mom today," I explained. "I figured it would be my turn next. Good to keep it handy at any rate."

He wrote it down and continued.

"We need tearless shampoo, too. And some kind of bath powder."

He paused again. "I already have those listed."

Simon had always done the shopping. He reveled in his inventory. We had spare everything on hand. Fresh bars of soap stood ready on the tops of showers. Toothpaste and floss lay in pairs in each bathroom. The pantry could rival any corner store. A week earlier, his utter thoroughness, his pervasive sense of order, would have irked me, but he was trying to work things out, so I tried to look at it from his perspective. He had a personal need to control his environment, to make order out of the chaos I brought to his life. I was probably next to impossible to live with the way I rushed from one obsession to another, ever self-centered. And there were many wonderful things about his orderliness. Many a woman would kill to have a husband who kept inventory, did the shopping, and made a point of dropping his dirty clothes into the laundry hamper.

He held the paper out to me. "Would you like to take over?"

"Sure, and face the firing squad when we come up short on asparagus? No thanks. But maybe we'll come with you."

"Come with me?" Another change. A small change in his routine.

"Yes. Sabrina loves shopping."

He winked at her. "I already knew that."

The blue church dress came to mind.

After I had run errands with Simon all afternoon, ballet was a welcome break. I led Sabrina to her classroom and took a seat in the waiting area. Most mothers left, but I remained, obsessed with worry about Ron abducting Sabrina.

I kept my seat long enough for her to settle into the class but had to reassure myself she was all right.

I peered into the ballet classroom through a viewing window. In the far corner, the teacher flicked a switch and music fluttered into the room. The row of little girls teetered on a black line—some giggling, some falling slack, some perfect for a split second—but I noticed them only with a flicker of my attention. My whole world settled around Sabrina. At the teacher's signal, she raised her arms in an awkward but earnest arc and followed the sweep of her tiny fingers with her eyes. Her knobby legs wobbled, her right foot stepped out of position, but she pulled herself back together and raised her dimpled chin. In her, I saw all the future of the world. She stood as clay to be molded. Solid, directed, yet free to make her own way. She might have some of her father's genes, but she was definitely her own person, full of drive and ambition. Life had just begun; even in the uncertainty of not knowing where her mother was, she had pulled herself up and gone on with all the hopes of life still attainable. My body flushed with an intense yearning to share her journey through all the trials of youth, school, teenage years, and beyond. At that moment I loved her as fiercely as if I had traveled the first five years with her.

At the end of the hour I had expected her to be worn out, but she skipped into my arms more invigorated than before. I hugged her. "Way to go, Fancy Feet. You were terrific."

"Teacher said I paid good attention."

"I saw. I'm very proud of you. Let's go home and tell Pai all about it."

"Will he take us out to celebrate?"

"Now, that's a good idea."

Simon thought so, too. We dined out, a picture-perfect family: Daddy, Mommy, daughter, and baby on the way. Then we returned home to reality.

Sabrina picked Taz up off the couch and went up to play in her room. We were left standing in the family room to play the happy parents. I thumbed through the CDs. Simon sank to the couch and watched me.

"The investigator called while you were out this afternoon," he said.

The CDs tumbled from my hands. "Well?"

"He's finally picked up her trail. It's a few days old, but he's hoping to catch up with her by the first of the week."

"Where is she?"

"He wouldn't say, yet. I also called a lawyer friend about Ron and custody. He advised waiting until we hear back about Phyllis, as to whether or not she's had second thoughts."

I couldn't keep living as I had today, looking over my shoulder, worrying about Sabrina every minute. I wouldn't give her up to Ron, no matter what. But I was too emotionally drained. I didn't want to turn this into an argument. I wanted to pretend everything was fine for a change. "I'm not going to even think about any of it till next week."

"You're working next week."

My heart felt like lead. "I know. The plant has probably fallen to pieces without me."

He looked around at the toys. "Well, the house certainly has."

"It's just a few toys." I gathered up Sabrina's puzzles, threw her dollhouse people into a nearby basket, and picked up my old dolly and fluffed up its dress. There was nothing pretty about it now, but it brought back fond memories. In the middle of such turmoil, memories were a treasure.

I picked up Sabrina's hairbrush and brushed Polly's nylon hair, straightening the knots. The work was therapeutic. It stilled my mind. Life could never step backward. I knew that. I couldn't regress into the youthful devotion Kevin and I once had. I couldn't force Simon and myself there, either. But I could make a choice on how to handle what had developed. My choices were clear. Leave with Kevin and hope what we'd had as children still existed. Or stay with Simon, which meant looking beyond his deceit, beyond his infertility, to remain faithful to our vows. Our vows weren't something to be taken lightly. I was a person of my word, and what more powerful statement was there than vows of marriage? I'd already compromised that by allowing Kevin to kiss me, but I hadn't gone so far that the harm couldn't be undone. I wanted to set things straight and get back on track. I wasn't one to give in or admit defeat. Maybe Simon was right about my tendency to persist, to see a thing carried through, be it a production schedule or a having a child. Or our marriage. I couldn't help it. It was the right thing to do. I didn't need religion to tell me good from bad, right from wrong. And I didn't choose one or the other because God was telling me to, but because in the course of nature, commitment was the right path. I thought briefly of my mother's attitude and how, despite her declaration of being Christian and praying for me, she had urged me toward Kevin. Obviously, claiming to be a Christian didn't make her perfect or even keep her steered clearly on course with God's teachings. Nevertheless, I knew even as I thought about it that I did see God at the center of it all, the center of the universe, the center of my vows. I just wasn't ready to admit it yet. I let myself believe I was intent on upholding my vows because it was my idea and my goal.

Then, a new thought came to me. Maybe doing the right thing was religion at its most basic.

As the idea welled in me, I saw myself in a new light, as a person who believed, who lived her life according to the commandments set forth by God himself thousands of years ago. It was hard to admit, but maybe everything that had happened to me was his doing, not mine. I may have taken the steps, but only because God had opened the doors. Whether it was just a new insight or a glimpse of faith, whatever it was, it opened the door to new possibilities, to reacting to Simon's faith with a different attitude.

I got up the next morning and put on a dress, a forest green silk with sleek lines and modest neck- and hemlines.

Simon kept glancing at me, but said nothing. I think he was afraid of breaking whatever spell had been cast over me.

Sabrina, unaware of the tensions, came right out and asked. "Are you going to church with us?"

"Yes."

"Pai said your faith isn't in church."

"No, but I have a few things to talk over with God today, so I thought I'd make a house call."

The church was a small gray stone building on the edge of Charlotte in a more populated area of town than our waterfront home, but not quite in the thick of things, either. Most members of the congregation were middle class: mothers with "fixed" hairdos, fathers with navy suits and burgundy ties, kids tucked into good outfits. Little girls pranced in with their hair in bows. The boys, dressed like miniature copies of their fathers, pushed and shoved under scolding eyes.

As I led Sabrina by the hand, I was glad I had taken the time to pull her hair into a stubby ponytail with a big pink velvet hair bow holding it in place.

Memories passed before me of the church my parents had taken me to. The Church of God's Holy People, a denomination thought up by some one-manned reformation, had been housed in a huge auditorium. Royal blue carpet had muffled our footsteps. The seats were stadium style, elevated around a circular stage area. The speaker system rivaled that of any concert I'd ever attended. The whole Sunday service, as I recall, was a show pleading for money in the name of Jesus.

Pastor Cassidy lived well in the name of Christ. We didn't go often. Dad rarely had money to spare that wasn't being dumped into cars.

I had pictured Simon attending a church like my parents', but his church was totally different, provincial with its warm oak-paneled walls, white wooden pews, and raised podium. Everything about it was more encompassing. Do I dare say it? It felt more Christian, though I couldn't define why. Moreover, it seemed welcoming and sincere. Simon moved among the pews, greeting people. They all seemed to know him by name. He was still his formal self, but more open among these worshippers than he normally appeared in public. I think that's why he fell for me. I'm outward. Not cuddly, but nothing phony or put on. I could keep company with anyone. The same with this church. The building and people were both welcoming, without any phoniness. He shook hands with a dozen men before he led us to seats near the front.

Sabrina picked up a hymnal and flipped through the pages as if she could read the words and had been doing so all her life.

The pastor had been recently replaced. I remembered Simon's comments on his first sermon: *Pastor Jones has a way of seeing into people. He talked to the entire congregation, but I felt like he was telling them my life story.* Simon never elaborated on exactly what portion of his life the pastor divulged, but I had assumed it included me. Curious to know more about this wizard, I asked Simon about the sermon the second week. He just shrugged. "If you want to know what he has to say, you'll have to come yourself." Obviously, I hadn't cared that much.

Pastor Jones was a small man, withered skin on a frail

frame with two bright spots of color on his cheeks. I pictured his bare legs as knotted and arthritic as his hands, which moved in slow, labored movements. I felt an urge to rush to the podium and give him a hand up. He looked no more a wizard than the man from Oz.

I waited, straining to hear wisdom from God, something that would straighten out my whole screwed-up life. I needed a sign that would tell me Sabrina would be safe from Ron, that my marriage would survive, and that my baby was not a perverted monster created by my desire to control my life.

Pastor Jones must have been talking to someone else that day. He kept going on and on about not looking for greener grass, but staying satisfied with the hay in the barn. I figured our whole situation was this pastor's fault. Simon resisted change because Pastor Jones told him to quit seeking a better life. How boring life would be if I didn't reach for change.

When Pastor Jones turned the sermon to sins of the flesh, I flushed. The pastor couldn't know about Kevin. Simon wouldn't have discussed our situation with him. I figured he was talking to the old man on the back row who looked like the type to have been cheating on his wife for years.

I shut out his droning voice and looked around me at the faces of religion. A young mother was struggling to hold her child still. Another was rocking her baby to the rhythm of the pastor's words. An old man sat nodding, eyes cast down. I wondered if he agreed with the words or just habitually bobbed his head. A middle-aged woman shrugged into a worn beige sweater. Her elbow caught in the sleeve. She twisted in her seat, trying to free it.

In the far front corner, a woman in a hat knelt, face hidden in folded hands. I thought she might be the type to put on the look of piety for the benefit of an audience. I kept watching her. Eventually, she raised her eyes to the heavy wooden cross behind the pastor, and I witnessed agony and pain draining down her face in tears. But as I watched, I saw her absorbing something. The pastor's words? Or inner illumination from some unseen source? I couldn't tell. Her expression changed. Her cheeks still glistened, but her tears quit flowing. Her face relaxed, gravity let go some of its hold upon her, and peace settled across her brow.

The change stabbed at me. Had I really witnessed this visible change or had it been a trick of the light?

Simon sat erect beside me, earnestly listening to the words from the pulpit. Did he know that peace? Had he experienced the lift I had just seen in the woman? Is that what he met when he closed his eyes on the aggravation I created? Is that what he had been trying to relay to me all these years?

Someone coughed. Another sniffled. A child dropped a book and kicked his seat in his efforts to retrieve it.

Not everyone here was at peace. That was easy to see. But some were. Maybe it only came in spurts. Maybe it was something you had to grasp and nurture.

I still didn't feel Simon's calling, but maybe I could understand it.

Simon's big hands lay splayed on his legs. I slid my hand under one of his. He squeezed it gently, a miniature hug.

Peace, however it came to a person, was something to grasp.

I was ready to reach for it, for my own sense of tranquility. I took a deep breath, closed my eyes, and after a few minutes managed to shut out the noises around me. I turned inward to the quietest place in my heart I could find, and I prayed in silence. *God, Simon wants me so badly to have faith in you. He's told me I have only to open my heart to you, and you*

will give me peace. Well, here I am. My life is a wreck. I'm plac-
ing it all at your feet, like he's always preaching. I'm ready for
your peace. If you're out there, show me your power. Set down the
stepping-stones and make this all work out.

My ears burned as if everyone in the room had heard my thoughts. I felt ridiculous for even thinking the words, yet strangely unburdened. I had delegated the problem.

Twenty-three

*T*uesday was the Fourth of July. Sabrina had already established plans for us.

"Oh, good!" she exclaimed. "We get to go to the park to hear the bands today."

Simon smiled smugly. They had hatched plans between them.

"We are?" I asked. It was tradition to have Mom and Babette's crew come over to eat. We grilled steaks, a gesture toward family togetherness that saved me from the two alternatives—the chaos of Babette's house or the claustrophobia of eight of us, now nine with Sabrina, being trapped in Mom's apartment without even a patio for a breath of air.

Simon nodded, and it was decided. "A new tradition is born," he said. "Someone at church told me about the program at Calvary Church. They have bands playing Christian music and set fireworks off at dusk."

I didn't reply. I solemnly envisioned the coming conversation with my mother. How would I explain the change in tradition?

"You do know that Phyllis always took Sabrina to the park to hear the bands, don't you?" he asked.

She had told me that. Simon was being mindful of her needs, and I was worrying about family politics. I bent down and scooped Sabrina into my arms. "Aren't you a smart girl for thinking up such a treat for us?"

In the end, we appeased everyone. We changed our annual supper to a late lunch. I kept the party focused on the back deck. The fresh air helped dissipate the children's noise and the adults' emotional eruptions.

Mom and Babette jabbered away in lounge chairs. I stood by the railing, sipping lemonade. Taz wove around my legs until I bent down and picked her up.

Babette joined me. "You didn't tell me you signed her up for ballet. You should have put her in Brooke's class. We could've carpooled."

I smiled weakly. Carpooling? What fun.

"Just look at how well they're getting along," Babette said. "Kindred spirits."

As I watched the two little girls holding hands and skipping across the patio, I felt like I'd fallen through a time warp. It seemed eons ago I had dreamed of raising my first child alongside Babette's third. Though I wouldn't face the idea straight on, I heard a whisper in my conscience—my prayers had been answered. I shook the notion away. That was Simon's declaration getting to me.

"I'd be careful, Baby," Mom said to Babette. "No telling what illicit lifestyle that child has been exposed to. I don't want to be mean to Sabrina, but we really have to put Brooke first at this point. We don't want any, um, inappropriate influences on Brooke."

"I can't believe you would say that," I said. "You don't even know Phyllis."

"I met her," Babette said. "She came home with you once. Remember?"

"Her father stalks my house, and you don't think I have

the right to make a comment about her background? And as for Phyllis, I can tell about people straight off. I know from things you've said that Phyllis has some serious problems."

"She got involved with the wrong people in college, but lots of kids do. That's not a crime. It's a misjudgment. I'm sure you've made a few in your day."

"What are you implying? What have I ever done that's shown misjudgment?"

"Nothing, Mom. Forget it."

"No, you're trying to make a point, so make it. I can handle it."

Where would I start? She constantly misjudged people and hurt others when she voiced her opinions. Comments about Simon, about Sabrina, about Kevin. And me. Always her judgment of me. "Boxes, Mom."

"Boxes? What on earth do you mean? I've misjudged boxes? I have no idea what you're talking about."

"Of course you don't."

"So explain yourself."

It wasn't worth the effort. "You wouldn't see it if I wrote it out in black and white."

She put down her cup. "Now, that's just mean—"

Simon emerged from the house with a platter of steaks. We rarely ate beef but made an exception for Independence Day to forestall derogatory comments from Mom.

"Oh my!" exclaimed Babette at the sight of them. "Come see, Barry."

Barry wouldn't be put out. "I'm sure they're the best. Simon always gets the best." He sipped his wine and kept his eyes on his magazine, as if the luxury were due him.

"We buy the best as a gesture of love," Simon graciously inserted.

"I'm not feeling a whole lot of love," grumbled Mom with her eyes on me.

Simon looked at me and sized up the situation quickly. "Disagreements are not for a lack of love, Mother," he said. "They are simply a matter of differing opinions."

She picked up her drink again. "People look beyond differences if they truly love one another."

What a statement coming from my mother. "Exactly my point, Mom. I love Phyllis. And I love her daughter." And I loved winning a debate. I excused myself to attend to the vegetables.

By late afternoon, I regretted having invited them along to the fireworks.

"Are we all driving separately?" Babette asked.

"Well, you're not likely to fit anyone in Carla's car, are you?" Mom said.

"Mama, can Sabrina ride with us?" Brooke asked Babette.

Mom wasn't done yet. "I know it hurts to hear this, Carla, but you're going to have to set aside that Porsche, finally. I always told your father it was no kind of automobile for a family person. You need a nice minivan, like Baby's."

"Actually, we're picking out a new car tomorrow. An Expedition."

"That figures," Barry said dryly.

Simon looked at me, surprised. We hadn't discussed it at all. I just couldn't let Mom get the upper hand. Besides, she was right. If Phyllis didn't show up, we would need a bigger car. The idea settled on him, and he nodded at me. He was probably just gladdened at the thought of retiring my Porsche to special occasions.

The women and children rode in Babette's minivan. Barry and Simon rode together in the BMW.

I thought the ride would be worse than the event. I should have known better. I should have foreseen problems.

"I didn't think to bring a chair," Mom said.

Babette spread a quilt. "We have plenty of room for you, Mom. Have a seat."

"Just listen to that music. I didn't know it would be so loud in real life."

"Live music is always louder," Blake explained. He didn't want to be with us, but his father had insisted. He was full of complaints. "But this music stinks. Let's leave."

"I like it," Brooke said. She and Sabrina had been dancing with twirls and leaps. "So does Sabrina."

Sabrina stopped for the tenth time and looked around. I thought she was afraid of losing me. "I'm right here, Fancy Feet. I'm not going anywhere."

"I'm not looking for you. I'm looking for my daddy."

I wrapped her in my arms. "It's okay, darling. I told you, we're here with you. We won't let anything happen to you." I couldn't believe my own words. My heart began pounding.

Simon squatted beside me. "Don't worry. If this were the public park, he might come looking, but he won't think about a church. That's why I chose it. Besides, we've only seen him the once and that was four days ago. He could be miles from here now."

Two hours later, we headed home. We hadn't seen a trace of Ron, but the reason was apparent early the next morning.

Twenty-four

The doorbell rang shortly after Simon had left for work. I was still getting ready. I had just pulled on a blouse and slacks. My hair stood on end, damp, as I rushed down the stairs and through the family room. Sabrina was hiding behind the couch. I paused, scared stiff.

"It's a policeman," she whispered.

Phyllis has been found, I thought. But not in the manner I'd hoped. The officer removed his hat as he stepped through the doorway.

"Carla Rochwell?"

"Yes," I replied. He was a middle-aged officer, rather dashing in his uniform. Peter Skyler, by his badge. He had big brown puppy-dog eyes that would have been beautiful if they hadn't been so morose. "Is this about Phyllis?" I asked.

His gaze arched over me to where Sabrina's pointed little face poked around the corner of the foyer.

I waved her away. "Sabrina, go to your room and fetch Taz down, please."

"I don't wanna."

"Now, Sabrina."

Weeks of being firm paid off. She scrambled to her feet and ran up the stairs.

"Ma'am, I always hate relaying bad news, but ..." He

looked to the envelope in his hand and took a deep breath. "You were listed as next of kin to Phyllis Samson."

I wasn't really kin, but we wouldn't argue details. "Yes, sir."

"A driver reported finding her car on the Blue Ridge Parkway at four forty-five yesterday morning. She apparently missed a turn in the road. I don't know if you've ever driven in those parts, ma'am, but the road twists and turns all sorts of ways, and the drop-off doesn't have guardrails in every case. The reporting officer feels she misjudged a turn. Went straight over the edge."

Tears trickled down my cheeks, but I felt numb. I had expected this, really. She hadn't misjudged the turn at all. Phyllis had taken the final escape from her life of confusion, of responsibility and recklessness woven together. That's why she had left Sabrina. She had planned to kill herself long before she dropped off Sabrina. That's why she sent the letter reconfirming custody.

He continued. "It took a right long time to get to the bodies, but it wouldn't have mattered. The coroner determined it was death on impact."

Bodies? Plural? If it had been suicide, there would have only been her. She wouldn't have killed another person.

I wiped away my tears. "Who else was in the car?"

"Her companion was male. His identification said Oliver Owens, but police records revealed him as Ronald Putnam."

Ron. She had taken Ron with her. That's what her letter had meant. *I can't escape my problem, so I'm going to face it head-on and finish it completely. I promise this is my last request of you. You won't have to bail me out ever again.*

The officer handed me the envelope—Phyllis's fate, my fate. He said, "I'm sorry to have had to bring you the news.

My heart goes out to you. Enclosed is the information from the coroner and the morgue address and such. If the county office can be of further assistance, please call."

I closed the door behind him and retreated to the sofa. Sabrina's voice came from behind me. "What's it mean?" She was standing in the living-room archway, still as a statue, with Taz clasped to her chest.

"How much did you hear?"

"Most all of it."

I beckoned her into my lap, and we shooed Taz away. Suddenly, I needed Simon desperately. He could be outwardly gruff and domineering, but he was compassionate on a whole different level, not on everyday issues, but when it came down to the line, he knew what to do. He knew how to handle death. When we met, my father had just passed away, which was what had brought me back to town. Our relationship was new and fragile then. He listened to my torrents of memories and regrets throughout many months of pain. He became my sounding board and my anchor. I can't recall one single thing he said to me, but I remember being engulfed in an aura of love that healed the deep, deep grief.

"You got the envelope, didn't you?" she asked.

I looked at the simple white envelope in my hand, not quite understanding her. "Yes, the police officer gave it to me."

"Mama said she would send it, and then you would understand everything. I thought she forgot to do it. She said after you got it, you would tell me it was okay to stay here with you. But Pai doesn't want me."

Poor child. I never imagined she knew about Phyllis's letter. I put an arm around her. "Do you mind being here with us?"

"My mommy isn't coming back." It was a flat statement.

"No, dear, she won't be coming back. Her car went off a

cliff." I squeezed her to me, wishing I could pull her inside and hold the hurt for her. "She's gone forever."

Her body felt bony and tiny in my arms. Such a frail thing entrusted to me. What had been speculation had become reality.

Her body trembled. "She told me I had to be brave, that I couldn't cry. I miss her. I want my mommy. I want my mommy."

I thought of her morning vigil at the window and realized that, like me, she'd kept hoping for the impossible, even though deep down she knew the truth even better than I. I clutched her to my chest and rocked her. We stayed like that for an hour, murmuring and rocking, until she fell asleep. I laid her on the sofa and took the envelope to the phone. First, I called Simon.

"They found Phyllis," I said quietly, afraid to hear the truth aloud.

"I told the P.I. to call me, not you."

"It wasn't him. An officer came by."

"So she'll be coming to pick up Sabrina?"

I sniffed away the tears that were brewing again. "No. She's dead. Ron with her. Off the side of the Blue Ridge."

The phone sounded as empty as the air around me for a long stretch. "I see," he finally said.

It was a lot to take in over the phone. I knew that. It changed the whole scope of my claim to custody.

"I have a client here," he said. "We'll talk tonight. Are you okay? Can your mother come sit with you?"

"I'll be fine. I'll see you tonight."

I sat a while, biting my lip. Simon would come through for me. At least, I hoped he would. I walked out to the porch and tried to gain some serenity from the beauty of the lake and yard, but my stomach churned and a deep ache settled at the base of my spine. I closed my eyes and let the warmth of the sun beat upon me till my face felt flushed and the heat penetrated to the core of my being. Limp with the humidity, limp with need, I found that the words, the prayer, came easier this time.

God in heaven, I know in my heart you're really there, and I'm finally ready to admit I can't do it all alone. I need you. I bend to you. I submit to your will. I can handle whatever you want to dish out, but it's Sabrina who's hurting more than any of us. I'll stand by my vows. I'll go to church. I'll raise Sabrina up to be Christian. I'll do whatever you lead me to do. But please, God, bring Simon around. Fix this up for her sake. Make us a family, and I will honor that role, and honor you, the rest of my life.

I opened my eyes slowly to the blue of the sky stretching above me. The brightness of it almost blinded me. His light over such a malevolent day.

My words floated away into the blueness of it, and I felt emptied of my burdens. I leaned on the railing, devoid of motivation until I remembered the envelope still sitting on the coffee table.

I sat stiffly on the sofa and read through it. Nothing but essential information. I retrieved Phyllis's will from the security box we kept hidden in a bottom kitchen cabinet. I had to take care of arrangements. Phyllis wanted to be cremated. That made things easier. I called the morgue and made arrangements, then called a funeral home to make an appointment to pick out an urn the next afternoon.

I called Mom. I gave her the officer's version of the event.

"A car wreck," Mom repeated. "Was she drunk?"

I didn't bother to tell her it was probably suicide. The reaction would have been worse. Instead, I explained about needing a sitter so I could work a few hours. I expected more sympathy this time. "So, can you sit with her tomorrow?"

"Carla, you just have to figure out some other arrangement. You are expecting your own baby. Have you forgotten?"

"What has that got to do with you watching Sabrina tomorrow?"

"You can't try to raise Sabrina with another child coming."

Is that where she'd gone wrong with me? She hadn't been able to raise Babette and me at the same time? "Lots of people raise more than one child."

"This is different. You've waited forever for your own."

Boxes, boxes. Sabrina was still in a box marked *Phyllis's Burden*. "Mom, the way I see it, Sabrina is now my own, too."

"She is not. She's an uninvited responsibility. You've got to think of your baby."

Did she really think I would abandon Sabrina to foster care or something? My head throbbed. "Sabrina's waking up. I'll talk to you later. Good-bye."

I looked at Sabrina's slumbering figure and dialed my last resort.

Babette answered.

"Hi. It's your favorite sis," I said. "I need to ask a favor of you." I explained about Phyllis's death and about my need to get out to the plant to catch up on some work. "I'm going to put Sabrina into camp. I already have her registered. I just can't send her off so soon, you understand. Not tell her Phyllis is gone from her life one day, then send her to camp the next. But if she could be with family, with you, then I won't feel bad going in to check on things."

My request met a heavy silence.

"I don't mind watching her, Carla. Brooke will enjoy having

a playmate. And if she's family now ..." Her voice faded a moment. "But I want you to think this through while you're at the plant tomorrow. You have Sabrina's future to consider. And, well, you know Mom told me about the baby ..."

The realization stabbed me. I hadn't told her! "Oh, Babette, I'm sorry. I should have told you. It's still so early. I'm not even trusting myself to think about it."

"It's okay. I never tell you right away, either. Plus, I know you and Simon are having problems, Kevin being here and all. And now Sabrina. Maybe you ought to think about what you're going to do. Maybe you ought to quit work."

Oh boy. Now we were at the crux of it. "I love my job. Just because you've chosen to be a full-time mom doesn't mean I'm going to do the same."

"Sure, I know. Lots of women work. But Sabrina has a big adjustment to make. And you've waited a long time for that baby. They aren't babies for long. It sounds like a long time, but it's gone in the blink of an eye."

I held my tongue.

She took a breath and plunged on. "You can tell me all kinds of things about the real world and business. I know you're a genius. But I can tell you about motherhood. I've been working at it for fifteen years. You think infancy and the toddler stage will last forever. But it doesn't. It's gone before you know it. And if you leave them in day care all that time, you don't even get a good grasp of it."

"How would you know that?"

"I worked at the grocery when Blake was a baby. Have you forgotten? Almost no money for all those hours, but we had to have the bit I earned. I cried every morning when I left him at day care."

"Actually, I'd forgotten you worked. I guess because I was

away at college." I thought about it a minute. "Why didn't Mom watch him?"

"She said she'd had her years raising babies. She went and got him out of day care some days, but she said she didn't want to be obligated."

The gulf of all that must have occurred yawned before me and gripped me with a remorseful ache. Obviously, much had transpired that my sister had never told me, or I had ignored. I had no idea things between her and Mom had ever been anything but ideal. "If it makes you feel any better, she won't watch Sabrina, either."

"I figured that, or you wouldn't have called me. You never call me unless you have to."

"That's not true."

"Yes, it is."

She was right. I really avoided her. What did we ever have in common? Nothing, till now. "It won't be true anymore, I promise."

I could almost hear her smiling. "We finally have kids the same age. Near enough, anyway."

"I always hoped we would, you know. And hopefully Brooke will help Sabrina get over Phyllis's death," I said.

"I'm sure she will. But I mean more than Brooke and Sabrina."

"Huh?"

"I'm several months pregnant already, Carla. I'm glad you never noticed. I did my best to hide it. I didn't want to make you resent me even more. That's why I kept asking and asking what was happening with you."

I stood there, stunned. "Congratulations." Nothing else would rise in my mind to fill the gap. "Oh, Sabrina is waking up." This time she really was. "I've got to go. I'll see you around ten tomorrow morning."

Sabrina was still weepy when she woke up. So was I. Too many pressures were mounting around me. I felt like I'd moved through a time warp and landed in an abstract version of my life.

I worked off some of my aggravations by cleaning the house for an hour, which I normally left for Abigail's Wednesday visit. But I had to do something constructive. Sabrina helped me straighten the toy shelves. I looked at them with new eyes, realizing they were here to stay. I planned to box up the old things and give them back to Babette. Sabrina would need more new toys, permanent things. So would a new baby.

Sabrina would be the big sister. Always.

I imagined the two of them that way, Sabrina in my role, and the baby trailing behind like Babette, but the image didn't fit. Sabrina was different. The baby would be different, too.

I couldn't fathom how I could work it out with Simon, keeping Sabrina and giving birth to another man's child. Even with Ron gone, I would still have to go through the formalities of Sabrina's custody process, which Simon had warned would be months long with court-date delays. Although I no longer had to worry about being challenged, things would go easier with a husband at my side, a show of a solid home environment. But I wanted more than a show. I wanted the dream to be reality. Unfortunately, the problems seemed insurmountable. Although Simon had stepped forward to help out, I knew he really didn't want Sabrina or the baby. I wasn't sure he wanted me, either. I didn't fit his lifestyle anymore. We no longer had the same goals. I wanted a family. I wanted noise and disruption and life careening into unknown territory. He wanted quiet evenings, travel, and simplicity. Life without change.

I wondered if God had heard my prayer, and if he would intervene.

I cast the thoughts away and kept myself busy. Sabrina helped me dust and vacuum the family room. We both felt lousy. Our bodies were slumped. Our faces looked haggard. The pall of Phyllis's death lay fully upon us. We needed my secret weapon. We ate a light lunch, then went out to the rose garden.

Sabrina remembered what I'd shown her. She took the trowel and knelt beside me. Carefully, she turned the weeds, shook the dirt from their roots, and tossed them into the bucket.

"Good job, Sabrina," I said.

Her face brightened just a touch. Soil and sunshine have a way of working on a person's spirit.

By two o'clock, I was exhausted. We showered, first her, then me. Refreshed, we sat at the coffee table sipping juice and putting together a hundred-piece puzzle. It was quiet. She had been silent most of the day. I'd expected a torrent of questions from her, but she matched piece after piece without comment until Simon walked in. We both looked up, surprised. It wasn't even three yet.

"I thought you might need me here. I couldn't concentrate, anyway."

Sabrina scrambled across my lap and ran to him, wrapped her arms around him, and sobbed. "Oh, Pai. Oh, Pai. Mommy's really gone now. The policeman told Mäe. She's left me forever."

Simon peeled her off his leg and squatted down. "I know. I know, Love. It'll be all right."

"But you said I couldn't stay here. Please change your mind, Pai. Don't make me go away."

He was fighting hard to keep tears from flowing. He squinted until his eyes were almost closed. His mouth pressed to a line. "I'm not making you go anywhere. Who else would call me Pai?"

I didn't know what to say. I looked at them and got up and walked outside to stare at the tranquility of the sky. Eternity. It stretched on forever, beyond the clouds, beyond our satellites, beyond the planets tracked by scientists. I stood there and shivered, not with cold, but with knowledge. And with lack of knowledge. There existed much more than logic could explain. I'd asked for proof, I'd opened myself to the possibility of God's power, and he had stepped forth and made the impossible happen. Who was I to doubt such supremacy? Who was I to take claim for my riches and the life that stirred within me? Who was I to think Sabrina had landed in my life by mere chance? A month earlier I would never have believed that Simon would accept someone else's child in our lives. God proved differently.

With my face turned upward, the sun cast away shadows and lay like God's own warm hand upon me. I drank in his power and surrendered myself to him wholly.

"Thanks," I whispered to the heavens. It was all I could manage at that point.

That put us halfway to the peak. If only Simon could accept the baby.

Twenty-five

The next morning when I pulled into Babette's driveway, Sabrina squealed when she saw Brooke at the red metal swing set. She unbuckled and ran to her side. Brooke would definitely be good medicine.

I sat looking at the house before getting out. I'd never really taken it in before: the roses climbing the trellis of the front porch where two white rockers gently rocked back and forth in the humid July breeze. The boxwoods stood rounded, carefully trimmed. A statue of a girl curtsied in the flower garden. Sabrina and Brooke were dancing around a big shady oak as if they were tree nymphs.

I'd always thought of myself as having more than my sister. Then I'd resented her for having children when I didn't. But here I was struck with the sameness of our lives. I thought we had striven for different things, but we both just wanted to be happy: to have a loving husband, a nice home, and a family. All the resentment I'd felt over her having children first drifted away. How had I ever considered that she'd intentionally been one up on me? I realized it wasn't something she had meant to do. I, on the other hand, had outdone her in many things and managed to flaunt those accomplishments in her face without even trying.

I went in the house and handed her my typed sheet of

baby-sitting instructions. "Take care of her. Here's my work number and stuff."

She glanced at the paper. "I've got your work number. You think I've been living on Mars or what?"

"Right. Sorry." I hugged her. "Thanks, Baby."

She didn't comment on my use of her nickname. She just smiled and walked me to the door.

Things went well the rest of the week. Babette kept Sabrina on Thursday and Friday. Sabrina seemed to accept her place with us. Simon quit challenging me on everything.

On Saturday evening Sabrina was playing with my old doll. She ascended the staircase, murmuring to Miss Polly lovingly. I was gazing at her dreamily, trying to remember my own games of doll baby, when Simon broke my reverie.

"So where'd you decide to put her?"

"Huh? Nowhere. I'm letting Sabrina play with her."

It wasn't often he caught me in outer space. He laughed. "Not the doll. Sabrina. What day-care center did you register her for?"

"None. I couldn't stand the look of them. Little rooms. Snotty-nosed kids."

"Okay, so where is she going? Babette's not watching her indefinitely."

"No, she can't, not full time. She has her hands full with her kids already. I'm putting her in camps. Swimming camp at the Y next week. Bug camp the following week at the science center downtown." I sounded like my secretary in her never-ending planning stage of what to do with her kids.

"And then?"

"Maybe computer camp."

"At five years old?"

"Well, something."

The news came back on, and Simon turned his attention to it.

I thought, at last, my life was in order.

A while later, Sabrina came down the stairs hauling the small pink suitcase I'd bought for her visit to my mom's and clasping Miss Polly in the crook of her other arm. Taz bounded down beside her. "I'm ready to go home, now," she said.

Simon and I were dumbfounded. "What?"

"I want to go home and tell Mommy all about my ballet class and hide-and-seek. Taz wants to meet her, too. We've been here a long time."

I fell on my knees in front of her. "Sabrina, darling. I thought you understood. Your mommy is gone. She's passed away, dear. She can't come back." I hesitated over saying the words, but she had to see the concrete image. "She's dead."

"I did what she said. I've been a big, brave girl. I haven't even cried 'bout it, 'cept once. But I want to go to her now. I miss her." She slipped from my grasp and went to Simon. "Take me to her, please."

Simon heaved her into his chair, half on his lap, half on the armrest. "Close your eyes, Sabrina, and imagine heaven and picture your mother there. That's where we hope she is, with the angels in the presence of God."

Tears flooded down her cheeks. "I want Mommy *now*." Simon scooped her into his arms and lugged her up the steps, singing the hymn Sabrina had learned in church the week before. This time I didn't smirk at his faith.

He came down the stairs a short time later. "Where are you?" he called out.

"In the front room," I answered. I didn't like the term "living room." We never *lived* in that room. It had its own atmosphere that prevented life from entering it. It was a museum, a showcase.

"She'll be all right," he said as he walked up behind me. "She was overtired. She hasn't been sleeping well."

I barely heard him. Phyllis's urn had all my attention. Simon had moved it from place to place in the house. It didn't seem to fit anywhere. Tonight it was on the antique end table, standing there like a soldier waiting for orders. *Ready, aim, die.* "Do we have plans for tomorrow?" I asked.

"Church."

Of course, church. We could be in the middle of a tornado and I could fill in that blank. The difference was that I no longer resented it. I, too, wanted to go. I had more talking to do with God. But I had other plans for the day, too. "What do you have planned for the afternoon?"

"I have a racquetball match. Why?"

"Chimney Rock. It's close by and it's beautiful. Let's take the urn to the top and let Sabrina set her free."

He nodded. "Okay, we'll do that, but next Saturday, not tomorrow. There will still be too many people on holiday from the Fourth."

"True. Next Saturday, then."

My own growing sense of God rumbled inside of me. "I wonder if she thought about God before she died."

"I hope so. Of course, we'll never know for sure what happened, but it sounds like she purposely killed herself and Ron. I hope her last thought was a prayer for forgiveness."

A knot settled in my stomach. *Thou shalt not kill.* "But she was protecting Sabrina. God won't hold that against her."

"I don't presume to know how God judges people. What I

do know is we have the chance to teach Sabrina about God's love for her and help her heal."

"I think spreading her ashes will be a step in that direction. She needs some finality."

"Don't we all."

Twenty-six

Macho men hike to the top of Chimney Rock. Pregnant women take the elevator.

We reached the precipice, all nicely fenced in for tourists to stand on, and gaped at the world below. Despite the guardrail and the mass of people milling around us, I stood as if alone on the top of the world. A breeze swept across my skin and made me feel like a kite flying high above the ground. Beneath me, roads spread outward through the little town, out into plaid farm fields and miniature barns.

I pulled juice boxes out of my pack and handed one to Sabrina. "What do you think?"

"It's just like the umpire skates building."

"The Empire State Building, you mean."

"That's what I said."

Simon snapped a few pictures of the scenery and some of Sabrina and me perched on a boulder with the world as a backdrop.

"Okay," he said. "Lunch at the little café over there, and then on to the top."

"The top?" I gasped. "You mean this isn't it?"

"No. We're only at the first overlook."

At least he allowed us lunch in between ascents.

I sat at the café, eating a roast beef sandwich and justi-
fying the climb. One part of me knew it was probably too
much exertion, being newly pregnant. Everything in me
screamed to protect this baby, my tiny miracle. But Simon
wasn't thinking in those terms. We had ignored the baby
issue for days. Maybe he'd imagined the baby had disappeared. Fear gripped me. Maybe it *had* disappeared.

I reprimanded myself for my paranoia.

But mentioning my condition would bring the turmoil to
the surface again when we were trying to bring peace to
Sabrina.

Worry built up in me with every mouthful. I couldn't
stand it. "Do you think it's safe to climb to the top?"

Simon pointed to the staircase. "Sure. There are staircases
for most of the way. And fences. See them? We'll have to keep
Sabrina between us, but she's not going to jump off the side.
Are you, Love?"

"'Course not." She picked at her french fries.

A constant flow of people ascended the steps. A young
father, sporting a baseball cap and short white socks, started
up with a toddler balanced in a backpack-carrier. Two elderly ladies, alike enough to name them sisters if not twins,
balanced on one another, with one gripping the railing. Four
teenage boys sprang past them, taking the steps two at a
time. A family of five stepped in slow rhythm behind the old
ladies. A beer-gutted fellow with a matching double chin
pulled himself up the first few steps with a mutt dog on a
leash leading the way. It nosed at the legs of the family
ahead until he yanked it back and waited for the procession
to speed up.

Surely, if two old ladies and an out-of-shape middle-aged
guy could do it, it couldn't be too difficult. I ran up and down

stairs every day. I opened my mouth to pose the statement aloud but stopped myself. Things were going too well.

I took it slow. Mr. Fitness, with Phyllis's urn in his backpack, took the steps at a steady pace. He paused on every landing, looking at Sabrina and me like we were anchors.

The first section wasn't bad. We reached a second lookout and rested. I felt fine.

The next section of the climb was tougher. Portions had been tamed with man-made staircases, but a large part was natural. Root-strewn dirt trails wove back and forth along the rocky ledge with chain-link fencing tacked here and there along the steepest ledges. Most looked less than sturdy. I grasped Sabrina's hand tightly.

As we climbed higher and higher, my legs began to shake. Sabrina didn't complain. She scrambled after Simon with determination, as if cut from the same mold. I watched them in profile. They looked like father and daughter in their tight-lipped concentrated efforts, their sinewy limbs and long faces. I called a rest. A throbbing pain had started in my side, but I gritted my teeth and said nothing. I couldn't ruin the moment. Instead, I reached out and asked for the camera. On the next incline I paused, gasping, clutched my side, and breathed deeply. The pain eased. I was all right. Simon and Sabrina gazed back at me. I captured them on film, two earnest faces striving for the top of the world.

The top seemed impossibly far away.

"Can you imagine the guys who put these steps here?" I panted out. "It's so steep. And they had to drag the wood up here, hold it in place, and build the steps."

Simon turned. "It would be a chore, wouldn't it? I wonder what inspired them?"

"Money. Look how much our tickets cost."

"But it didn't generate money for ages." He struck out again, sharing an increased appreciation for every set of steps he came to, as did I.

Finally, I had to stop them. With every step, my anxiety rose. The baby became paramount in my mind. "I need a rest. I'm pregnant, remember?"

Simon stopped short and stared at me. I could almost affirm he had actually forgotten, put it out of mind.

We were at a rocky ledge with a chain-link fence ten feet away, breaking the path from the sheer drop. Simon leaned against the rock cliff and pulled drinks out of my bag for each of us. I swallowed deeply and brought my heart and lungs back to a normal pace as I stared, with drooping shoulders, at the ground.

Figures passed us. A dozen pair of shoes. Tennis shoes, loafers, a kid in flip-flops. Who lets a kid climb a mountain in flip-flops? I didn't look up.

My hand rested on my abdomen. I pressed my stomach, thinking maybe I could feel the baby, which, of course, I couldn't. I would have sat there forever, but I had to finish the climb. We were almost there. One more grade, from the looks of it.

Simon recapped the bottles and swung the backpack onto his shoulders. "Do you think you can make it?"

"I don't think I have a choice at this point."

"It was your idea, remember?"

He was right.

He extended his hand to me and pulled me up. The ache had ebbed away. I felt somewhat recovered. Once more, I put one foot in front of the other, slowly, but steadily. People continued to pass us. Skinny girls with pimply faced boyfriends.

A huge Mexican family—aunts and uncles, grandmas and preteens—all chattering away in Spanish. I let them pass. Simon stopped and held Sabrina's hand, waiting.

Then we came upon it. The summit. It lay before us like a mountaintop patio, smooth black rock soaking up the sun's heat and radiating it back up at us. Sabrina stood at the center of the rock and gaped at the scene. Land fell away from us as far as we could see. The world below was a model set of tiny cars and mountain shacks. Wispy clouds were caught among distant trees, and grassy fields stretched out below us. We were standing in the sky, with all of creation spread at our feet.

"This is it, isn't it?" she asked.

"I sure hope so," I said, collapsing. I could feel the throbbing again but tried to turn my mind from it. I stared in awe at the wonder of the world stretching before me. I let the peace of the landscape settle over me a moment, then laid back and stretched out flat, but the pain became a dagger stuck in my side. I drew in long, deep breaths, resolving to begin a slow walking regimen back home.

"I never dreamed it was so beautiful. No wonder Mommy wanted to come here."

"Your mother said she wanted to come here?"

Sabrina turned from the scene to look at me, puzzled. "Pai said everyone wants to come to heaven."

I nodded. "Yes, everyone wants to go to heaven, and this feels like heaven. In fact, this may be exactly how it looks in heaven, but it's not heaven. It's the top of a mountain."

"But Pai said we were coming here for Mommy."

Simon was standing under the shade of a tree behind us, off the rock ledge where the mountain sprawled with scraggly shrubs and spindly evergreens. He was staring out over the world, lost in thought. I sat up and waved him over. With exaggerated panting, I said, "It's time, hon. Explain it to her."

Simon squatted beside me and pulled the backpack into his lap. A few other climbers approached, claiming a spot on the rock ten feet away to gasp and share in the majesty of the view. Simon glanced at them and hesitated. Was he embarrassed? Maybe. He wouldn't do anything to attract the attention of onlookers, I knew. But the strangers seemed to be ignoring us, so he pulled the urn from hiding and handed it to me.

I stroked the intricate design. It reminded me of Phyllis's complexity—her artsy nature—but she was also like the pewter itself, made of good stuff that had been molded into a new shape by life.

I imagined her as I had last seen her, her hair straggling around her shoulders in an array of loose frizzy curls. Her mouth wide with laughter and good cheer despite the sadness in her eyes.

Sabrina noticed the urn and stooped to touch it. "What's that, Mäe?"

There was no easy explanation. Simon stared into the sky. It wasn't his place to tell her; I knew that. He hadn't even known Phyllis. I took a deep breath. "Everyone dies. You know that, don't you? We'd like to live forever, but it's not planned out that way." My stalling technique failed. Her eyes began to glaze. "Some people get buried in the ground when they die. That's what graveyards are."

"But they don't stay in the yucky ground. Pai told me so. They turn into spirits and fly up to heaven to be with God. What's that got to do with that fancy jar?"

I propped the urn between us. "Well, some people don't want to get buried in the yucky ground, even in a fancy casket with satin pillows. They believe their spirit flies out of their body the minute they die, and they don't need their old skin and bones anymore. Your mother was that way."

"I know. Pai told me she was up here with Jesus and looking down at me to be sure I was pleasing him, being good and all."

The preacher was pouring out of her, complete with quotes from Simon. The old agnostic in me cringed, but God had answered my prayer in Simon's acceptance of Sabrina. He had proved his existence, despite my antagonism. I wanted to believe in heaven and life after death. Especially thinking of my father. I couldn't bear to think of him as being gone from me forever. How comforting to believe we would be reunited one day.

Phyllis, her ashes cold between my very hands, had been so full of spirit. It was inconceivable to think of people as no more than body parts, all the knowledge and love and good-ness in them dissipating into nothingness. Something had to be carried on beyond life as we knew it. That meant God and heaven and life after death. I welcomed the soothing thought of a spiritual life and hoped Phyllis's spirit had risen to heaven, to a blissful eternity. I let the peace of it wrap around me. "Yes, that's right. Your mother became a spirit and didn't need her body anymore. She didn't want her old body to be buried. She was cremated." Sabrina scrunched her eyes in confusion. I tapped the urn. "Your mother's ashes are in here. We're going to toss them out to the wind, to be blown across the mountain."

Her face screwed up into a knot. "My mommy is in there?"

Simon leaned close behind me, watching her. I could feel his breath on my neck. Then he plopped on his bottom and held out his hand to Sabrina, who not only took it, but also fell into his lap and grasped his shirt. "Your mother isn't in there, Love. Just her ashes."

Even though I knew it didn't coincide with Simon's theology, I had to say something to soothe Sabrina, and I knew how Phyllis would want Sabrina to imagine death. "She's around us in the blue of the sky and the green of the trees. She's one of God's beautiful creations. And she wants us to cast her ashes out, so her spirit can be free to fly."

"I want my mommy." Tears poured from her. My arms ached to hold her, but Simon pulled her into him, letting her cry into his shoulder. I couldn't understand how she could turn to Simon for comfort instead of me. Wasn't I the one who held her every night while she fell asleep?

The pain in my side eased. I ran my fingers down Sabrina's back as she curled against him, so tiny and helpless, like the infant in my womb that I couldn't touch with my fingers or see with my eyes. I knew love. I already mourned the idea of ever being parted from my child, and I'd not even seen his face. The anguish Phyllis must have felt as she fled, knowing she would never hold Sabrina again, washed over me and choked me. Tears flowed uncontrollably. I cursed Ron for returning, for carrying Phyllis down a path that made her feel death was the only escape. How had she had the strength to take her own life? She must have felt that Sabrina was in danger. She must have taken her own life with Ron in tow to protect her child. Love stronger than life. "Your mother loved you very much, Sabrina. She didn't want to die. She didn't want to leave you. We have to believe she's still here with us, watching you right now. And she's waiting. Waiting for you to spread her ashes."

She cringed from the words, curled tighter, and burrowed

into Simon. The light seemed to shift on Simon's face. A
pained look crossed his features. He wrapped his arms
around her, smoothed her hair down her neck, kissed the
crown of her head, and whispered, "We're here for you,
Sabrina, and we're not going anywhere. I promise. Hold on
just as tight as you need to."

We sat there on that peak, the sun beating down on us,
the rock hard and hot beneath us, and waited for her to turn
around on her own. She hadn't mourned until then. She was
facing the fact of life without her mommy for the first time.

I think that's when we faced it, too. Although I'd contemplated the idea of Sabrina being our daughter forever, I hadn't
really focused on the depth of that commitment until right
then, with her sorrow arcing around us. I saw us as a family,
with bonds and love and meaning behind our words and
actions. She was there in Simon's lap, relying on us for everything in life.

Simon felt it, too. I could see it in the way he held her, his
big hands clasped across her back, his head leaning against
hers. He could feel her need for him, her dependency. I
leaned against his shoulder and laid my hand on his leg. He
dropped one hand over mine. As my heart leapt, he squeezed
my hand gently, a silent communication of union.

A steady tread of climbers arrived behind us, awestruck at
the peak; the same comments played time and time again
before each hiker passed on to the return trail. A few people
motioned toward us and whispered. A bent old man—how
had he managed the climb?—shuffled in front of us to offer a
friendly greeting and point out where he had eaten lunch as
if we hadn't looked at the scene below.

From the next group, a spunky little boy decked out in red
bandanna, cowboy hat, and fancy black boots stomped

around us and said, "What's wrong with her?" I shook my head and fixed my eyes on the horizon.

Sabrina uncurled and twisted around to face him. "Go away."

"You don't own this mountain, crybaby."

She swiped her sleeve across her face, smearing the tears. "I'm not a crybaby."

"Are too."

"Am not."

"Then why are you crying?"

Her eyes spit fire. Her spirit was winning out over her sorrow. "'Cause I gotta throw my mommy off the mountain."

The boy's mother reached his side and took his arm while talking to another adult. He wiggled out of her clutches. "You're lying."

The other adults had turned an ear toward the youngsters. She pulled herself together for the audience and sat up straight. "Am not lying."

She heaved the urn into her tiny lap. "My mommy's in here, and I'm gonna throw her out to the air like she asked me to." Sabrina had their attention now. I had wanted it to be private, quiet, just the three of us alone with the solemn majesty of the moment like in the movies, but we had an audience now. At least they had pulled Sabrina from her shell.

She laid her baby fingers on the top of the urn. I nodded at the question in her eyes and helped her lift the lid. I'm not sure what she expected to see, but she stared into it as if she couldn't fathom what she was seeing.

"It's ashes," I whispered, "like in the fireplace." Maybe I should have explained the whole cremation scheme at home, taken the process in tiny steps. Too late.

Simon caught the urn as Sabrina scrambled to her feet.

The ache in my side had subsided to a throbbing knot. I pushed myself to stand. We stood there, all three, staring at the urn, a freak show with these strangers' curiosity flaring around us.

A man's voice erupted from between the women, deep and gruff, matching his beard and tattered baseball cap. "Leave 'em be, Mabel. Ain't ya got the manners to allow 'em to make their peace?" He strode across the rock ledge, onto the path. The others trailed after him, little cowboy in tow.

Simon raised the urn. "May God bless you with a place in his heavenly kingdom."

I nodded to him and took Sabrina's hand. I closed my eyes to ward off the welling tears, but they came again, dripping down my cheeks, puddling on my lips and eyelashes. My nose ran.

As the ashes fell from the urn, a wind stirred around us and swept them up in a cloud of dust. Sabrina stared in wonder, until a few ash flakes landed on her arm. She shrieked and clasped my leg. "Mommy, Mommy ..." over and over. I pulled her up into my arms, ignoring the snatch of pain it caused. She cried into my hair, changing her chant. "Mãe, Mãe ..."

I touched her cheek and whispered, "Look."

The ashes rose and wafted out on the breeze, swirling in a miniature tornado-like twist and sifting down to the scene below.

"Your mother is free, sweetie. She's flying all around us."

Sabrina said, "Like an angel."

I sighed, settling, coming to terms. "Yes, an angel. A beautiful angel."

With the urn emptied, Simon put his arm around us.

"Angel dust, Mäe. She's waving with magical angel dust."

Sabrina watched the ashes drift down against the deep green of the trees, the blue of the sky, the majesty of the valley below, and the rise of the land beyond. She lifted her chin and began to sing, first quietly in a little girl voice, but rising with confidence. "Angels we have heard up high, singing way up in the sky, on the mountains u-up high, where the angels like to fly. Glo-o-o-o-o-o-o-o-o-o-ria, an ex-cell-ent Day-o."

Okay, so she didn't have the words quite right, and she'd combined two songs. Her sweet voice cut through my sorrow, and I smiled. Simon joined her, and I chimed in, too. "Glo-o-o-o-o-o-o-o-o-ria, in excelsis De-e-o."

We remained knotted until the last of the ashes danced away and then a bit longer. If other groups passed behind us, we were oblivious.

"I'm thirsty," Sabrina said, and the ethereal mood was gone. Our minds returned to the present, to our aching legs and dry throats.

"Come on," I said. "Let's move into the shade, and I'll get out a juice box for you."

We walked on down the trail, each lost in our own thoughts, mine being solely to get home for a soak in the tub.

The trail was easier in that we were descending, but there were fewer wooden steps. The going was rocky and rough. My side still throbbed, but I forced my mind away from it. What good would it do to complain when there was no way to get down but to put one foot in front of the other?

Ahead, though we couldn't see it for the thick of trees, we heard the rushing of water. At the last ridge, we came to a small waterfall pouring into a clear rocky pool. A dozen people had slipped off socks and shoes to totter along the stepping-stones and wade in the knee-deep water.

Sabrina squealed with delight, "Can I go in the water?"

Simon stooped to help with her shoes. I trudged to the middle of the walking bridge and leaned on the railing to watch them. My stomach churned and told me it was close to five, time to head home or somewhere to eat. I felt light-headed.

The notion of the baby drawing from my reserves came to mind just as another pain gouged my abdomen. I doubled over.

A warm sensation gushed in my crotch. "Simon." I meant to yell it, but it came out mumbled as my grip slipped from the railing, and I crumpled to the wood planks.

Voices clambered around me. Hands touched my shoulder and forehead. Strong arms heaved me up. Familiar, musky sweat. Smooth face. Long white neck. Simon. I gave into him and cried for the second time in a day, another mourning—one only I would ever understand.

Behind me, someone else hollered that they were bringing the little girl, my Sabrina.

No one could navigate a woman down the remaining steps. They were impossibly steep. I've been back time and again to that very spot. How Simon got me down, I don't know, but the next thing I knew I was strapped into our new Expedition. We flew around the hairpin mountain curves before I fully breathed and faced what was happening.

"It's too late," I said. "No need to rush."

"Who made you a doctor?" he replied, speeding up and pulling the cell phone from the glove compartment.

"Let's not all die over this. Is Sabrina buckled?"

"Are you going to die?" Her voice wavered.

I reclined the seat as far as I could, then reached for Sabrina's hand. I knew her fear. "I'm not dying, Sabrina. You just sit and relax. I just need some rest. That mountain was too much for me."

In my heart, I thought of Phyllis. I was carrying her baby home. And she was carrying mine to the top of the mountain. To the sky. To heaven. A year ago, two weeks ago, I would have railed at Simon's God and blamed him, but I closed my eyes in exhaustion, thinking the trade had been justified, numbly wondering why I'd not been given the choice beforehand: baby or Sabrina. Listening to her quiet sobs, I knew. Beforehand I would have chosen incorrectly. *All in God's time,* Simon had said. I had to see the plan from hindsight.

A road sign proclaimed our distance from Charlotte. Sixty-five miles. It could have been eternity. As I gripped the seat and listened to the tires spin over the pavement, I contemplated the confirmation of my loss.

Twenty-seven

*S*imon hoisted me from the car and led me into the hospital. With all the times I had been to see Dr. Freeman, my heart aching, wishing Simon would be there for the creation of our child, I felt hollow now.

Simon had phoned Mom. She and Babette were at the emergency-room entrance. Brooke and Bette were twirling around one of the thick columns as if it were a maypole.

"Oh, my darling," said Mom as she stepped off the curb to help me to the door. "What have you done to yourself?"

That's me, her constant failure.

Sabrina scrambled out of the car and stood stock still right on the narrow curb, poised as if on a balance beam. The girls called out to her as they continued around the post, their free arms flapping like injured bird wings. Simon and I progressed across the entranceway, with me leaning against him. "Sabrina, you go with Babette," he said. "We'll call you in a bit and let you know how Mäe is after the doctor has seen her."

I wanted to stop and hug her. As distressed as I felt, I needed the comfort of her little body against mine, but I hadn't the strength to speak my mind.

The doors swished open, and we passed through with Mom shuffling up behind. "I'm staying right here with you, Carla. Babette can keep Sabrina."

Maybe she meant well, but I was too filled with grief to listen to her platitudes. I shook my head and turned pleading eyes at Simon.

"You'll have to stay here, in the waiting room," Simon said.

A thin brunette nurse who had to be twenty-something but looked sixteen, if that, chatted nonstop while she settled me on the bed, interrupting herself every few sentences with a breathless laugh that sounded half-mad. Simon retreated to the back corner and watched.

"Have you had a Doppler exam done before? It finds the heartbeat, like a stethoscope, but magnifies it." She held up a tube of jelly. Before I could respond, she squirted a dollop of it into my navel. It was so cold I sucked in my breath, which raised another howl of laughter from the young nurse just as Dr. Freeman arrived. He stood at the end of the bed, his eyes serious over his professional smile. "I thought we'd decided I wouldn't see you until Monday?"

I met his wit with my own. "I just couldn't bear the idea of you playing a full game of golf."

He chuckled.

Simon reached out from his spot in the corner. "Hello, Dr. Freeman. Simon Rochwell."

The two of them shook hands, assessing each other in their protective roles, curiosity rising in their eyes and passing on with some previous blank filled in.

"Glad to finally meet you," Dr. Freeman said. He crossed his arms. "Bleeding doesn't always indicate a miscarriage. It's quite possible, but not absolute. What were you doing when it happened?"

"Climbing Chimney Rock."

Dr. Freeman blinked and stared at me. I felt like crawling under the sheets.

He washed his hands and took the Doppler from the nurse. "Anything yet?" he asked her.

She shook her head and backed up a pace to give him room.

The jelly on my navel felt nasty. He gripped the cylinder in his right hand and the palm-sized speaker box in his left and moved the device slowly across my abdomen as the machine emitted an irritating wave of static.

He clicked it off. The nurse wiped off the jelly while he switched to a stethoscope. Again, he listened in several places. He stood back and talked through his smile, even more fixed than before. "I couldn't find a heartbeat, but that's not unusual. It's still so early in your pregnancy." He turned to the nurse. "Vaginal scope." He turned back to me. "We're going to do an internal ultrasound with a vaginal scope. It may not show us anything this early, but for peace of mind, we'll try."

The nurse rolled in another piece of machinery: a blackish viewing screen with an instrument attached. It wasn't exactly a comfortable procedure, but it didn't hurt. If I'd been the coy type, I would have been embarrassed beyond measure, but years of being prodded and poked had removed every shred of modesty I had. I stared at the screen, trying to fathom what Dr. Freeman saw.

Simon stepped up and held my hand.

Finally, Dr. Freeman pointed to a dark area. "I see something here. I can't be positive this early, but it looks like a sac."

"You mean I'm still pregnant?"

"It's just a guess at this point, but I think so."

Simon spoke up. "Then what caused all the blood?"

"Could be one of several things. It could be that she did

miscarry, and I'm seeing something else here. It could be that the corpeus luteum burst—a cyst that provides progesterone to the body during the first ten weeks of pregnancy. Or it could be she was pregnant with more than one fetus, and one remained viable. The latter is my best guess. It's quite common."

The words didn't sink in at first. I still had a baby. I'd lost a baby. I couldn't join the fragmented ideas. I couldn't decide which to think about. They were like arrows pointing in opposite directions.

Simon's hand in mine felt unreal. He'd expected the baby to be gone, I'm sure, but here was Dr. Freeman telling us a baby still survived.

Slowly, Simon's hand withdrew from mine, and he crossed his arms. "So what does this mean?"

"We'll boost her progesterone considerably. I won't restrict her to bed rest, but she needs to avoid anything strenuous and allow for as much extra rest as possible."

I let my head flop back. I would rest. I promised my baby and myself total rest.

Dr. Freeman wrote out a prescription for the increased progesterone and instructed the nurse to give me an injection before discharging me. "I want you to stay here for the next few hours. Let's make sure that temperature goes down. If it's down by nine, you can leave. I'll see you in my office in a few days."

When we were alone again, Simon remained distant. "I'd better pick up Sabrina. I'll feed her and come back for you tonight."

"Okay."

He walked to the door, stopped, and came back to the foot of the bed. He tried to look at me, but couldn't. He stared at his feet. "I didn't want you to lose the baby, you know."

I nodded, but I couldn't speak. Neither could he. He turned and left.

Kevin and Gina entered together a half-hour later, him holding the door and ushering her in. I tried to picture Gina in his truck or him in her Cadillac. Neither seemed like a fit. "Well, hello," I said. "How'd you two get here?"

"Up the elevator and down the hall," Kevin quipped, hanging his hands in his pockets.

Gina laughed as if he were a stand-up comedian. "Your mom called and told me," she explained. She handed me a white teddy bear wearing a bright red polka-dot bow tie. It still bore the price tag from the hospital gift shop. "You're going to be okay, huh?"

I took the bear and messed with its ears. I wondered what she had been told. "The doctor thinks I was carrying two babies and miscarried one. The other, we hope, is okay."

She sat on the edge of the bed. "Why didn't you tell us you were having a baby?"

It was *us* now, was it? At least from Gina's lips. "I just found out the other day."

Gina frowned at Kevin. "The girl tries everything under the sun to get pregnant for two years, and then she doesn't call her best friend when she gets the news."

Her statement startled me. I guess she was my best friend, yet we didn't seem that close now. In retrospect, we hadn't really chosen to be friends. I had more or less fallen into the habit of hanging around with her. I hadn't confided in Gina about any of my recent problems, certainly not about the insemination. She was only asking about the baby now because it was appropriate. I couldn't imagine her caring about the progression of my pregnancy.

Babette would, though.

Kevin sprawled out in the ugly vinyl chair in the corner and slung one leg over his knee. He obviously hadn't told Gina that he knew about the baby.

"Could you get me something to drink, Gina?" I asked.

She looked from me to Kevin and back again, measuring the situation, then shrugged. After all, what competition could a pregnant woman in a hospital bed be? I imagined what a fright I was with my hair stuck out in all directions and a pallor of death that reached down through to my bones. My eyes felt like they had shrunk to unappealing slits, with, no doubt, telltale black shadows of stress.

Gina, of course, stood there radiant in a beige little thing that hugged her very unpregnant body. I didn't even have to be showing yet to feel the difference yawning between us. She spun around and darted out the door like a deer flicking her tail behind her.

Kevin leaned forward. "So what does Simon say?"

My hands went instinctively to my tummy. *How quickly things change,* I was thinking. Life kept going forward, us making choices, taking steps, and being carried along full force, but our minds could sit back where they were for days, unmoving, not grasping the changes. That's how I felt. My life had gone on, all this happening to me so quickly that I couldn't place where I was anymore, like a tornado twisting around me, and I was stuck in the eye. Kevin still had us discussing whether he or Simon would raise the baby.

"Simon hasn't said anything."

Kevin mashed his lips together, something he had done

for ages, a habit of frustration. What had he expected? He would show up with Gina, and I would say, "It's over between Simon and me, so come pick me up at noon?"

Gina returned with a cup of ice and a single-serve bottle of apple juice. "Here you go." She settled on the edge of the bed. "So give us the details. Due date. Sex. All that stuff."

The cold, wet bottle felt good in my hands, something simple and real to concentrate on. Gina struck me as being more like the cup of ice: a frivolity that would melt away if left too long. I tried to imagine her cooing over a baby. "March twenty-third. Too early to know the sex, but I keep thinking of it as a boy. Either way, I'll always wonder about the other one, whether they were the same sex or different. Whether they would have been alike or not." In the car, I'd thought of the child itself, that one individual I would never know. A new image came to me as I began to think of my lost baby in terms of its living twin. The living child would always have a shadow. A shadow with an unseen face. Perhaps they would have been different, opposites but still tied together by their birth, one dominant and the other a follower. I wondered if life and death had reversed their roles, that the dominant one may have been the one who died, the one who would now live forever as the shadow.

"I was a twin," Gina said. "Same deal. My sister died in childbirth. Well, I guess we better go and let you get some rest."

I was too stunned by her comment to grasp that she was leaving. That was the deepest secret Gina had ever exposed about herself. Not a frivolous confidence like getting drunk and barfing on a date. Or other girlfriend confessions, like the night she had been deep into her fifth margarita when she admitted in laughing hysterics that she'd stolen her dad's putter and sold it to buy a dress. This was something deep and serious that she must have carried in her heart for years, yet she slapped it on the table like a headline. Somehow it evened things out, which must have been what she intended, as if to say I wasn't some special case for Kevin to get worked up about because she'd had it worse; she was the living twin.

I'm not sure Kevin heard what she said. He followed her cue and pulled the door ajar. "If you need anything ..."

I nodded.

Gina slipped her delicate fingers around his arm. "... just give us a call."

Kevin's lips were still mashed into a flat line. I couldn't tell if he was pleased with the reference or irritated. Either way, the idea of her hooking her claws into him made me cringe.

As the room fell silent behind them, I lay in bed, wondering if he would dump Gina if I said I wanted him. It wasn't a matter of wanting him anymore. I just wanted him to want me. It was pure jealousy—a useless, pitiful emotion.

The thoughts rolled around in my head as my eyelids became heavier and heavier. The progesterone had felt like fire coursing into my cells when it was injected, but the pain subsided and I slept a while.

A nurse came in at shift change to check on me. "Do you think it would be all right if I got up and walked around a bit? My bottom is getting sore from lying here."

She checked my vital signs. "Supper will be rolling in here in a few minutes. Why don't you eat, and then you can stretch your legs. You aren't scheduled to check out until nine."

An hour later, I walked gingerly out of my hospital room and wandered down the hall as carefully as if the floor were made of glass. I had no intention of bringing any more harm to my baby.

Down the hall and around the corner, I came across something I wasn't looking for. Or maybe I was and hadn't consciously known it. The chapel.

I hesitated with my hand on the door handle. *Come in and visit.* I stepped inside. It wasn't large, just a soft blue room with some folding chairs and a picture of Jesus hanging on the far wall. A woman was sitting in the front seat. A wave of familiarity swept over me. It couldn't be her. I stepped farther in. She must have felt my eyes on her because she turned to face me. I gasped. It really was her. The weeping woman from Simon's church.

"Come in," she said. "He welcomes everyone, you know."

I took a seat. "I've seen you at church."

She nodded. I could see up close that her cheeks were tear stained, but she was smiling.

"Are you feeling okay?" she asked.

I nodded.

She enfolded my hands in her two cool, bony ones, wrinkled with age but light and gentle. She didn't say anything but returned her gaze to the portrait of Jesus and closed her eyes. Her breaths were slow and steady, easy. I looked at the picture. Really looked. I could see compassion in that picture, whether it was his or the artist's, I couldn't argue now, but I saw it right then. I could feel the peace emanating from the woman. I wanted it so badly for myself. I closed my eyes and tried to wish it into being, but it wouldn't come. I envisioned the wonders of the world: the perfection of a summer sunset, the peak of a majestic mountain, a winter wonderland of snow-laden branches and a hushed world, the miracle of spring rising from moist earth. My heart slowed. My quaking stopped. My brain quit whirring. I felt calmer, but I couldn't grasp the peace, the same serenity I saw in the woman. I could almost see the circle of light, but I was outside it, stuck in the shadows.

I don't know how long we sat that way, but when my eyes opened, hers opened simultaneously, still locked on his image.

"He feels such tremendous love for you. He only wants you to trust him, to put yourself totally in his care."

"I have. Really, I have."

"No, you're still trying to manipulate him. Let go. Let God put things in order for you."

I closed my eyes again and shut out the world. Again, I envisioned his light and stepped toward it. I could see it, but I was still outside it. The woman was right. I was still holding back. I had let God into my life, but I still had one hand on the steering wheel. *I* wanted to decide if I ought to side with Kevin or Simon rather than to simply trust God to heal my family. I sighed and stood to leave. "I hope whoever you are praying for is okay."

"He's fine. God's will isn't always easy to accept. John and I spent our whole lives together. It was hard to say good-bye. But I see now why he timed it so. I was meant to carry on, to touch someone else." She looked up at me. "He knows you'll always love your daughter."

"Yes, I will, but she's not legally my daughter, yet."

She smiled wistfully. "Not that one. The one God holds."

My hand flew instinctively to my abdomen, and my heart jumped. Did she mean the baby in my womb or the one I miscarried? How could she know? I couldn't begin to fathom it.

"Go now," she said. "Your husband needs you."

Simon and Sabrina were in the room waiting when I returned. My temperature was normal. I was ready for the comfort of my own bed.

Sabrina picked up the teddy bear. "Where'd this come from?"

"Kevin gave it to me." One look at Simon and I could have knocked myself in the head. "And Gina," I added too late. "They came together."

The nurse came in with my release papers and declared that I had pulled through fine. I wasn't sure Simon and I had. His demeanor declared he still had more than a few questions about Kevin. The peace of the chapel faded away.

Twenty-eight

imon treated me like a porcelain doll. He helped me up the stairs to bed, and I lay there all evening and night. We talked only pleasantries. His response to the situation was all in his actions. He brought me food and drinks and checked on me periodically. He tucked Sabrina into bed.

When he came to bed late in the night, he lay still on his side for some time, then rolled over and eased one arm around me, his hand coming to rest on my tummy, as if touching the baby.

The next morning, while the sun was still a rosy cloudburst, Sabrina crept into our room and crawled under the sheets, between us.

"Tell me how my mommy died," she said.

Simon nodded at me. Quietly, with images of trees and owls and soaring eagles, I told her about the Appalachian Mountains and a car that missed a turn.

She didn't ask any more questions. She wiped away her tears, curled into my side, and fell back to sleep.

We woke her at nine and got dressed for church. I was stir-crazy. I had to get out of bed. I actually wanted to go, though I wouldn't admit it aloud.

Sabrina seemed to have recovered. She seemed content. In fact, at church she seemed more sedate than usual. I saw her head bent in prayer for a long time and wondered if she was actually finding consolation talking to God the way Simon did. If it helped her come to terms with Phyllis's death, it was worth whatever Simon had said to her.

I thought about the hospital chapel and tried to find that center, that light I had sensed there, but it wouldn't come. I felt shattered and distracted. Maybe I didn't pray the right way. I don't know. I wished I could listen in to Sabrina's prayer, to hear what she prayed to see if it would work for me, too.

I expected her reflective mood to continue after the service, but she popped up from her seat with her face full of smiles.

"Can I go get doughnuts with the other kids, Pai?"

Normally we said no. We visited in the reception area with the other families, but we didn't allow her to eat doughnuts. I can't say why Simon gave in to her, except for the determined eagerness about her and the melancholy morning we'd shared in bed.

"Just this once," he said. "Don't start asking every Sunday."

"I won't. Thanks, Pai." She ran off to join the girls she'd met over the past weeks, and they headed to the table of doughnuts, little girls in yellow, green, and blue, like a bunch of brightly colored butterflies hovering over a flower patch.

I still didn't feel comfortable among the other church members. I stood beside Simon, offering empty greetings and nodding to the trivial conversations.

"See you Friday, Simon," said Mrs. Dylan, a little old woman in a bright red blazer with matching lipstick, shoes, and pocketbook. I tried my best to imagine her exercising at the club on a Friday evening in a Spandex outfit. The image didn't fit.

Simon waved at her. "Yes, ma'am."

A young boy approached. "Preacher said to give you this list, Mr. Rochwell."

Simon stuck the paper in his pocket without looking at it. "Thank you, Johnny."

I spotted the crying woman, the woman who had knelt and prayed with fervor on my first visit and who had spoken to me in the hospital chapel. I searched her expression to see if rapture still showed on her face this morning, but she looked ordinary. Cheerful, but ordinary. I smiled and waved at her. She nodded and smiled back.

When we reached the house, Sabrina insisted she keep the dress on. "Just for a while. Please? I want M'issa to see it."

"It's time for lunch. You'll mess it up," I said.

"I don't want lunch. My stomach hurts."

"That's not surprising. I shouldn't have given in. No doughnuts next Sunday for sure," Simon said. She continued to plead with him about the dress. "You can't play in it," he decided. "You may sit on the front step and watch for Melissa. As soon as she gets home, you come in and change."

"Thank you, Pai."

He ate his salad and left. Sabrina wandered in and lay on the sofa.

"What's wrong?" I asked.

"My tummy still hurts."

Illness. I hadn't had to deal with this before. My first instinct was to call Kevin. After all, he was a pediatrician. I picked up the phone and dialed all but the last number before I hung up. If I wanted Simon to mend things, I couldn't keep setting Kevin between us. I tapped the phone a moment and then called Babette.

"Does she have a temperature?"

"I don't know."

"Well, check that first. Then, put a hot-water bottle on her stomach and give her a cup of warm tea."

"I don't think we have a water bottle."

"Then soak a kitchen towel with hot water and put it in a plastic bag."

"Okay. I'll try that."

I tried the oral thermometer. Sabrina couldn't hold it in her mouth.

"I need an ear one," she said.

"An ear thermometer? Like at the doctor's office?"

She nodded.

Her forehead didn't feel too hot, so I gave up on that and went for the hot towel and warm tea.

"This tea is yucky."

"There's no sugar in it. Just sip a little bit."

"I don't want any. It's going to make me puke."

She started sobbing then, not her usual spoiled cry, but moaning tears. I laid the hot towel across her abdomen, covered her with a blanket, and rubbed her back. She curled into a knot. I turned soft music on the radio and rubbed her back until the tears subsided and her breaths came steadier. I left her to sleep and stepped out to my garden.

The sun was hot, but gardening would allow me time to think. There was so much I had to sort out, still. And if I were meant to relax, this was the best medicine.

I settled in a shady patch. As I turned the warm earth between my fingers, I thought of how much I knew about flowers and how little I knew about raising children. My thoughts flickered from the present to a picture of the future: Sabrina and the new infant, with me caring for them both. I basked in the visions. I realized the changes I would have to make. I ticked off a list of all the things we needed. A high chair and crib, a playpen, more toys, outlet covers, baby bottles, and—I laughed at the thought of me ever admitting it—plastic dishes. And an ear thermometer. The sun had shifted. Sweat trickled down my neck. It was time to quit and check on Sabrina.

As I stood, my head spun. I'd overdone it. Again. I steadied myself on the fence a moment, then slowly made my way across the grass to the safety of the house. The cool air slapped me in the face. I crossed the room, expecting to find Sabrina asleep on the sofa.

She was gone.

Twenty-nine

For a moment, I forgot Ron was dead. The blood drained out of my face and settled in the soles of my feet. My heart pounded in my head, and I couldn't catch my breath. I didn't know what to do first—phone the police or run out the door to see if I could see my precious little girl being dragged across the yard.

Just as I turned to grab the phone, the door opened. Simon entered. At that very same instant, Sabrina came pounding down the stairs. "Mäe! Oh, Mäe, I got changed. I want to help with the roses. I'm all better, now."

Simon frowned. "All better?"

I felt my face flush as I sank with relief onto the sofa. She was safe. Ron was dead, and she was safe. But the enormity of the life ahead as a mother loomed with wider definition. I would constantly be on guard. I would constantly be on alert for keeping her safe, and my baby safe and healthy. Did mothers ever stop worrying? I flopped flat out and took in long breaths.

Simon bent over me and felt my forehead. "You were outside gardening? In this heat? I thought this baby was the most important thing in the world to you."

I closed my eyes. "I thought some fresh air would help relax me."

"It relaxed you all right. You're lucky you didn't get heat stroke. And how about you, Little Miss? What do you mean you feel better?"

"I was sick, but Mäe fixed me."

"Mäe fixed her," I whispered.

"Doughnuts," he muttered. "How many of those doughnuts did you eat?"

"One of each. Chocolate, iced, sprinkly, and one had little white things on it, but I didn't like it much."

"Four? Sabrina! No more doughnuts. Don't even ask next week. And you," he pointed his long, bony index finger at me, "you're not moving off that sofa all afternoon. Here's the remote. Watch a movie." He brought me a glass of ice water, still complaining. "How's a guy supposed to take care of a crazy pregnant woman and a silly little girl when neither one has the sense God gave them?"

I smiled through my stupor. He wouldn't discuss our future, but he took prime care of us.

"You're an excellent nurse, Simon," I told him. "I think you missed your calling."

"No, I didn't." He sat on the side of the sofa. "I'm just careful not to overlook any symptoms." Then he delved into a story he'd never before told me about his little sister falling ill. "I thought it was just a stomachache. I forced her to go to school. I had a test that day, and I didn't want to miss it. Mom was at work, and there wasn't anyone else to watch her. She didn't tell the teacher she was sick. She pushed herself to sit through class until recess. When the other kids ran out to play, she couldn't stand because the pain in her side was so severe. It turned out she had appendicitis. I'd sent her to school with appendicitis! Her appendix could have ruptured. She could have died because

I let a dumb science test distract me from paying attention to what was ailing her."

I rubbed his back and thought of the strain it must have been taking on the responsibility of siblings and feeling his every decision weighed like that of an adult. "It wasn't your fault. You were a kid, not their father."

"They counted on me. That's what I've tried to convey to you. Children are an awesome responsibility."

He didn't say it with derision as he had before. He had a gleam of pride this time, like he knew he was up to the challenge.

His intent care continued over the next week, me doing my obligatory resting, Sabrina clamoring for activity and attention. If God's intention was to steep Simon in the full responsibility facing him, he accomplished it. Simon became an outstanding father and husband, going far beyond necessity.

One evening, I sat up in bed startled by a pounding noise. My heart leapt to my throat with fear of some horrible accident, but then I heard another sound, a guttural sound, human, but strange, followed by squeals of glee. I crept to the bedroom doorway and peered over the banister. Simon had Sabrina on his back and was prancing around on all fours like a horse, trying to neigh. Sabrina was hanging on for dear life and laughing so hard she finally lost her grip and they both tumbled to the floor in a fit of giggles.

A carefree little boy. I knew he was in there somewhere.

I crept back to bed wrapped in happiness.

I don't know if it was because the role of father had begun to appeal to him or if he just had to know where we stood, but either way, he came to my second ultrasound.

The amniotic sac was intact. The heart was beating. He stared at the screen and held my hand and didn't let go. Simon was trying his hardest. He wouldn't verbally admit to accepting the baby, but he wasn't a man of many words. His actions said it all. He was determined to make it work, make *us* work, to create a future together as a family, and I was following his lead.

I decided I had to officially end it with Kevin. I wanted to formally tell him Simon and I had worked things out, that we were going to make it, and that I couldn't be caught going to lunch with him or walking in the park holding hands.

I told myself it was for his benefit, but it was for mine. I needed closure.

His truck was in front of Grandpa Norris's house. Sabrina ran off like a shot to the nearest fence to gaze at the horses in the field. I stood at the door, buzzing the bell and knocking. He didn't answer.

"Come on, Sabrina. He's not here."

"Look, Mäe. A stable. Can we look? Please."

The stable stood a hundred yards away, a huge brick affair with black-barred doors and windows and private paddocks leading off each stall, which emptied further into the rolling pasture. Inside, I knew, the walls were built of wide, thick boards. The stall doors slid on wheeled runners. The tack room was like a small house, with running water, a tiny kitchen, and a bunkroom off one end. The cows were housed separately, in a barn across the way.

The smell of hay beckoned to me. I had never been one for riding horses, but many a good time was had in the hayloft, where bales of hay were stacked like huge bricks, walling in the most intimate rooms with a bit of arranging. Loose hay leavings formed a bed for lovers seeking solitude. I shivered, remembering, and for the first time, feeling ashamed, wishing it had never happened, wishing Simon had been my one and only. How much simpler life would seem.

"I want to see the horses, Mäe!"

I remembered one special horse—King, a huge black stallion, with not a bit of white save one stocking, sire to many a fine foal. Curiosity tugged me along. I had to see if he still reigned over the herd.

I waved Sabrina ahead. "Okay. But don't reach your fingers into the stalls. Horses bite, you know."

She skipped through the grass, across the gravel, into the lair of my teenage years. My past called to me. I was the old *me*: an entire life looming ahead with Kevin at my side, except this time I knew the outcome. I took a step and then another and forced myself to enter.

My eyes didn't adjust immediately. The aroma of sweet hay overwhelmed me, perfume over manure. Sabrina was midbarn, talking to a man. As I walked forward, I thought the shape leaning on the rake was hired help, but then I heard the voice.

"Sure you can ride one, but you timed it wrong today. They're feeding right now."

I slowed my steps.

"What brings you here?" he asked.

I wasn't sure how to say it, especially in front of Sabrina. It had been easier in my head. "I wanted to tell you everything's all right."

"Everything?" He cast me his most charming smile, a look that radiated from him and triggered a memory. He had used his wide-eyed blank puppy face on my mom all those years, and she still bought it. I'd been on the other side with him. He'd forgotten. Or he was too much in the habit of duping folks to remember not to use it with me. I answered anyway. "Yes, everything has worked out, the baby and all."

A horse whinnied, and my resolve shifted. I didn't know what else to say to him. "Where's King?" I asked.

"You're kidding. You remember King?"

"Of course I do. Where is he?"

"Come see." He propped the rake against the wall and led me to the very end, to the largest corner stall with a huge private grazing area, high fenced and well kept. The penthouse of the stable. There stood the stallion in all his splendor, the sheen of his coat glinting in the sun. He reared and neighed. The mares in the barn whinnied back.

"I can't believe it! He's still beautiful."

Kevin shook his head. "I can see how much horse management stuck in your head. King was seven when we graduated. That was twenty years ago. He'd be quite a guy if he could still kick up his heels like this."

He had played me for a fool. "Humph. I figured he'd learned a few tricks from your grandpa."

"King and Grandpa both held their own, that's for sure." He pulled a carrot from a bucket and held it out to the horse. "I'd say their grandsons didn't fall too far from the apple tree, either."

My hands itched to reach out and touch the bit of chest hair where his collar opened. Instead, I walked past him into the sunshine. "It's as beautiful as I remember it." I turned to face him and laughed. "Still stinks, too."

"Come on, City Girl. I'll buy you a drink."

"Sabrina," I hollered.

"Leave her. I'll send my kids out."

"They're here?" I had forgotten they were coming.

"All this room to run, and they're plugged into Nintendo, fighting aliens."

I yelled out to Sabrina again, and she walked out of a stall with an armful of tomcat. Of course, she hadn't held Taz in three days, but this was someone else's cat, a new toy.

"You'll find kittens up in the loft," Kevin offered.

Just what I didn't need. Another kitten.

I told her we would be in the house and followed Kevin up the path. We were doing that reacquaintance routine, acting all jolly and laughing over the smallest thing, so he could grab at me, chase me, touch me. Our hands brushed one another, but I stepped away. I had to find the words to tell him it was over.

We entered through the back, past the pool of my previous misadventure, into the family room. Sure enough, his kids were sprawled on the floor with eyes and ears focused on the bleeping game playing on the television. The boy, a skinny fellow with thin hair and glasses—quite the opposite of the hefty halfback son I'd imagined—worked the control like a courtroom stenographer recording events. All I could see of the girl was a head full of blonde curls and pudgy, dimpled legs.

"Hey, Ruby, Matt, I want you to meet a friend of mine, Miss Carla."

Eyes flickered at me and spun back to the screen, the delayed "Hi" coming like some out-of-sync soundtrack.

"She brought someone for you to play with, a little girl named Sabrina. She's waiting for you in the barn."

He remembered Sabrina's name this time.

That brought the girl back around. "Is she five?"

I nodded. "Exactly five."

She jumped to her feet, punched the power button on the machine, and shot across to the door. "Come on, Matt!"

"I oughtta whack you for that! You didn't let me save." He scrambled to his feet and ran after her, his knobby knees almost clanking together in his effort to catch up.

"They've been a bit lonely. The novelty of horses and cows wore off after the first forty-eight hours."

I could understand that. There's only so much you can do with a horse. I had never understood the junior high school horse craze of my peers.

"A drink?" he asked.

Now we were doing the formality steps. Why was everything in life so predictable? "Water would be great."

I toured the family room while ice clinked into glasses. Potato-chip bags lay on the table and floor. A red sock without a mate poked out from under the sofa. A Monopoly board and money were shoved to one side, with the top half of the box knocked into the far corner. Remnants of pizza had shriveled on abandoned plates around the room. Shirts and pajamas lay draped on furniture. The carpet was a minefield of Lego blocks.

I'd never considered myself a clean freak. I did my part at home because it was the easiest way—no, the only way—to live with Simon, but I guess I had become used to an orderly home. The mess of the place disgusted me. I tucked the Monopoly game into its box and retrieved the lid. I gathered the nasty plates and carried them to the kitchen.

Kevin was tapping his foot and staring at the microwave.

"I prefer my ice water cold," I said.

He whirled around. "I had some doughnuts left."

"Remember, no doughnuts."

"Oh yeah."

The trashcan was one of those tall ones with the flipping tops, except this one was overstuffed. Some greasy tinfoil hung out the top, gumming up the works. I had to set the plates on the counter and take the top completely off it to mash it all down before I scraped the old pizza in.

Kevin didn't seem to notice. He had gone back to watching the seconds count down on the doughnuts. "I find a few seconds of nuking makes them just like new again."

The sink was full, too. I wasn't tackling that job. I pushed a pot and mixing bowl to the side and stacked the plates on the counter, then rinsed my hands. There wasn't any soap, or I would have washed properly.

No towel, either. I shook my hands, then wiped them on my jeans. Two dark handprints of dampness hung on my thighs. He pulled a plate from the microwave. The thought of reheated day-old doughnuts was as appealing as Mom's meatloaf.

"Leave the doughnuts. I want to look around the old place."

He handed me a jar of water. "Hope this is okay. We seem to be out of regular glasses. You know how it is with kids."

A jar. I lifted it toward my mouth and stopped. It smelled faintly of pickles. I thought of all the crystal in the front dining room. In the past, I had seen the huge dining table set for meals—candle tapers, gleaming silver, gold-rimmed wine goblets, antique plates. I had dined with Kevin's family the night of our graduation while wearing my best dress and a corsage from Kevin. I doubted Kevin even entered that room nowadays. The room was untouchable, like Mom's four china plates kept interminably on display but never used. They might get broken. And—gasp—they had to be hand washed.

"I wasn't very thirsty anyway." I left it on top of the microwave and took his arm. "Give me the tour."

He stroked my hair as if I were a cat. "You've seen it all before. Nothing's changed here in fifty years."

"But I've forgotten it all."

I tried to look beyond it, but every room was the same. Mess everywhere. Even the dining room had overflow from the study, papers and books stacked on the ivory linen tablecloth. I had become more like Simon than I thought. There was something to be said for cleanliness.

Upstairs, I headed to Kevin's room. Even though he'd lived within driving distance, his grandparents had set up a room for him so he could spend weeks at a time here during the summers. Football posters on the wall and model airplanes suspended from the ceiling. I remembered every detail.

All the memorabilia was gone, now. The walls were blue and blank. The same twin bed, covers jumbled at the foot. Hotwheels cars and Star Wars figures were strewn around, paused midgame it appeared. He walked in behind me. "Matt sleeps in here."

"Oh, of course."

Time kept marching on. Why did I repeatedly turn to the past, old haunts, old friends, and expect them to be the same? Nothing ever stays the same. I am different right now than I was a moment ago. Yet I grasped the old and remained shocked at its change.

And I did it again.

He took my hand and led me down the hall to Grandpa Norris's room. An imposing four-poster bed dwarfed the room. He stepped around the bed to sliding doors and a patio. "Everything seems quiet," he said, staring toward the stable.

Even in my limited experience, I knew quiet wasn't necessarily a good thing with kids.

Then he walked across the room and looked out the front windows toward the road as if he expected to see them marching around like little soldiers. I was surprised he didn't know that kids remained invisible unless you were on the phone and accidents couldn't be prevented whether you were in the same room with them or not.

"I'm sure they're fine," I said.

He returned to my side. His hands went to my hair and down my shoulders. "You wanted to come here, didn't you?"

I was such a stupid little girl; I felt fourteen. Why couldn't I find that even line—the border one explores as friends and steps back from? Maybe Kevin and I had erased our borders too well, too long ago, to ever gain them back. We were all or nothing.

We both had children playing outside. A baby was stirring within me. I was working things out with Simon. I didn't want anything from Kevin, but here I was, still hung up on him. None of it made sense.

The bed loomed beyond him. Something caught my eye. White silk dangled off one corner.

His fingers gently brought my mouth around. His lips met mine, talking between nibbling kisses. His eyes took on a desperate look, eager for affirmation, like days gone by. "I knew you'd come back to me. You just had to get it worked out. That's why I backed off, left you alone. I had to let you come to me when you were ready. I'm so glad you're ready now."

I tried to open my mind, to focus on that quiet center, Simon's peace, the elusive tranquility I'd looked for in the chapel, the serenity of the old woman. That's what I'd come here to settle, to set this one bit in line so I could step into that circle and move forward.

"I've always wanted you, Carla."

I opened my mouth to tell him it was over, but he put his lips over mine and kissed my voice away. I went off center, again. His words, his touch, fed the spark I'd nurtured through the months. I had tried to extinguish it, but it smoldered within us both. The need burned and grew. The sweet ache, the insatiable hunger.

I ran my hands up his back. His mouth closed on mine, ending conversation. I fell onto the bed. He toppled down on me, the whole weight of him. For a moment, I was buoyed by the sheer energy we produced. So easily, we slid back into the place we'd been, the *us* of then. I wanted so desperately to be transported to that carefree state, to transfer that undefeatable bliss to the *us* of now.

Children's voices emerged from the stable to the open air of the field and moved up the path to the house.

I wasn't solving my problem.

I pushed at him.

He ignored me, his lips working more fervently against mine.

I turned my head and pushed him again. "The kids are coming."

"They won't come in here. They know better." His lips moved to my neck.

I pictured Sabrina standing outside the door wondering why Mäe wouldn't let her inside. I imagined her telling Simon, after all we had been through, all we'd recovered between us. Why was I here playing with fire? Time *had* gone on. I could never recapture what I'd had with Kevin. All that had passed. "Stop, Kevin. I can't."

"Just once, Carla. He'll never know. Just once. I can't get you out of my head. I know you feel the same."

Their voices were in the house now.

"Not now. Not like this." I had to think. I had to breathe and clear my head.

"You're killing me. You were easier in high school." He chuckled and searched for my zipper.

Easier in high school? Were we still operating on how many bases he could advance in one go?

I pushed his hands away and sat up. "I wasn't ever easy." I stood up and straightened my clothes.

A car turned in the driveway.

His son's squeaky voice broke through the walls. "Dad! Gina's back with the food! Dad!"

Gina's back with the food?

Kevin smoothed his hair, tucked in his shirt, and loped out of the room.

Slowly, I stepped around the bed and examined the white silk. A woman's negligee. Gina's no doubt.

Even when something is so obvious in hindsight, it still has the ability to waylay me. Insanely shallow didn't begin to describe me. Idiot, maybe. I actually thought I was special enough to be the center of two men's lives when I had a hard enough time staying focused on one.

Evidence lay all around the room. A lipstick on the dresser. A romance novel on the floor by the bed. Panties and a sweater tossed in the corner of the closet. I peeked in the master bath. Hairspray, two toothbrushes, perfume, a curling iron, a plastic hair cap.

I walked down the hall and into the family room with my professional smile ready. "Gina! What a dear you are running out to buy dinner for Kevin and his kids."

I know when I'm being evaluated. She wasn't so firmly entrenched in that bed that she'd written me off completely.

"It was my turn. He went last time."

Touché. She couldn't have stated it more clearly: She had become a fixture in his life. They had developed a routine and a history already.

I felt faint. These were my best friends, both confidants. Both had hoodwinked me. They were sleeping together, living together. Had they assumed I knew?

Sabrina set a jar of some kind of red drink down on the coffee table. I watched her, my mirror, my latest measurement of success. I had new commitments—Simon and Sabrina and my baby. And I had almost betrayed them all.

Gina unfolded a wrapper. "Cheeseburger, ketchup, no mustard or pickle. That's you, Matt Sprat."

Nicknames even? Knew their orders? Perfect Gina cast into the disarray of Kevin's life. The idea whirled around, too hard to realistically connect.

"Nuggets for Little Chickie," chimed in Kevin.

"With orange soda," added Gina, handing a drink to Ruby.

"Time to go, Sabrina," I said.

She settled her little fingers in my outreached hand, and we walked down the long hall toward the front door.

Kevin caught up to us in time to open the door. He was licking mayonnaise off his fingers. I thought I could see that boy of old times shining out through his eyes, a little bit in his smile. Maybe he was still there. Maybe he was 100 percent original. Maybe I was the one who had moved on.

"Just once," he whispered earnestly. "Meet me."

I'm sure my smile must have looked watered down. I hadn't the presence of mind to deal with his proposition. I only wanted to escape to myself again.

"School starts back in a week," he said. "The kids will be gone."

"Sabrina won't be," I replied. *Will Gina?*

"Carla—"

"It's over, Kevin. That's what I came over to tell you. We've already had our once." I progressed down the steps with Sabrina.

I was glad I had driven the Expedition. As I buckled Sabrina into her booster seat, its bulky frame shielded me, a dome of parenthood. Foreign and clunky as it felt after years of driving my daddy's Porsche, I was getting used to it, taking it on like a new skin, a new *me*.

"Mäe, I sure am hungry."

"Me too. Let's have a Friday-night date. Where would you like to go?"

"It's Friday?"

"Yes."

She sat up straight, ready to go. "The soup place."

It took some thinking to figure out where she meant. "Soup place?"

"Where Pai works."

"Simon is a lawyer."

"Not that work. The other one. The place he feeds people."

I was totally stumped.

"Lots of people at church work there, too."

"The soup kitchen?"

"That's what I said!"

"Simon doesn't work there."

"Yes, he does. We had to pick up a bunch of bread and drop it off there that day he babysat me. He told me he works there on Fridays, taking care of God's people."

Images of all the months past shifted. That made sense. That sounded much more like Simon than late games of racquetball. It wasn't hard to guess why he had never told me. I would have mocked him for it. I had been as bad as my mother about putting people in boxes. I'd put my own husband in a box marked *Uncaring* and considered another marked *Promiscuous* that wasn't even close to representative of him.

"Why didn't you tell me before?"

She shrugged. "Didn't think about it. It wasn't never Friday."

I laughed at this music smarty who didn't know the weekdays. "You really want to go eat there?"

"Yes."

I tried to imagine eating supper among the homeless. "Really?"

"Yes."

I weighed the situation a moment, wondering if she had the story straight. I didn't want to walk into a soup kitchen full of strangers.

I closed the passenger door and climbed behind the wheel. I swear I felt the baby move right then, a little fluttery movement, like bubbles in my abdomen. Anyone else would claim it was gas. "This is a first." And I meant it on both counts as I pulled away from Kevin and headed downtown to the shelter.

I felt all the eyes of the world on me as I clasped Sabrina's hand and climbed the cement steps into the large room echoing with voices and the clank of dishes. I held Sabrina at my side while I got my bearings. I couldn't see Simon at first. Men, women, and children walked to and fro carrying trays. Half the tables were filled. Nearby, five women sat chatting and nibbling. The ringleader could have been my mother—curly hair, flamboyant gestures, loud voice. It seemed more like a party than a soup kitchen. At the next table, two boys talked while an old man stared silently into his plate. Three greasy-haired guys who smelled heavily of tar wolfed down their food without pause.

I scanned the line of workers behind the counter. I recognized a lot of faces from church, including Mrs. Dylan, the plump lady who had said she would see Simon on Friday. She hadn't actually said she would see him at the club. I'd assumed that's what she meant. She must have meant here. I kept looking, concentrating on the busy figures until I spotted him at last. He was at the end, dishing peas onto plates. My heart lurched. Sabrina was right. He was here. All the Friday nights I had suspected him of drinking with buddies or sleeping around with some woman, he had been doing charity work.

Sabrina and I maneuvered around the tables and into the kitchen area. "Need some help?" I asked him.

His mouth fell open. "What are you doing here?"

"I could ask the same thing."

He grinned. "Putting my actions where my Bible is," he said, feeding me my own words.

"You've forgotten *Thou shall not lie* again. I thought you spent Fridays at the club."

He shrugged sheepishly. "For a bit, after I'm done here. Same on Tuesdays. Got to keep fit."

Sabrina spoke up. "I want to eat with Jethro again."

Simon laughed. "Sure thing." He waved to a heavy woman stirring a pot and checking something in the ovens behind us. "Rachel, can you scoop a kid's plate for me, please?"

"Jethro?" I asked.

"He's a regular. Funniest guy. Works picking up trash all

day long at the park. Not paid, of course, but that's what he does."

An image came to me, the skinny old man walking in circles at the park with a plastic bag in his hand. He had waved at Sabrina, not me. Imagine my husband being friends with him! I felt off kilter.

The heavy woman worked like the wind, bustling like my mom, scooping things from here and there, and presenting a plate in seconds. "Well, land sakes," she said, "who're these fine young ladies?"

Simon tousled Sabrina's hair. "Carla and Sabrina."

"I figured you fer a bachelor much as you're in this place, Simon. You ain't gonna tell me they's your kin, are ya?"

He nodded. "My wife and my daughter. And we have a baby on the way."

That's when I felt it. It's not with me always, and rarely ever as strong as it was at that moment, but as he laid claim to all three of us, a halo must have been hanging around my head. I felt this wholeness, this swelling fullness in my heart that extended through my entire body and soothed my mind of everything but pure love. Not just happiness, but a completeness. I had finally admitted there was something bigger in control of my life. I had conceded that God was greater than I. I had let go, put everything in his hands, and it had been handed back to me. In the midst of all those strangers and the steam rising off of flat trays of vegetables and barbecued chicken, in the harsh florescent light, in the most improbable place in the world, I felt God caress my soul. For the first time, I glimpsed the peace that Simon knew, the peace of heaven. With the baby stirring within me, Simon, Sabrina, and I stood together in a circle of light.

Thirty

By November, the baby was showing. I had reached that terrible pudgy state before the baby is actually a nice round ball out front. I looked more fat than pregnant. Thirty-eight years of being thin as a stick, and I had to look dumpy at my class reunion. I was tempted to wear one of those T-shirts that says BABY and points at the belly. Simon disagreed. He said I finally had a round bottom and my breasts were bigger and I ought to be glad. Who would have guessed pregnancy would turn him on?

The hall was decorated to a tee. Thank heavens Gina had stepped up for the job and not Betsy. The lights were dim, the music live but not overwhelming. A mirror ball cast flashes of light around the room.

It sparkled off my new necklace, too. Simon had given it to me that evening. I'd just pulled on my pantyhose. What an ugly pose to be caught in, especially in maternity hose with their wide span of dark brown stretched across an expanding belly. My bra was just as bad—a conventional white one, not a black lacy thing that I wouldn't mind being approached in. Simon couldn't wait for me to descend the steps, feeling beautiful. He stood there fully dressed, looking his part in his black suit, and rummaged in his pocket. He pulled out a blue velvet box.

"I got this for you," he said, handing it to me and standing there, like a gawky schoolboy, watching me.

Definitely not a grapefruit this time. I rubbed the velvety finish before I opened the box. A penny-sized aquamarine hung on a gold chain.

"It made me think of your eyes, that clear kind of blue."

I sniffed. My eyes aren't at all pretty. They are too narrow, and they aren't the dark riveting blue of innocence. They are an empty blue, as pale and transparent as my hair and skin. "I hate my eyes."

He kissed my cheek. "Nonsense. They're like a piece of the sky."

Then he left me alone to finish dressing, to think of what he saw in my watered-down blue eyes and how I'd found God in my own wonderful piece of the sky. To think of how differently I saw things nowadays, of how I had begun to see the good in him and in the whole world again.

My mother had come around, too. Maybe all she'd ever been worried about was my happiness and could see that I was finally and truly happy, or maybe she'd reflected on her own actions, but whichever the case, she'd pulled me aside during our Sunday dinner a couple of weeks after the episode at Kevin's house. "I just heard that Gina has moved in with Kevin."

"I've known for a while, Mom."

"You didn't tell me."

"That would be gossiping, wouldn't it?"

She fell silent a moment. "Baby told me Simon took Sabrina and Brooke to the Asheboro zoo last week. She says he's like a changed man, really taking to the role of father to Sabrina."

I let her words hang there, thinking she wasn't done.

"And he actually seems happy about the baby."

"He is, now."

She hesitated, then continued in a rush as if the words were bottled up and had to explode out in a single breath. "Look, Carla. I've been thinking about it a lot. I shouldn't have been pushing you at Kevin. It wasn't very Christian of me. You made the right decision sticking with Simon. I know that now."

"I took a vow, Mom. For better or worse. Didn't you and Daddy set a good example, always working out your differences? Did you think I wasn't capable of doing the same? Simon and I just had to get through a portion of bad stuff to find the better part again."

She nodded. "You're a strong woman, Carla. You're everything your daddy wanted you to be. He'd be proud." Tears welled in her eyes and mine. I reached out and took her into my arms. It felt good to hug her.

"You and I, we're only tough on the outside. We're both soft on the inside. That's what Simon says."

"He does?"

"Yes. Like M&M's candies, he says."

"Smart man," she said with a smile and leaned into my shoulder.

Walking into the reunion, I touched the blue aquamarine gem and tensed on Simon's arm. I knew I would see Kevin. He would be dressed in a black tux, everything sucked into place and looking too tempting to avoid. My classmates would shake their heads in wonder that I had ever let him go.

He would ask me to dance.

I wasn't sure what I would answer. Despite all the changes, despite having a faithful husband and an officially adopted daughter, I was still human. I might dance with him. But I knew I could dance and keep it just a dance. My eyes weren't wandering anymore because my heart was home.

I hugged people as I made my way to the punch bowl and turned to find a girl I could barely remember watching me. I wondered what I represented to her—valedictorian, scholarship winner, former girlfriend of the most popular boy in school? Or just a face in the crowd? A person worth no more or less than anyone else.

This girl, Sheila Hill, a person once a part of my childhood, stood an arm's length from me and cocked her head like an eager pup. She had the blandest, flattest face I'd ever seen on a woman. She was the last classmate Mom had found on her search for far-flung students—the one Mom had called me about, flabbergasted to hear she had become a model. Gina reached my side and whispered, "She models her hands. Jewelry, soap commercials, and nail polish." We both laughed. It was good to laugh with Gina again.

I expected Sheila to use exaggerated gestures as she talked, but she kept her hands folded in front of her. "So tell me, Carla. What did you end up doing with your life?"

The words hung there, waiting for the same wise validation I searched for upon first seeing Kevin way back in June. What, of all these years, did I choose to display as my success, the consummation of my life? Did I end up a businesswoman? A wife? A mother? I wasn't about to be labeled and stuck in one of my mother's boxes. I'd grown up in her boxes and realized I'd been sticking people into those same confines, defining them before I even knew them—and sometimes even after I knew them. I'd stuck my own husband in a box of sorts to the point that he had to lie about his Friday nights and his infertility. I'd learned I had to be more open to the world and to myself. There were so many new adventures still left in life that I couldn't define myself, let alone the strangers around me.

No more boxes. No one can be catalogued so easily. A businesswoman? A wife? A mother? None of those summed up all I'd done and all I had yet to do. I thought of my single patch of perfect peace in an otherwise bumpy life and considered whether I would ever be able to call it back as some seemed to. I thought of Sabrina, of Simon, of Kevin, of my unborn child, and the one I'd lost. I thought of my job and of the possibility of leaving it, of life with my daddy and now without him, of dealing with my mother on the new grounds of her being grandmother to my children, of what I must have meant to Phyllis and never fully appreciated, of my blossoming relationship with my sister, and of where my footsteps would carry me tomorrow. Oh, there was so much still to strive toward. Which path, when given the opportunity, would I choose to take?

What had I ended up doing with my life?

The truth dawned on me as I looked at Sheila. "I don't think I've *ended up* anywhere, yet. Every day is a new beginning."

Readers' Guide

*For Personal Reflection or
Group Discussion*

Readers' Guide

Most contemporary movies and stories portray a marriage in trouble, making the spouse look mean-spirited and introducing a new love on the horizon as the answer to the main character's problems. *A Piece of the Sky* attempts to set the reader on that same trail but with a different outcome: a character who resists breaking her vows. Despite her attraction to Kevin, Carla knows she ought to honor her marriage to Simon, and in the end she does. What is initially lacking in her commitment is faith in God, a turning point she can't be cajoled into but comes to in her own way through God's intervention in her life.

Infertility is the catalyst to the breakdown of the Rochwells' marriage; faith in God is the solution, and through him, honesty, trust, and fidelity are revealed as the building blocks of a lasting marriage. In the end, Carla is blessed with a family, but how would her story have differed if she'd ended up childless? Is financial security worth such cost?

As Carla's story evolves, so does her relationship with her mother, sister, and friends, revealing how life views and circumstances affect those interactions. Perhaps it made you reflect on your own life, your own relationships, and how others perceive your attitude, words, and actions.

The questions below may provide fodder to guide your reflections.

1. As the story opens, Carla depicts Simon as being controlling, stubborn, and self-serving. Ironically, the same can be said of her. She is a woman with a plan who is intent on doing what it takes to reach her goals. In what ways does she manipulate Simon, her mother, her sister, and her friend Gina for her own means?

2. Carla says that driving causes a complete change in Simon's personality from being bound in limitations to being adventurous. She, too, gets a thrill from driving her Porsche, but if Simon accompanies her, she feels she's being judged and loses the ecstasy of the ride. How does this symbolize her overall relationship with Simon? Do you ever feel like a different person when you are with your spouse than when you are venturing out alone? Does your confidence increase or decrease?

3. Much of Simon's personality is skewed by Carla's bitter viewpoint. Were there scenes in which you saw through Carla's bitterness and took away a different personal view of Simon?

4. Carla isn't a typical sympathetic character at the opening of the book, but she softens as the story proceeds. How is this reflected more personally through first-person narration? What would have been lost in the story if it had been told through third-person narration?

5. With her edgy attitude, Carla expresses thoughts that are often too crass or injurious to say aloud. How did you react to her blatant comments and observations? Have

you ever been guilty of thinking one thing while saying another? What drives the difference between thoughts and words? Are your verbalizations affected by your mood or who is within earshot? Is the same true of Carla?

6. In what ways does Carla's attitude change as the story progresses? Is this change revealed in her narration?

7. a. During their phone conversation, Carla and Phyllis refer to the childhood game of Rock, Paper, Scissors: *scissors cut paper, rock smashes scissors, paper covers rock.* Carla explains that she is the rock and Phyllis is scissors. How had those roles played out in their lives up to that point?

b. Phyllis suggests that Simon and Sabrina must be paper. In what ways do Simon and Sabrina dominate Carla? How does Phyllis "cut" Sabrina and Simon? Do the slogans have the same connotations by the end of the story?

8. Carla takes on a dreamier, creative persona in Phyllis's presence. Is there anyone in your life who has a similar affect on you? Why/how can another person's presence affect our self-image and personality?

9. Carla comments on the "boxes" in which her mother categorizes people: Phyllis as being flighty and undependable, Sabrina as being a burden, the host at the restaurant as being Asian and nothing else, Carla's old classmate Sheila as being mousy. Despite resenting her mother's comments, Carla is also guilty of classifying people. Who does

she initially define in one way and later discover is something else altogether?

10. Carla feels her mother treats her more brusquely than her sister, Babette. Do you agree, or is it Carla's distorted perception?

11. The pastor at Simon's church gives a sermon against *the grass is always greener* mentality of not being content at home. As a result, Carla blames the pastor for making Simon resistant to change in their lives. Why would it have been more apt for Carla to apply the sermon to herself?

12. As Carla, Simon, and Sabrina leave Chimney Rock in a rush to reach the hospital, Carla has her own revelation of what Simon meant by *[God] doesn't promise to give us what we want as much as what we need. Sometimes those aren't the same things.* What has she received that she didn't foresee wanting or needing, and how does she feel about it?

13. Carla and Simon have both been dishonest with each other—Carla by using a sperm donor and Simon by hiding his low sperm count. Do their motives justify their untruths? How does their lack of honesty affect the trust and fidelity between them?

14. Seated in the dining room early one morning, Carla watches her neighbors embracing in the shower. How does Carla's interpretation of their romance compare to her own marriage at that point? How does her willingness to spy on them embody her own desperation?

15. Although the story explores honesty, trust, and fidelity, the underlying theme is that no one is in ultimate control of her own destiny. Carla's attempts to control her life are all brought up short by unforeseen incidents: Sabrina's arrival, Simon's intransigence, and Phyllis's death. Carla realizes all her careful planning could not foresee the twists in fate. Do you feel that the impact of events and other people on our lives is merely random progression through life or is it God's influence?

16. Simon and Carla discuss the story from the book of Genesis in which God made Abraham and Sarah bide their time until old age before blessing them with Isaac. How does the Bible story compare to Simon and Carla's struggle?

17. Simon and Kevin are almost opposites in terms of physique and personality. Simon is lean, orderly, and dedicated to his faith. Kevin is heavyset, daring, and spontaneous. How is it possible for Carla to be attracted to both of them? Do you think her faithfulness to Simon goes deeper than mere obligation? Did you want her to stay married to Simon? Did your opinion change by the end of the story? Why or why not?

18. Initially, Carla's desire to have a child comes as a natural progression in life: career, marriage, and then child. Do you feel the desire for motherhood is something that naturally wells up in a woman, or do environment, society, friends, and family play a strong role? Have you felt these effects in your life?

19. Simon's father passed away when he was a young boy, leaving Simon responsible as the man of the house. In what ways did Simon's childhood role as a father figure impact his desire for children? How was Carla's experience as an eldest child different from Simon's?

20. How does Sabrina go from being a wedge between Simon and Carla to being the tie that binds their marriage? Would the outcome have been different if Phyllis hadn't committed suicide? How important was Sabrina's presence to Simon's eventual acceptance of Carla's pregnancy?

21. At the outset, Carla resents Simon's evangelizing. In contrast, she is surprised to learn that her mother prays every night. Based on Carla's viewpoint and your own life observations, do you think it's important for Christians to express faith both in actions and words? If so, to what extent?

22. Carla was obviously closer to her father than to her mother. She shares memories of working with her father on his many car projects and playing sports with him. She tells us he treated her as a person, not a girl, capable of achieving whatever she desired. How did this affect her career ambitions and, in turn, the outcome of her marriage?

23. Carla laments that Babette has a nickname because she does not. Her mother says that nicknames are something earned through relationships. How does this mind-set pertain to Simon's endearment "Love"? Why does the title "Mäe" doubly satisfy Carla?

24. After an officer arrives to announce Phyllis's death, Carla finally acknowledges she isn't in control of life and seeks God's help. Her prayer is answered when Simon accepts Sabrina into their family. Carla walks outside, where she looks to the blue sky and the heavens beyond to offer thanks. At the end of the novel, Simon remarks that Carla's blue eyes are his own *piece of the sky*. How do these two scenes reflect upon each other to justify the title of this book? With Carla's high expectations in life and her obsession to conceive, what other connotations could be tied to the expression *a piece of the sky*?

25. At the story's conclusion, Carla is asked what she ended up doing with her life. Why is she reluctant to answer? How would you answer that question in terms of your own life journey?

With today's medical advancements, in-vitro fertilization, cloning, and stem-cell research have all built upon one another. The questions below broach these subjects. *Caution*: Although careful consideration of these issues is vital for the future development of medicine and humankind at large, these questions may cause heated debates and should be approached with prudence.

26. In today's society, women trying to conceive are bombarded with many moral issues regarding conception and pregnancy. By Christian standards, as the writer of Hebrews states in 13:4, married couples should not abuse the sanctity of their marriage or defile the marriage bed. The sacredness of intercourse is also upheld in the Ten

Commandments by the declaration against adultery. In the story, Simon defines intercourse as the conjugal union that binds husband, wife, and God—meaning artificial insemination (sperm introduced to the uterus through a medical procedure) denigrates vows because it interferes with the physical union that unites husband and wife as one flesh. Do you agree that artificial insemination violates the marriage covenant? Why or why not? How about in-vitro fertilization, which bypasses the unitive act by fertilizing oocytes (eggs) in a laboratory and then implanting the zygote into the uterus?

27. Simon and Carla also discuss their infertility in terms of God's will. When humans assume control over fertility, are they violating God's will by thwarting his providence over the creation of life?

28. Do you believe that a soul comes into existence at the moment of conception? If so, does this hold true for in-vitro embryos created in a laboratory? What should be done with unused embryos?

29. Acceptance of artificial insemination and in-vitro fertilization has led to cloning, which is the creation of a being from DNA cells—cells culled from a host body. Do you think cloning is acceptable? Why or why not? How does it compare to in-vitro fertilization and artificial insemination? Since clones are not created through fertilization, do they have souls?

The Word at Work Around the World

A vital part of Cook Communications Ministries is our international outreach, Cook Communications Ministries International (CCMI). Your purchase of this book, and of other books and Christian-growth products from Cook, enables CCMI to provide Bibles and Christian literature to people in more than 150 languages in 65 countries.

Cook Communications Ministries is a not-for-profit, self-supporting organization. Revenues from sales of our books, Bible curricula, and other church and home products not only fund our U.S. ministry, but also fund our CCMI ministry around the world. One hundred percent of donations to CCMI go to our international literature programs.

CCMI reaches out internationally in three ways:

• Our premier International Christian Publishing Institute (ICPI) trains leaders from nationally led publishing houses around the world.

• We provide literature for pastors, evangelists, and Christian workers in their national language.

• We reach people at risk—refugees, AIDS victims, street children, and famine victims—with God's Word.

Word Power, God's Power

Faith Kidz, RiverOak, Honor, Life Journey, Victor, NexGen — every time you purchase a book produced by Cook Communications Ministries, you not only meet a vital personal need in your life or in the life of someone you love, but you're also a part of ministering to José in Colombia, Humberto in Chile, Gousa in India, or Lidiane in Brazil. You help make it possible for a pastor in China, a child in Peru, or a mother in West Africa to enjoy a life-changing book. And because you helped, children and adults around the world are learning God's Word and walking in his ways.

Thank you for your partnership in helping to disciple the world. May God bless you with the power of his Word in your life.

For more information about our international ministries, visit www.ccmi.org.

Additional copies of *A PIECE OF THE SKY*
and other RiverOak titles are available
wherever good books are sold.

If you have enjoyed this book,
or if it has had an impact on your life,
we would like to hear from you.

Please contact us at:

RIVEROAK BOOKS
Cook Communications Ministries, Dept. 201
4050 Lee Vance View
Colorado Springs, CO 80918

Or visit our Web site:
www.cookministries.com